RANDOM
HOUSE
LARGE
PRINT

Dear Friends,

Many series that are on TV these days are so much fun to watch and have so many fans, who become addicted to their favorites, that I became intrigued by the idea of writing about one. There are so many people involved in the production and some terrific actors.

And as always, there are underlying themes and subplots in the book as well—one of them being a challenge that many parents face more and more often, the empty nest, with our children taking jobs they love in other cities and moving far away. Often, if your children "do well" now, it means they got a job they love, somewhere else. It can be very lonely once your kids move away and you can't do things together spontaneously. You wish you lived closer to your adult children but no longer do, and visits are too rare. And for a single parent, it can be a real heartbreak to have children who live far away. We wish them well, but miss them fiercely. It would be wrong to hold them back, so we don't. But then we, as parents, have to face the challenge of filling our time and keeping our own lives satisfying and interesting, in a city where we once lived with our children and saw them every day, and don't anymore. It's an art form for parents to make the best of it, and it can be very challenging.

In some ways, this book is about reinventing yourself, at any age. The heroine of the novel has a successful career writing for a magazine. And after a chance dinner party she attends, an opportunity presents itself to write a TV series, which opens new doors, and gives her fabulous new experiences she never dreamed of before. Suddenly the void left by her children moving away to their own lives and careers (to San Francisco, Dallas, and London, while she lives in New York) is not so devastating, as she explores a whole new career and all it entails. She meets fascinating people, makes new friends, discovers her own talent in a different field, and builds a whole new life for herself.

It's an opportunity many of us wish we had, and as The Cast unfolds, we discover all the exciting elements of writing and filming a hit TV series, and all the people who are part of it. It sounds like a lot of fun to me!

The doors to a whole new world open for the people in the book, and for us. I hope you thoroughly enjoy The Cast, and all the interesting characters portrayed. Have a great time reading it—I loved writing it!

Love,
Danielle

The Cast

Accidental Heroes
Against All Odds
The Apartment
The Award
Blue
Country
Dangerous Games
The Duchess
Fairytale
Fall From Grace
First Sight
Friends Forever
A Good Woman
Happy Birthday
Hotel Vendome
Magic
The Mistress
One Day at a Time
Past Perfect
Pegasus
A Perfect Life
Power Play
Precious Gifts
Prodigal Son
Property of a Noblewoman
The Right Time
Rushing Waters
Undercover
Until the End of Time
Winners

DANIELLE STEEL

The Cast

A Novel

RANDOM HOUSE
LARGE PRINT

Copyright © 2018 by Danielle Steel

All rights reserved.
Published in the United States of America by Random House Large Print in association with Delacorte Press, an imprint of Random House, a division of Penguin Random House LLC, New York.

Cover illustration: © Tom Hallman

The Library of Congress has established a Cataloging-in-Publication record for this title.

ISBN: 978-0-5255-9038-5

www.penguinrandomhouse.com/large-print-format-books

FIRST LARGE PRINT EDITION

Printed in the United States of America

10 9 8 7 6 5 4 3 2 1

This Large Print edition published in accord with the standards of the N.A.V.H.

To my much loved, wonderful children,
Beatie, Trevor, Todd, Nick, Samantha,
Victoria, Vanessa, Maxx, and Zara,

May your lives be full of new adventures,
new chapters, new beginnings,
with each chapter better than the last.

May you give each other strength,
remember the good times,
and may you embrace life!

I love you with all my heart and soul,

Mom/d.s.

The Cast

Chapter 1

The sounds of the office Christmas party drifted into Kait Whittier's office through the partially open door. She paid no attention to it as she sat bent over her computer, trying to finish the last of her work before the Christmas break. It was Friday afternoon, Christmas was on Monday, and the offices of **Woman's Life** magazine would be closed until after New Year's. She wanted to get her column in before she left, and she had lots to do before two of her children came home on Sunday morning to spend Christmas Eve and Christmas Day with her.

But for now, her entire focus was on what she was writing. It was for the March issue of the magazine, but the time of year didn't matter. She tried to keep her subjects of general interest to women, about the difficult issues they dealt with, at home, in their relationships and marriages, with their kids, or in the workplace. The column she wrote was called "Tell Kait," and it was hard for her to believe she had been writing it for nineteen years. She responded to some letters directly, on particularly sensitive personal subjects, and included others in the column that were of broader scope.

She was often cited as an expert, and invited to be on panels about women's issues, or to appear on TV shows on all the major networks. She had majored in journalism in college and went on to get a master's in journalism at Columbia. And a few years after she started writing the column, in order to gain greater credibility and insight, she had gotten a master's in psychology at NYU, and it had served her well. The column was at the front of the magazine now, and many people bought **Woman's Life** primarily to read her. What had originally been referred to as her "agony column" in editorial meetings was now a huge success and treated with dignity and seriousness, as she was. And best of all, she loved what she did and found it rewarding.

In recent years, she had added a blog to her repertoire that included excerpts from her column. She had thousands of followers on Twitter and Facebook, and had contemplated writing an advice book, but hadn't done it so far. She was mindful of walking the fine line of not overtly giving delicate advice that would leave the magazine open to lawsuits or herself to being charged with practicing medicine without a license. Her responses were intelligent, carefully thought out, sensible, wise, and full of common sense, the kind of advice one would hope to get from a smart, concerned mother, which she was in her private life with her three children, now grown up. They had been very young when she began writing at **Woman's Life,** as an entry path into the world of women's magazines.

She had really wanted to work at **Harper's Bazaar** or **Vogue,** and agreed to write the women's advice column as a stopgap while she waited for a more glamorous position to open up elsewhere. Instead she had discovered her niche and her own strengths, and had fallen in love with what she was doing. It was perfect because she could do the work from home when she needed to and went into the office for editorial meetings and to deliver her finished columns. When her children were young, it was a schedule that allowed her a lot of leeway to spend time with them. And now she was free to be in the office more, although she did much of her work by email. She had faced many of the problems herself that her readers wrote to her about. Her fans were legion and the magazine had been quick to realize that they had a gold mine on their hands. Kait could do whatever she wanted at **Woman's Life,** and they trusted her gut instincts, which had been infallible so far.

Kaitlin Whittier came from an aristocratic Old Guard New York family, although she was discreet about it, and had never traded on that fact. And her upbringing had been unusual enough to give her an interesting perspective on life at an early age. She was no stranger to family problems, or the

vicissitudes of human nature and the disappointments and dangers that even blue blood couldn't
protect you from. She was fifty-four years old, with
striking good looks. She had red hair, green eyes,
and she dressed simply but had a style of her own.
She wasn't afraid to voice her opinions, no matter
how unpopular they were, and she was willing to
fight for what she believed in. She was a combina-
tion of courageous and quiet, dedicated to her career yet devoted to her children, modest yet strong.

In nineteen years, she had survived the transi-
tions of several regimes at the magazine. She kept
her focus on her column and never played political
games. Her attitude had won the respect of manage-
ment. She was unique, and so was her column. Even
her colleagues loved to read it, and were surprised to
find many of their own challenges addressed there
as well. There was a universal quality to what she
wrote. She was fascinated by people and their relationships, and spoke about them eloquently, with a
touch of humor now and then, without offending
her readers.

"Still working?" Carmen Smith asked as she
poked her head in the door. She was Hispanic, a
native New Yorker, and had been a successful model
a dozen years before. She was married to a British
photographer she'd fallen in love with when she
modeled for him, although their marriage was tur-
bulent and they had separated several times. She
was the magazine's beauty editor. She was a few

years younger than Kait, and they were good friends at the office, although they never got together outside work, their home lives were very different. Carmen ran with a racier, arty crowd. "Why am I not surprised? Figured I'd find you here when I didn't see you falling into the eggnog or rum punch with everyone else."

"I can't afford to drink," Kait said, grinning without looking up as she checked the punctuation of the response she had just written to a woman in Iowa who was being emotionally abused by her husband. Kait had sent her an individual response as well, not wanting her to wait three months to see her concerns addressed in the column. She had advised the woman to consult an attorney and her physician, and be honest with her adult children about what her husband was doing to her. Abuse was always a hot topic to Kait, which she never failed to take seriously, and this time was no different. "Ever since that electric facial you tried out on me, I think I've been losing brain cells," she said to Carmen. "I've had to give up drinking to compensate for it." Carmen laughed and glanced at her apologetically.

"Yeah, I know, it gave me a headache, and they took it off the market last month. But it was worth a try." The two women had made a pact ten years before, when Carmen turned forty, never to have plastic surgery, and had stuck to it so far, although Kait accused Carmen of cheating because she got

Botox shots. "Besides, you don't need it," Carmen continued. "I would hate you for it if we weren't friends. I'm the one who's not supposed to need any help, with olive skin. Instead, I'm starting to look like my grandfather, who is currently ninety-seven, and you're the only redhead I know with fair skin and no wrinkles, and you don't own a moisturizer. You're a disgusting person. Why don't you come and join the rest of the office getting smashed around the punch bowl? You can finish the column later."

"I just did," Kait said as she hit the send button to email the piece to the editor in chief. She swiveled in her chair to face her friend. "I have to buy a Christmas tree tonight. I didn't have time last weekend. I've got to put it up and decorate it. The kids are arriving Sunday. I only have tonight and tomorrow to get the decorations up and wrap the presents, so I can't hang around the punch bowl."

"Who's coming?"

"Tom and Steph," Kait responded.

Carmen didn't have children, and had never wanted them. She said her husband acted like a child, and one was enough, whereas Kait's children had always been vitally important to her and were the center of her world when they were younger.

Kait's oldest, Tom, was more traditional than his two sisters, and his goal had been a career in business from his earliest years. He had met his wife, Maribeth, at business school at Wharton, and they had married young. She was the daughter of a fast food king in Texas, a financial genius who had made literally billions, and owned the largest chain of fast food restaurants in the South and Southwest. He had one daughter and had always longed for a son, and had welcomed Tommy with open arms and taken him under his wing. He brought him into the business when Tom and Maribeth got married after grad school. She was smart as a whip, worked in marketing in her father's empire, and they had two daughters, who were four and six and looked like little angels. The youngest had her father and grandmother's red hair and was the liveliest of the two. The older one looked like her mother, a pretty blonde. And Kait hardly ever saw them.

Tom and his wife were so active and involved in Maribeth's father's life that Tom only saw his mother in New York for lunch or dinner when he was in town on business trips, and for major holidays. He was part of his wife's world now, more than Kait's. But he was obviously happy and had made a fortune of his own, thanks to the opportunities his father-in-law had shared with him. It was hard to compete with that, or even find room in his life for her now. Kait accepted it with grace and was happy for him, although she missed him. She'd gone to see them in Dallas several times, but she always felt like an intruder in their busy life. Aside from work in his father-in-law's fast food empire, Tom and Maribeth were engaged with philanthropic activities, their two daughters, and their community, and he traveled constantly for business. He loved his mother but had little time to see her. He was on his way to a success of his own, and she was proud of him.

Candace, her second child, was twenty-nine, and had chosen a different path, as the middle child. Possibly to get attention, she had always been drawn to high-risk pursuits, and danger in various forms. She had spent her junior year in college in London, and never came back. She had gotten a job at the BBC and worked her way up to producing documentaries for them. She shared her mother's passion for defending women struggling from abuse in their cultures. She had worked on several stories in the Middle East and underdeveloped countries in Africa, and had caught various diseases in the process, but thought the hazards of her job well worth it. She was frequently in war-torn countries, but she felt it crucial to put a spotlight on the situations women were in, and was willing to risk her own life on their behalf. She had survived a hotel bombing and a crash of a small plane in Africa, and always went back for more. She said she would have been bored working at a desk or living in New York full-time. She wanted to become an independent documentary filmmaker herself one day. In the meantime, her work was meaningful and important, and Kait was proud of her as well.

Of all her children, Kait was the closest to Candace and had the most in common with her, but she rarely saw her. And as usual, Candace wasn't coming home for Christmas, she was finishing an assignment in Africa. She hadn't made it back for the holidays in years and was always severely missed. There was no important man in her life. She said she didn't have time, which seemed to be true. Kait hoped that one of these days, Candace would find The One. She was young and there was no rush. Kait didn't worry about that for her, only about the places she traveled to, which were dangerous and very rough. Nothing frightened Candace.

And Stephanie, Kait's youngest, was the family computer genius. She had gone to MIT, gotten a master's in computer science at Stanford, and fell in love with San Francisco. She got a job at Google as soon as she got her master's, and met her boyfriend there. She was twenty-six years old and in seventh heaven at Google, and loved everything about her California life. Her siblings teased her about being a geek, and Kait had rarely seen two people better suited to each other than Stephanie and her boyfriend, Frank. They lived in Mill Valley in Marin County, in a tiny ramshackle cottage, despite their long daily commute to Google. They were crazy about each other and their high-tech jobs. She was coming home to spend Christmas with her mother, and after two days was planning to meet Frank and his family in Montana to spend a week with them. Kait couldn't complain about that either. It was so obvious that her daughter was happy, which was what she wanted for her, and she was doing brilliantly at her job. Stephanie was never going to come back to New York either. Why would she? She had everything she wanted and had ever dreamed of right where she was.

Kait had encouraged all of them to pursue their dreams, she just hadn't expected them to do it so successfully and so far afield from where they'd grown up, and to plant their roots so deeply in other places and different lives. She never made an issue of it, but she missed having her children nearby. But in today's world, with people more mobile and less firmly anchored, they often moved far away from their families to establish their careers. She respected her children for it, and to avoid dwelling on their absence, she stayed busy herself. Very busy. It made her column even more important to her. She filled her life with work, and was diligent about it, and loved what she did. Kait was happy in her life, and there was a certain satisfaction in knowing she had brought her children up to work hard to achieve their goals. All of them had found rewarding work, and two of them had found partners they loved, who were good people and the right mates for them.

Kait herself had been married twice, the first time right out of college to her children's father. Scott Lindsay had been handsome, charming, fun loving, and young. They had a great time together, and it had taken six years and three children to figure out that they had none of the same values and very little in common, except that they both came from old, established New York families. Scott had an enormous trust fund and Kait finally realized that he had no intention of ever working and didn't have to. He wanted to play for the rest of his life, and Kait thought everyone should work, no matter what their circumstances. Her indomitable grandmother had shown her that.

She and Scott had parted ways right after Stephanie was born, when he announced that he wanted the spiritual experience of living with Buddhist monks in Nepal for a year, was thinking of joining an expedition to climb Everest after that, and thought that the mystical beauty of India would be a great place to bring up their kids, after his adventures. They divorced without animosity or bitterness after he'd been gone a year, and he thought it was for the best too. He stayed away for four years and was a stranger to his children by the time he got back, and then moved to the South Pacific, where he married a beautiful Tahitian woman and had three more children. He died after a brief tropical illness, twelve years after the divorce from Kait.

She had sent the children to visit him in Tahiti, but he had very little interest in them, and they didn't want to go back after a few times. He had simply moved on, and had been a poor choice of mate for a husband. Everything that had made him

charming and seductive in college made him anything but later on, once she grew up and he didn't.
He never really had and didn't want to. She was
sad for her children when he died, more so than
they were. He had spent so little time with them
and showed so little interest. They had almost no
connection to him. His parents had died young
as well, and had no contact with the children before they did. So Kait's children had grown up with
their mother as the hub and only support system
in their lives. She had shared her own values with
them, and all three of them admired how hard she
worked, while still being available to them at all
times, even now. None of them needed her help
particularly. They were well on their way on their
chosen paths, but they knew she would have been
there for them in a minute if they needed her. It
was who she was, with her priorities clear about her
children from the moment they were born.

Kait's second attempt at marriage had been entirely different, but no more successful than the
first. She waited until she was forty to marry again.
Tom had left for college by then, and both of her
daughters were teenagers. She met Adrian just as
she started a master's in psychology at NYU, he
was ten years older, completing his doctorate in art
history, and had been the curator of a small but respected museum in Europe. Erudite, accomplished,
fascinating, intelligent, he opened new worlds to
her, and they traveled to many cities on museum

trips: Amsterdam, Florence, Paris, Berlin, Madrid, London, Havana.

In retrospect, she realized she had married him too quickly. She was worried about facing an empty nest in a few years, and anxious to establish a new life of her own. Adrian had endless plans he wanted to share with her, had never been married before, and had no children of his own. It seemed like a good fit, and it was exciting being with someone with such a rich cultural life and extensive knowledge. He was very reserved but kind and warm to her, until he explained to her a year after they married that his desire to marry her had been an attempt to go counter to his nature, and in spite of his good intentions, he had fallen in love with a younger man. He apologized profoundly to Kait and moved to Venice with him, where they had lived happily for the past thirteen years, and her marriage to him had obviously ended in divorce as well.

She had been gun-shy about serious relationships ever since, and distrustful of her own judgment and the choices she'd made. Her life was happy and satisfying. She saw her children whenever possible when they had time. Her work was rewarding, and she had friends. When she turned fifty, four years earlier, she convinced herself that she didn't need a man in her life, and hadn't had a date since. It just seemed simpler like this. She had no regrets about what she might be missing. Adrian particularly had taken her by surprise, and nothing in his behavior toward her had suggested to her that he might be gay. She didn't want to fall into someone's trap again, or make a mistake. She didn't want to be disappointed, or possibly encounter something worse. Although she was a great proponent of relationships in her column, they had begun to seem too complicated for her. She always insisted she was happy on her own, although friends like Carmen attempted to convince her to try again, and said she was too young to give up on love at fifty-four. Kait was always startled by her age. She didn't feel it or look it, and had more energy than ever. The years had flown by. She was fascinated by new endeavors, the people she met, and her children.

"So are you coming out to get drunk with us?" Carmen asked her from the doorway, looking exasperated. "You make the rest of us look bad, working all the time. It's Christmas, Kait!" Kait glanced at her watch, she still had to get the tree, but she had half an hour to spare, to hang out with her colleagues and share a drink.

She followed Carmen to the area where the eggnog and rum punch were set up, and took a sip of the eggnog, which was surprisingly strong. Whoever had mixed it had a heavy hand. Carmen was drinking her second one by the time Kait slipped away, went back to her office, looked around, and picked up a thick file off her desk, filled with letters she was planning to answer for the column and a draft of an article she had agreed to write for **The New York Times** about whether discrimination against women still existed in the workplace, or was simply a myth and a relic of the past. It wasn't, in her opinion, it was just subtler than it used to be, and it depended on what field. She was looking forward to finishing it. She slipped the file into a tote bag Stephanie had given her with the Google logo on it, quietly made her way past the revelers with a wave at Carmen, and got into the elevator. Her Christmas vacation had begun, and now she had to get busy decorating her apartment for her kids, who would be there in two days.

She was planning to cook the turkey herself on Christmas Eve, as she always did, and would have all their favorite treats on hand. She had ordered a Yule log at the bakery, and had already bought Christmas pudding from a British grocery store she liked. She had Bombay Sapphire gin for Tom, some excellent wine for all of them, vegetarian dishes planned for Stephanie, and the right kiddie treats and breakfast cereal in pastel colors for her granddaughters. And she still had to wrap all their gifts. It was going to be a busy two days until they arrived. Thinking about it, she smiled as she got into a cab for the ride uptown to the Christmas tree lot near her apartment. It was beginning to feel like Christmas, and even more so as it started to snow.

*   *   *

Kait found a handsome tree that looked about the right height for her ceilings, and they promised to deliver it later that night when the lot closed. She had the stand she needed, and the decorations and lights. The snow was sticking to her red hair and lashes as she picked the tree out and then walked the four blocks to her apartment. People looked festive and happy with Christmas Eve only two days away. She had also picked out a wreath for the door, and some branches she could use to decorate the fireplace mantel in the living room. After she took off her coat, she started to unpack the boxes of decorations she had used for years and her children still loved. Some of them, from their childhood, were a little tired and battered, but those were their favorites, and if she failed to put them on the tree, they noticed and complained. The souvenirs from their early years were important to them. It had been a time filled with love and warmth.

She lived in the same apartment she'd had when they were growing up. It was a generous size for New York, and been perfect for them when she bought it twenty years before. There were two decent-sized bedrooms, one of which was hers, a living room and dining room, a big country-style kitchen where everyone congregated, and, since it was an old building, three maids' rooms behind it, which had been her children's bedrooms when they were young, and were big enough for them as kids. The second bedroom next to hers she used as a guest room now when needed, and an office for herself. It had been the children's playroom when they were growing up. She was planning to turn over her bedroom to Tom and his wife while they were there for their brief visit. Stephanie would have the guest room/office. Tom's two little girls would have one of the former maids' rooms their father and aunts had grown up in, and Kait was going to sleep in Candace's childhood room, since she wouldn't be home. She hadn't moved to a smaller apartment because she loved having enough space for her children and her granddaughters to visit. They hadn't all come home at the same time in several years, but they might again one day. And after twenty years, she loved the apartment, and it was home. A housecleaner came to tidy it twice a week, and the rest of the time, she fended for herself and cooked her own meals, or picked something up on the way home.

With the salary she made from **Woman's Life,** and money her grandmother had left her, Kait could have afforded a slightly more luxurious life, but chose not to. She didn't want more than she had, and had never been inclined to show off. Her grandmother had taught her the value of money, what it could do, how ephemeral it could be, and the importance of hard work. Constance Whittier had been a remarkable woman who had taught Kait everything she knew about life, ideals she still lived by and in turn had demonstrated to her children, although Constance had been less successful with her own children, or maybe just not as lucky. She had saved the family from disaster more than eighty years before, and had been a legend in her time, and set an example for them all of resourcefulness, sheer grit, business acumen, and courage. She had been Kait's only role model growing up.

From an illustrious aristocratic family herself, Constance watched her own family and the Whittiers lose their entire fortunes at the same time in the Crash of '29. She'd been young, married, and had four young children at the time, including a new baby, Kait's father, Honor. They had lived in a golden world of enormous houses, vast estates, unlimited wealth, beautiful gowns, spectacular jewels, and armies of help, all of which vanished and turned to ashes in the crash, which destroyed so many lives.

Unable to face what would come next, Constance's husband committed suicide, as their entire world was liquidated, and she was left alone with four young children and no money. She sold what she could, they had lost the rest, and she moved with her children to a tenement apartment on the Lower East Side and tried to get work to feed them. No one in her family or immediate circle had ever worked, they had inherited their fortunes. She had no skills other than being a charming hostess, a beautiful young woman, a good mother, and a devoted wife. She thought of taking in sewing, but had no skill for it. So instead she did the only thing she could think of and knew how to do. She made cookies, which she loved doing for her own children.

They'd had a fleet of cooks and servants to conjure up whatever delicacies they wished, but Constance had always enjoyed making cookies for her children, when the cook would let her into the kitchen. Her parents' cook had taught her to make cookies as a child, and it served her well. She began making them in the one-bedroom apartment on the Lower East Side. And taking the children with her, she brought her cookies to food stores and restaurants in plain boxes, where she wrote on them "Mrs. Whittier's Cookies for Kids," and sold them to whoever would buy them. She got an instant positive reaction, not just from children, but adults, and grocery stores and restaurants began to place orders with her. She could barely keep up production for the orders, and what she earned helped to sustain her and the children in their new life, where survival and making enough money to support her children were constant concerns. She added cakes then, and began researching recipes she remembered from Austria, Germany, and France, and the orders kept growing. She saved her money and within a year was able to rent a small bakery in the neighborhood, and continued to fill the ever-increasing orders.

Her cakes were extraordinary, her cookies said to be the best. Other restaurants farther uptown heard of her, and added their orders to her first customers', and she was soon supplying some of the best restaurants in New York with her baked goods, and had to hire women to help her. Ten years later, she had the most successful commercial baking business in New York, which all began in her tiny kitchen, in desperation, to support her children. Her business increased in the war years, when women joined the workforce and had no time to bake at home. Constance had a factory by then, and in 1950, twenty years after she began, she sold the business to General Foods for a fortune that subsequently helped support three generations of her family and was still doing so. The trust she had established had provided a nest egg for each of them that allowed them to pursue an education, buy a home, or start a business venture. She had set an example to them all, born of necessity and her own resourcefulness and refusal to be beaten.

Constance's sons had proven to be a disappointment to her, only too happy to ride the coattails of their mother's fortuitous success and be idle themselves. She admitted later that she had spoiled them, and one of them had been unlucky. Her oldest son had had a passion for fast cars and faster women, and died in a car accident before he married or had children. Kait's father, Honor, had been lazy and self-indulgent, drank and gambled, and married a beautiful young woman who ran off with another man when her daughter Kait was a year old. Kait's mother disappeared somewhere in Europe and was never heard from again. Honor died a year later, somewhat mysteriously in a brothel while traveling in Asia, when Kait was two and left with nannies in New York. Her grandmother had taken her in and raised her, and they adored each other.

Constance's older daughter had been a talented writer, and had written successfully under the pen name of Nadine Norris. She died in her late twenties of a brain tumor, childless and unmarried. And Constance's younger daughter had married a Scotsman, lived a quiet life in Glasgow, and had nice children who had been kind to her until her death at eighty. Those children were Kait's cousins, whom she liked but rarely saw. Constance's pride and joy had been Kait, and they shared wonderful adventures living together as Kait grew up. Kait was thirty when her grandmother died at ninety-four, after a remarkable life.

Constance Whittier had lived a wonderful life to a great age with all her faculties intact and a sharp mind. She had never looked back with bitterness or regret over what had been lost, nor resented what she'd had to do to save her children. Constance had treated every day like an opportunity, a challenge, and a gift, and it had helped Kait to do the same in hard times, or when faced with disappointments. Her grandmother had been the bravest woman she'd ever known. She had been fun and exciting to be with when Kait was a child, and even into her nineties. She had stayed occupied until the end, traveling, visiting people, keeping abreast of new developments in the economy, fascinated by business and learning new things. She had learned to speak fluent French in her eighties, and then took Italian classes, and spoke it well.

Kait's children still remembered their great-grandmother, although the memories were dim now, since they had been young when she died. She'd had dinner with Kait on her last night, and they had laughed and had a lively conversation afterward. Kait still missed her, and smiled whenever she thought of her. The years they had shared had been the greatest gift in her life, other than her children.

As she set the Christmas decorations carefully on the kitchen table, she saw a few from her own childhood, and she remembered hanging them on the tree with her grandmother when she lived with her. They brought back a flood of memories, and even though the ornaments were faded now, Kait knew the memories never would. Her grandmother would live on forever in the love and joy they had shared, which had been the foundation of the life she lived. Constance Whittier had been an inspiration to all who knew her. And the cakes and cookies she had baked out of necessity to save her children became household words. The cookies were simply called 4 Kids, and the fancy cakes and baked goods were Mrs. Whittier's Cakes and had fed them all. General Foods had wisely preserved the original names of the products, which were still popular, and big sellers for them. Constance Whittier had become a legend, an independent, resourceful woman ahead of her time, and Kait still followed her example every day.

Chapter 2

Knowing that her children would be home for only a short time, Kait wanted everything to be perfect. The tree, the house, the decorations, the meals. She wanted them to leave two days later on a cloud of benevolence and good feelings toward each other. Tom was sometimes dismissive of his younger sister and teased her. She lived on another planet in a world defined by computers, and Tom thought her boyfriend was weird. He was a nice guy, but hard to talk to, and was interested only in computers. He and Stephanie were among the bright lights of Google, and were classic geeks. And Stephanie had often commented privately to her mother that it was strange to think that her brother's father-in-law had made billions selling fries and burgers, and chicken wings with barbecue sauce and secret spices they wouldn't reveal. But Hank, Maribeth's father, was a brilliant businessman and had been wonderful to Tom, giving him every opportunity to share in his success and make a fortune of his own. Hank

Starr was a generous man, and Kait was grateful for the chance he had given Tom. And Maribeth was a smart woman and a good wife.

Stephanie was successful in her own pursuits, and had found the perfect mate for her. Kait couldn't ask for more. Only Candace still worried her, with the dangerous locations she went to, to make her documentaries for the BBC. Her siblings thought she was crazy to do it, and couldn't understand what drove her. Kait had deeper insight into her middle child. Faced with her brother's huge financial success as the crown prince in his father-in-law's realm, and her younger sister's brilliant mind, Candace had chosen a path that made her a star in her own right, and garnered the attention and respect of the world. Her deep concern for the plight of women had inspired Candace to become their voice and champion, and she brought attention to them with her documentary specials, no matter what it took for her to do it. It made what Kait did seem very tame, answering letters from distressed women around the country, and advising them on how to solve their ordinary daily problems and strive for a better life. She gave them hope and courage, if nothing else, and the feeling that someone cared about them. It was not a negligible accomplishment, and accounted for the success of her column for two decades.

Kait was no crusader like her middle daughter, or her grandmother, who had turned a tsunami that nearly drowned her into a wave they'd all ridden for many years. She had been a trailblazer for women, which was unheard of and rare in her day. She had proven that a woman with no training and no skills, brought up to do absolutely nothing except to look beautiful and be a companion to her husband, could actually succeed with the limited resources at hand. Children were still eating and loving her 4 Kids cookies all over the world. Kait had always loved them herself, although the commercial ones weren't as good as what had come out of her grandmother's oven when she was a child, but they were still delicious and sold well. She occasionally followed her grandmother's old recipes for one of her fancier cakes, particularly the Viennese Sacher torte that was her favorite as a child, although Kait made no claim to being a talented baker or chef. She had other skills, as evidenced by her column for **Woman's Life**.

She decorated the tree that night long after midnight. She put the prettiest, more recent ornaments closer to the top for the adults to admire, and the treasured sentimental ones of her childhood and her children's on the lower branches where her granddaughters could enjoy them. She finished, and stood back to admire the result at three in the morning, and went to bed with a long to-do list for the next day.

She was up and busy at eight o'clock, and by late afternoon on Saturday, the house looked perfect and she was happy. She went to the supermarket to buy the last of what she needed. She set the table, checked their bedrooms, and spent the evening wrapping their gifts, with a DVD of her old favorite television series, **Downton Abbey,** playing in the background. The show had gone off the air several years before, but she still enjoyed it, and the characters felt like old friends. It was nice to hear voices in the room, and it gave her a sense of someone with her. She'd watched it so often that she knew much of the dialogue by heart. Her children teased her about it, but she loved the way it was written. It was a family saga that had originated in England with a British cast and become a huge hit in the States by its second year. And the grandmother in it sometimes reminded her of her own.

The gifts she had chosen for her family were as varied as they were. She had bought Tom a beautiful leather jacket that was just jazzy enough for his life in Texas and he could wear on weekends. And she found a handbag and a big gold necklace from a trendy designer she knew Maribeth loved. She'd gotten Stephanie and Frank fleece-lined denim jackets, and hiking gear, since they lived in jeans, and owned only hiking boots and running shoes. Stephanie always stared in horror at the stilettos her sister-in-law wore. Kait had bought them all books and music as stocking stuffers, and American Girl dolls for both of her granddaughters, appropriate to their ages, with all the accessories that came with them.

She'd had a ball buying the dolls a month before, and watched what children their ages were begging their parents for when she picked them. And Maribeth had given her some hints, which helped her. Kait and her daughter-in-law had always gotten along, although they couldn't have been more different. And Kait was well aware that Maribeth had made a concerted effort to turn Tom into a Texan. He wore cowboy hats in Dallas, and had custom-made cowboy boots in every possible exotic skin, from alligator to lizard, given to him by his father-in-law. Tommy had entirely blended into his adopted world, which would have been hard to resist, given the accolades and benefits it provided him. He adored his wife and children, just as his mother had loved him and his sisters as children, and still did. At times she missed them all fiercely, but she never let herself dwell on it. It was enough knowing they were happy, and she had a good life too. She followed her grandmother's example, celebrating what she had and never complaining about what she didn't.

She opened her eyes on the morning of Christmas Eve, filled with anticipation, excited to see them in a few hours. She tried to call Candace on her cellphone, but couldn't reach her. Kait showered and dressed, put on black jeans, a red sweater, and ballet flats, checked the apartment again, and turned on the tree lights. She was ready. Tommy and his family were arriving in the early afternoon, on his father-in-law's plane, and on Christmas night, they would be joining him at an enormous property he had rented in the Bahamas, to spend the rest of the vacation with him. Tommy and Maribeth and the children spent the Christmas break with him every year, after spending the actual holiday in New York with Kait. It had been their tradition since they married seven years before.

Kait was too excited to eat lunch, and read through some of the letters she still had to answer. And after that she updated her blog, which was enormously popular. She had children's Christmas carols on the stereo for Meredith and Lucie Anne. It was Lucie Anne who looked so much like her father and grandmother, and was a Whittier through and through. She was a little fireball with huge green eyes, red hair, and freckles, who was polite to adults, but fearless and asked amazingly intelligent questions for a four-year-old. Meredith, Merrie, was shyer, more cautious, more demure, and very southern, like her mother. She loved to draw and wrote poetry for school. Both were bright, interesting children, and Kait wished she had the chance to spend more time with them and get to know them better, but the children's lives were so full, with school and extra-curricular activities, that even when Kait was there to visit, the girls hardly had a spare moment for her. A couple of visits to Texas during the year, sandwiched into their parents' hectic schedule, and their annual Christmas visit never seemed like enough.

Stephanie had taken the first commercial flight out of San Francisco, and would be at the apartment by three P.M. Stephanie had no interest whatsoever in marriage or children, and Kait wondered if she ever would. Stephanie thought that marriage was an antiquated tradition that was no longer relevant, and she had never been attracted to the idea of having kids. She preferred the company of adults with similar interests, and Frank agreed with her. They were in love with their work and each other, and there was no room in their life for children. And Candace was light-years from settling down with anyone, given her work for the BBC and her own career goals.

Kait listened to other women talk about the time they spent with their grandchildren, and how much they enjoyed them, but it wasn't part of her life in the same way, or maybe her destiny. Kait regretted that she wasn't as engaged with her grandchildren as her grandmother had been, but she saw them too seldom and for too little time to connect deeply with them. All she could do was spoil them a little and try to get to know them. She was busy with her column and her own life, and her grandchildren felt like someone else's children.

When the doorbell rang at two o'clock, she was prepared. The moment the door opened, her son hugged her and strode into the room in a suit, Maribeth took off her coat and couldn't stop admiring how beautiful the tree was, and the decorations, and Merrie and Lucie Anne danced in looking like little fairies. Lucie was wearing her favorite tutu under her red coat, and she told Kait immediately all about her ballet lessons and the recital she was going to be in in June. Kait brought out sandwiches and cookies, she had eggnog for the adults and hot chocolate with whipped cream and marshmallows for the two girls, and they all chattered excitedly as Kait glowed. She loved it when her children were home.

Stephanie arrived an hour later, in jeans and hiking boots, and a heavy plaid wool jacket of Frank's she'd borrowed for the trip. She was happy to see her brother as he hugged her, and the two girls were delighted to see their aunt, who was always fun and loved getting up to mischief with them. As soon as she set down her suitcase in her small childhood room behind the kitchen, they came in to bounce on her bed, and she let them.

It was a wonderfully warm, cozy afternoon, which they all thoroughly enjoyed, and that night they dressed for dinner. The two little girls wore smocked party dresses that Kait had sent them that looked like the ones their aunts used to wear at their age. Maribeth had on a sexy black cocktail dress, and Stephanie arrived in a white sweater with her jeans, and didn't change the hiking boots she had on, since she had forgotten to bring shoes, as she always did. Tom was properly dressed in a suit and tie. Kait had worn black silk pants and a lace blouse and small diamond earrings that had been her grandmother's and she loved.

The conversation was lively at the table and afterward Kait helped the two little girls set out a plate of cookies for Santa, with a glass of milk, carrots and salt for the reindeer, a ritual they followed every year. Kait helped Maribeth put them to bed, and read them a Christmas story, while Stephanie and her brother discussed the new computer system they were switching over to in his father-in-law's business, and she warned him of things to watch out for, which he found very informative. His sister was more knowledgeable about computers than anyone he knew, and he trusted her advice.

The adults sat up until long after midnight once the children were in bed. They used to go to midnight mass before Merrie and Lucie Anne were born, but they had no one to leave the girls with, and they were too young to join them for church late at night, so it was no longer part of their routine, for now anyway. And just as they were about to go to bed, Candace called them on Skype. It was already Christmas Day for her, and they all talked to her and caught up on what she was doing and where she was. Tom held the laptop so she could see the tree, and she told her mother that it looked beautiful, and she wished she was there with them. It brought tears to Kait's eyes to see her, and she promised to come to London to visit her, as soon as Candace got back from her current assignment. It gave her something to look forward to, and Candace teased her younger sister and asked if she was wearing hiking boots or shoes, and Stephanie laughed and held up a foot to show her the boots, and they all laughed with her.

"I forgot my shoes," she said with a big grin.

"Yeah, right. Tell me about it. I don't think you own any. You always borrow mine when I come home for Christmas," she reminded her, and Stephanie laughed harder. "How's Frank? Did he come with you?" Stephanie shook her head.

"I'm meeting him in Montana day after tomorrow. He's fine. We're going to spend a week with his parents. His dad's been sick so he wanted to visit with him." The two sisters didn't talk often, so they took advantage of the holiday call, and they were on with her for half an hour before they ended it.

Kait looked nostalgic afterward. "I hope one of these days you all come home at the same time," she said. They had all noticed that Candace was thinner, and the area around her was rugged, but she seemed happy, and she said she'd be back in London for a few weeks, but probably not for long. They were all moving ahead at full speed in their own lives, and Kait had her own. She couldn't imagine what she would have done if she didn't. She would have been lost if she didn't have a job she loved that filled her time, and she was reminded again that you can't hang on to your children, and they're only on loan to you for a short time.

After the call, they all went to their rooms and went to bed. Maribeth apologized to her mother-in-law for taking over her room, and Kait assured her that she was happy to give it to them. She liked sleeping in Candace's old room, next to the girls. And she had told them when she went to bed to wake her in the morning, which she knew they would.

She wrote letters from Santa for them to find in the morning, along with the stockings she filled with Christmas candy, lollipops, and small toys and little books and things to keep them busy. It had been a tradition with her children too, like all the others they followed.

The apartment was quiet after that, until the two girls pounced on Kait's bed in the morning, squealing with delight over what Santa had left them in their stockings. And she read the Santa letters with them, which praised them for being such good girls all year and assured them that they were at the top of Santa's "Nice" list.

When the other adults got up, in bathrobes and pajamas, they opened the gifts from Kait under the tree, because the girls couldn't wait a moment longer. Everyone loved their presents, and Tom and Maribeth gave Kait a beautiful antique gold heart-shaped locket on a chain with photographs of Merrie and Lucie Anne in it. Stephanie gave her a new computer, which she'd had delivered before she came. It was supposed to be state-of-the-art and much better than the one Kait had at home now. Stephanie set it up for her and showed her all the applications she'd added, and she had bought her the latest phone to go with it. Tom and Maribeth brought out the gifts from Santa that they'd brought with them, and a few from them for everyone.

And then they all had breakfast together, went to get dressed, sat in the living room while the girls played with their dolls, and had a casual lunch in the kitchen. The day sped by, and Kait had an ache in her heart at six o'clock when Maribeth dressed the girls in their traveling clothes, and at six-thirty they left the house, after endless hugs. They were on their way to the airport in New Jersey where Maribeth's father's plane was waiting to take them to the Bahamas. Kait sat in the living room talking quietly to Stephanie after they were gone, trying to fight back tears. In a single day she felt closer to her granddaughters, and then they were gone again.

"It all goes so quickly," Kait said softly. Stephanie was leaving at six o'clock the next morning. For Kait, Christmas was almost over, and it had been very sweet.

"At least we still come home, Mom," Stephanie reminded her, and Kait knew it was hard for them to understand how much it meant to her, and how different her life was without them. Letting go was a fine art she'd had to learn once they grew up, and it was far from easy. Being with them always made her regret again that they didn't live in the same city.

Life would have been very different if she could see them any time and have lunch or dinner with them. She had been given back her own life to fill and reorganize once they grew up, and she knew from the letters she answered in her column that it was a challenge other women struggled with as well. One minute you were a family, and the next you were alone, in some cases, although she never whined about it or complained to her children or even her friends. She tried to make it look easy, out of pride and respect for them. But the ache in her heart was almost tangible after Tom and his family left. She never wanted any of them to know how much it hurt to be apart from them. She felt that her happiness wasn't their responsibility, but only her own. She reminded her readers of it too, and told them to take charge of their own lives, and fill their time proactively.

"Frank wanted me to spend Christmas with him and his family this year," Stephanie added, and Kait was grateful she hadn't. "But I didn't want to do that to you. I knew you'd be disappointed."

"Yes, I would," Kait confirmed to her. "Very much so. Our holidays together mean the world to me." She looked forward to them all year, but she didn't want to sound pathetic to her daughter.

"I know, Mom," Stephanie said quietly and patted her shoulder, and then they went out to the kitchen to eat leftovers and talk about how cute Tom's daughters were. Stephanie commented that he was a very good father and seemed surprised by it. "It's so time-consuming. I don't know how he does it."

"It's worth it," Kait explained to her.

"I guess that's why Frank and I don't want kids," Stephanie said seriously. "It's too much to deal with. I can't see myself ever doing that."

"You might feel differently about it later." Stephanie was only twenty-six.

"Maybe," she said, but she didn't look convinced. They finished dinner and cleaned up the kitchen, and Stephanie put the dishes in the dishwasher for her mother. "It's so odd in a way," she commented. "I never think of you as old, or as a grandmother. You're still so young. It must be nice to have your own life back and have all of us grown up and out of the nest while you can still enjoy it." Kait looked at her and realized how little her daughter understood of motherhood, and what a void it left when kids grew up and took off, no matter how young you were.

"My happiest years were when you were all young and still at home. I enjoy my life now and my work, but nothing ever compares to that. I guess some people are relieved when their kids leave. But you all spoiled me, and were damn nice to have around," she said ruefully, and gave her daughter a hug. "I was never in a hurry for you to leave, and I love it when you come home." Stephanie nodded, but still had no concept of how much her mother missed her, even if she had a good life of her own.

"You should get a boyfriend, Mom. That would be fun for you. You're still great looking. Frank thinks you're hot," she said sincerely, and Kait laughed.

"Tell him thank you for the compliment. And where do you suggest I find one? Place a personal ad? Send out a mailer? Pick up guys in bars?" Kait was teasing her. Life seemed so simple at Stephanie's age, and she lived on her own planet, where other people's lives weren't real to her. She had always been that way, and now Frank had joined her in their limited universe, where they related better to computers than people.

"You must meet a lot of cool guys," Stephanie continued.

"Not really. And I'm actually happy like this. I'm busy with the magazine, my blog, Twitter, Facebook, and the rest. I'm happy to come home and collapse at night. And when I read the letters I get, I'm relieved I don't have the problems that go with most relationships. I've been married twice. I don't want the headache of someone screwing up my life, arguing with me, maybe cheating on me, wanting to change the way I live, telling me what to do and how to do it, and being angry about my career and how much I work, or hating my friends. People put up with a lot to make relationships work. I don't want to do that again. I kind of have it all the way I want it, except for you guys being spread all over the map in three cities, on two continents, but I'm used to that too now." She looked content as she said it. "I miss all of you, but I'm fine on my own."

"You're not old enough to give up on romance." Carmen had said the same thing, but Kait hadn't been in love in years, and it hadn't gone well when she was. Her life was comfortable just the way she had it. "You don't need to get married again, just have a guy you can go out with when you feel like it."

"That sounds more like an escort service than love," her mother teased her. "I don't think men like being on call. They expect more than that, and they should. I think the whole era of social media has given people the impression that you can use an app to conjure up a guy whenever you want, and then dismiss him like an Uber car when you're tired of him. And I know there are people who do that, but that's not me. There's no substance to that. I can't see the point of it. I like the old values and relationships. I just don't know if I want one for me, and when I think about it seriously, I realize I don't."

"That's too bad, Mom. You're too nice and too much fun and too smart to sit here by yourself. I think you should start dating." She made it sound like a sport Kait should take up again, like tennis or golf. But Kait knew it was a lot more work than that. After her last marriage, and her totally misjudging Adrian and being taken in by him, she had no desire to try again. And she hadn't met a man in several years who caught her fancy anyway. It was an easy sacrifice to make.

"Thanks for the suggestion," Kait said, and hugged her again as Stephanie glanced at her watch.

"I'd better get to bed early. I have to leave the house at five A.M. tomorrow to catch my flight. Don't bother getting up to say goodbye. We can say it tonight." But Kait immediately shook her head.

"There's no way I'm going to let you leave without giving you a hug and saying goodbye. What else do I have to do? I can go back to bed after you leave." She never let her children leave without seeing them off, she never had, and wasn't about to start now.

"You don't have to," Stephanie said generously.

"I know I don't. I'd feel cheated if I didn't get a last hug in before you go," she said, smiling at her, and Stephanie laughed.

"You're still a mom," she said, looking as though the concept was a mystery to her, and Kait suspected that was the case. Maternal instincts did not appear to be part of her daughter's makeup, although she was sweet to her brother's kids, and acted like a child herself with them.

"Of course I'm a mom." Kait smiled at her. "That's forever, it's part of who I am, no matter how old you get." It was particularly meaningful to her, since her own mother had abandoned her as a baby. Years later, her grandmother had made a concerted effort to discover what had happened to Kait's mother, thinking Kait had a right to know, and had learned that she had drowned in a boating accident in Spain when Kait was about ten years old. But her mother had never attempted to contact her or see her after she left, in the nine years before her death. Motherhood hadn't been part of her skills either, and she'd made no attempt to grow into it. Kait's grandmother was the only mother she'd ever had, which was part of what drove Kait to be so dedicated to her kids. She never wanted to be even remotely like her own mother.

"Well, my feelings won't be hurt if you don't get up," Stephanie assured her, but she knew Kait would.

Kait set her alarm for four-thirty when she went to bed, back in her own bedroom. The next morning she knocked on Stephanie's door with a cup of coffee and a piece of toast, and set them down next to Stephanie's bed. Twenty minutes later, Stephanie emerged, in Frank's plaid jacket with her carry-on, looking fresh-faced, with her dark hair still damp from the shower. She'd had a good Christmas with her mother, but she was excited to be joining Frank in a few hours. He was her real life now. Her mother was a piece of history, an important landmark, and an anchor for her, a touchstone she could come back to whenever she wanted.

The two women hugged for a long moment, and Kait kissed her and took a last long look at her as they waited for the elevator. Then with a broad smile and a wave, Stephanie thanked her mother for a wonderful Christmas, and she was gone when the elevator door closed. Kait stood staring at it for a long moment, and walked slowly back into her apartment. She felt lost for a minute, looking around, as though recognizing her own life again, the life where she was an adult woman alone, and her children were gone. And no matter how she filled it, denied it, or tried to ignore it, she was what her readers talked about with such poignancy. She was an empty nester. And after Stephanie left, in the silence of the apartment, Kait walked back into her bedroom, got into her bed, and cried, missing them fiercely.

Chapter 3

The week between Christmas and New Year's was bitter cold, and it snowed twice. Stephanie texted Kait from Montana to say she had arrived safely, and Tommy sent a text from the Bahamas to thank her for a nice time and their gifts. After the initial shock of their departure after the time they'd spent together, which always hit her when they first left, Kait got back into the groove of her own life. In some ways, it was pleasant being the parent of adult children. She could do whatever she wanted, work, relax, sleep, read, watch TV, see friends, or do nothing at all. She could eat at any hour and not worry about entertaining anyone, or making sure they were having a good time.

There was always a balance, and sometimes a conflict, between wanting to spend time with her children, missing them when they were gone, and liking time to herself. It was a luxury she had never had as a single parent when they were growing up. She was always doing something for them then, or worrying about them, helping with homework, keeping an eye on who their friends were, consoling their broken hearts, helping them fill out college applications, or talking to them about the important things in life. And at the same time juggling her professional obligations and doing her work and meeting deadlines. She had often thought of her grandmother during those times, who had gone from opulence and grandeur, with unlimited money and no responsibilities, to a one-bedroom walk-up apartment, taking care of four children herself without the help of maids, governesses, or nannies, and starting a business making cookies and cakes for neighborhood restaurants so her own children could eat and have a roof over their heads and new shoes. And on the days when the obstacles ahead seemed insurmountable, Kait remembered what her grandmother had accomplished, and knew that she could do it too, in much easier circumstances than her grandmother had wrestled with at a far more difficult time.

Kait did her work for her column, did a Q and A interview for the **Los Angeles Times** by email on her new computer, and, as a reward to herself, watched another episode of her favorite series again. It was always enjoyable for her, no matter how many times she'd watched it. The situations in **Downton Abbey** usually resolved satisfactorily after an episode or two, you knew who the good people were and the bad guys, and what to expect of them.

She was surprised by how much comfort it gave her. Carmen had a whole other list of favorite shows that she liked for different reasons and they talked about over lunch. She preferred mysteries and wasn't bothered by violence, and shows that had a science-fiction quality to them were the ones that she loved best, which Kait didn't like at all. Everyone seemed to have a favorite show these days, on the cable channels or by streaming. The era of sophisticated series on television had come into its own.

Four days after Stephanie left, Kait got a call from the friends who invited her to their New Year's Eve party every year. It was always something of a haphazard gathering of people who had nothing else to do and didn't want to spend the night at home. She had already decided not to go this year, she didn't want to venture out into the cold and battle for a cab to get there, and it was supposed to snow again. It seemed like a perfect time to stay home, and she had declined their invitation two weeks before. She didn't have a date, and didn't want to spend another New Year's Eve watching other people kiss at midnight, while she pretended not to care. Normally, she didn't, but on special nights like that, she hated feeling like a loser or the odd man out. New Year's Eve seemed designed for that.

Kait was surprised when Jessica Hartley called her herself to convince her to join them. She worked in the art department at a rival magazine and was a talented artist. Her husband ran a hedge fund on Wall

Street. They weren't close friends, but the Hartleys invited her to their New Year's Eve party every year. And she had gone many times.

"Come on, Kait. It's a tradition, you can't skip it this year." But that was precisely what she wanted to do. A night in bed in her pajamas watching television and eating takeout sounded more appealing than getting dressed up and risking life and limb on icy streets in bad weather. But Jessica was persuasive, and Kait was annoyed at herself when she ran out of excuses to decline and finally accepted. She was even more so when it took nearly an hour for a car to come to pick her up, while she waited in the lobby, wishing she hadn't accepted. The car finally arrived and took her downtown to the Hartleys' West Village apartment. Like her, they had grown children, both of theirs were in college, and Jessica had said they were home for Christmas break and had plans of their own that night. She complained that they hardly saw them while they were in town. They were always out with friends.

Jessica and Sam were delighted to see Kait when she got there, and welcomed her warmly. There was a group of people standing around the fireplace, trying to get warm. And as they did every year, the women were wearing long gowns or dressy cocktail dresses, and the men had worn black-tie. It was the one night of the year when all the Hartleys' friends agreed to dress up. Kait had worn an old black velvet skirt with a white satin blouse, and she tried to get into the mood as she accepted a glass of champagne from Sam, and stood near the fireplace with the others. It was the coldest night so far that winter, breaking some kind of record for miserable weather, which made Kait long for her bed again.

Although she only saw them once a year, she recognized nearly everyone there that night, but there was one unfamiliar face in the crowd. His name was Zack Winter, and Sam said they had been college roommates. He was a TV producer from L.A., Jessica whispered, and she told Kait that he produced several award-winning series, and coincidentally was single, and had just gotten divorced. She realized then why they had insisted that she join them, since she was the only single woman in the room, and she was being offered as some kind of blind date for the night, which made the evening seem even more arduous before it began. He was wearing a dinner jacket with a black T-shirt, jeans, and black suede loafers, and he was very L.A. The only thing missing, Kait thought to herself, was a gold chain around his neck. And he looked like he hadn't shaved in a week, which made him appear more unkempt than trendy at his age. Kait didn't bother trying to make conversation with him since she had noticed on the seating chart that they would be next to each other at dinner. She wasn't looking forward to it, no matter how successful his shows were.

She would have been more impressed if he'd worn a pressed white shirt, the bottom half of his suit, and shaved. He was about the same age as Kait.

But by the time they sat down to dinner an hour later, everyone had relaxed. The food they served was always delicious, and people were anticipating a good dinner and a pleasant evening, with a congenial group of people.

"I used to read your column. I'm an avid 'Tell Kait' fan," Zack told her pleasantly after they sat down. "I tried to save my marriage with it, but I think my ex-wife was a little beyond your scope. We're having a custody battle over the dog. I still read your blog and follow you on Twitter," he said, as a waiter from the Hartleys' caterer set down cold crab in front of them, and Kait wasn't sure if she should be sympathetic or laugh. But he seemed good humored, and she decided to be honest with him, no matter how unkempt he looked. He was like a stereotype of an L.A. producer, or what she imagined one would look like.

He asked her what her favorite shows were and she admitted to being a **Downton Abbey** addict, and he smiled. "Whenever I have a bad day, I watch two of my favorite episodes, from the last two seasons, and the world feels like a better place again," he said. The woman on his other side overheard them, asked which show it was, and admitted to being hooked too, and then went into rhapsodies about one of his shows, a modern-day family saga set in Australia, and Zack seemed pleased. And the man seated across from them started talking about the police drama he had been devoted to for the last three years. Within five minutes, half the table was talking about which series they liked best, and Kait listened to them, amused, as Zack leaned toward her and laughed too.

"It's a national frenzy," he said to her. "You just hope you come up with the right show at the right time, there's always an element of luck involved in a big show." He was modest about his success, and an avalanche of comments and heated discussions had started at the table about their favorite shows, several of which were Zack's. Kait had seen two of them but didn't watch them regularly. "We have three hit shows on the air at the moment, and we're starting a new one in January about a Chinese family in Hong Kong. I'm not sure it's your cup of tea, though, it's edgier than the others, with a fair amount of violence in it," he said to Kait.

"You're right, that's not my thing," she agreed. "I love my nice, cozy family show. I've watched a couple of other series, and they always stress me out more than when I started watching. I enjoyed seeing two of yours, though."

He laughed. "Some people like violence and high stress. It's like shock therapy, it distracts them from real life."

"Real life is distracting and shocking enough. I don't need more on TV." They chatted more about

his next show, and what shooting on location in
China was like, which he said had been difficult.
He was knowledgeable about his subject and well
traveled. She found him personable and intelligent
to talk to, despite his somewhat shaggy appearance,
which would have gone over better in L.A. than at
the Hartleys' New Year's Eve party. There was nothing trendy or avant-garde about them, and Zack
stuck out like a sore thumb, but he was so likable
that no one cared. And for most of the guests, his
success balanced out his trendy L.A. look. And after
a while Kait forgot about it too. They talked about
their kids then, their jobs, L.A. vs. New York. He
had grown up in New York and had started out producing Broadway shows, and had gone to London
to work in TV and then L.A., and had done well
at it. He was one of the most important producers
in television, but he seemed quiet and unassuming.
And Sam startled her over dessert when he spoke
directly to Kait, loud enough for Zack to hear him.

"You should write a TV show, Kait. You could
base it on your family."

"Any drug lords in your family, or famous crimi-
nals?" Zack teased her and she laughed and shook
her head.

"Hardly. I think Sam is referring to my grandmother, who was a remarkable woman. The family
lost everything in the Crash of '29, and my grandfather committed suicide. She moved to a walk-up
apartment on the Lower East Side with four chil-

dren under five and no money, and she had never worked in her life. She started baking cookies, and then cakes, and sold them to restaurants, and kept them all alive, and provided for them. Fast-forward the film, and she sold the business to General Foods years later. Mrs. Whittier's Cakes, and the cookies were abbreviated to 4 Kids. You've probably eaten them."

"Are you kidding? They were the mainstay of my diet all through my childhood, and still are. That was your grandmother?" He looked vastly impressed. "She must have been quite a woman," he said admiringly, and was suddenly even more interested in Kait. He had enjoyed talking to her all through dinner, and liked her looks and understated elegance.

"She was," Kait said. "I grew up with her. But that's another story. My mother disappeared when I was a year old, and my father died a year later, so I grew up with my grandmother. We had a great time together, and she taught me all I know about life."

"I smelled a strong matriarch there somewhere when I read your column. I never made the connection, though, between Kait Whittier and Mrs. Whittier's Cakes. She must have made a fortune when she sold it," and then he looked suddenly embarrassed. "I'm sorry, that was rude. But I love stories like that, of people who take life by the throat and refuse to be defeated, especially women, and in those days, that was a major accomplishment."

"She believed that you can do anything you want to, or have to do. She was the bravest woman I've ever known. I always tell myself I'll write a book about her, but I haven't yet."

"What about a bible for a TV show instead?" He threw it out as a random idea off the top of his head, referring to the synopsis used to tell the basic story of a TV show. She knew what he meant. "Not necessarily about her cookies and cakes, but a woman like her, who has lost everything and doesn't just survive, but creates a whole new life. Stories like that inspire people. It's why you love the show you watch. People need role models and inspiration. And it's even more impressive when you think she did it in the early thirties when women like her didn't even have jobs or know how to work. There were a few women scientists then, and in the arts, but no businesswomen, especially from what I have to assume was a very elitist world. Weren't the Whittiers related to the Vanderbilts and the Astors?"

"Cousins," she confirmed. "I'm not sure they spoke to my grandmother once she started baking. 'Commerce' was very poorly viewed then, and wasn't considered an option for women, or even for most men in her world."

"That's what I mean, and what I love about it," Zack said, his eyes alight with interest, and Kait smiled, thinking of her grandmother. She had been a small, elegant, dignified, erect woman who was every bit a grande dame for most of her life, and wore beautiful hats when she went to her office. She stopped doing the baking herself after the first few years, although she created the recipes or found them in old European cookbooks.

It was five minutes to midnight by then and the time had flown, talking to each other. Sam began the countdown as they left the table and wandered back to the living room.

"Happy New Year!" Sam shouted, and pulled his wife into his arms to give her a kiss to start the new year. The other guests did the same with their partners, and Zack looked at Kait sympathetically. It was an awkward position for them to be in, chatting with a stranger at midnight on New Year's Eve, while everyone else embraced.

"I'd kiss you, but you might slap me," he said playfully. And he didn't look as though he wanted to. But he had enjoyed talking to her. "Happy New Year, Kait," he said softly. "I hope you have someone more exciting to spend it with next year," he said ruefully, and she laughed.

"This was exciting enough. Happy New Year, Zack," she said as he took out his wallet, extracted a business card, and handed it to her.

"I know this is incredibly rude at a dinner party. But if you ever decide to write something for dramatic purposes about your grandmother, or a woman like her, give me a call. We can always use stories like that." He sounded as though he meant it, and she slipped his card into her bag.

"I don't think I could write a screenplay. At least I never have. It's not something I'm familiar with."

"You don't have to. All you have to write is the bible. The producer would find a screenwriter for you and you could work together. You'd just have to write the overview, and some ideas for thirteen episodes if you sell it to a major network, and anywhere from six to twenty on cable. They make their own rules. And then pray they come back for more. I hope you do write something, Kait. You know enough about people, and women, from the column you write, to come up with some great ideas and story lines. I love what you have to say, because it's sensible and smart, real and direct. There's nothing phony about it. You write things anyone can relate to, even a man. I learned some things about women reading your column." She could tell that he was serious, and she was touched.

"So, have you two come up with a hit TV series?" Sam asked, when he walked up to them. He had noticed that they had talked animatedly all through dinner, and he wondered if Zack was going to ask her out. Sam knew Kait wasn't his usual profile. Zack liked younger women, mostly actresses, and sometimes the stars in his shows. But Kait was beautiful and intelligent, and would have made more sense than the starlets he normally went out with. But Sam couldn't tell if there was chemistry between them or not. Kait was too polite to show it, and Zack kept his game to himself and always had, even in college. He was one of the few guys Sam knew who didn't brag about his conquests. He could have, but it wasn't his style.

"We're working on it," was all Zack said to his former roommate, as Kait drifted away to talk to her hostess and the other guests. "Interesting woman. Fascinating background," Zack commented and then wandered away himself.

Zack came to say good night to Kait just before he left. He was flying back to L.A. the next day on an early flight. He reminded Kait to call him if she had any ideas, but she doubted she would. She couldn't imagine what she could think of for a bible for a TV show. And as she had said to Zack, she wanted to save her grandmother's story to write her biography one day. She would be an inspiration even to modern women, and had been decades ahead of her time, by sheer necessity, if nothing else.

Kait left a little while later, and was glad she had come. She had enjoyed meeting Zack and talking to him. She was sure they would never meet again, there was no crossover between their worlds, but it was fun to meet new and different people, and suddenly his Hollywood aura was of no importance. Clearly he had talent, or a good eye for what worked, with so many successes on TV. His many victories were proof of that.

"What did you think of Zack?" Jessica asked her

once Kait had her coat on and was about to leave. She looked at Kait meaningfully, who ignored the innuendo and answered her sincerely.

"He's terrific to talk to, and was a great dinner partner. Thank you for seating him next to me," she said politely, but meant it.

"That's it? You didn't find him fatally sexy?"

"I'm sure I'm not his type," she said simply, and he wasn't hers either. He was pure L.A., part of the entertainment world, and could have any star he wanted at his feet, Kait was sure. And he seemed like the kind of man who'd prefer very young, sexy women, since he had easy access to them.

"Well, I'm glad you liked him," Jessica said as the other guests began to leave and Kait slipped out. She could see there was a long wait for an Uber, so she asked the doorman to get her a cab. She stood outside for a few minutes, waiting for him to return with one, and by the time he got back five minutes later, her face, ears, and hands were numb. She slid in gratefully and gave the driver her address up-town. He was relieved to find her sober and almost hadn't stopped for her on his way back to the ga-rage. New Year's Eve was a hard night to drive.

"Happy New Year," the driver said in a heavy Indian accent. He was wearing a bright turquoise turban, and Kait smiled when she saw it. It had been a nice evening, much more so than she had expected, thanks to Zack, and she was flattered that he thought she should write a bible for a show. And it pleased her that he liked her blog and followed her on Twitter. She put a lot of time and thought into what she wrote. She loved helping people, but had no instant inspiration for a TV series. She didn't think she had anything more in her than "Tell Kait." She didn't want to do anything more exotic than that, even if she enjoyed what she watched on TV herself.

And as the perfect end to the evening, she put on a DVD from the last season of **Downton Abbey** and watched the final Christmas special on her laptop when she got home. She knew she'd be up late if she did, but she could sleep in the next morning. And she was going back to the magazine the day after. Her Christmas break was over. It had been a nice one, and she'd caught up on her work. She was starting the new year fresh, with a clean slate. It was a good feeling, and as the theme music of the show came on, she sank back onto the mountain of pillows on her bed and settled in to enjoy it. Despite her reservations, it had been a very nice New Year's Eve after all, and she was glad she'd gone. The episode she'd chosen of **Downton Abbey** was one of her favorites. And before it was over, she had fallen fast asleep as the new year began.

Chapter 4

When Kait woke up on New Year's morning, the DVD had finished, her laptop battery had run out, and the lights were on. She got up to plug her computer into the charger, looked out her window, and saw that it was snowing heavily outside, and almost everything had come to a standstill. A few buses were running, and there were one or two cabs moving slowly. The snow was deep.

She went to make herself a cup of coffee, and sat down at the new computer that had been a gift from Stephanie. She still wasn't totally at ease with it, it had more options and fancy frills than her old one, but she loved it. She wondered what to do for the rest of the day. She was caught up on the letters she had to answer for the column, her tweets, and her blog, and she didn't want to go out in heavy weather. She thought of Tommy and his family in the Bahamas, and Stephanie in Montana with Frank. She wondered where Candace was and what she was doing, and she sat staring at the blank screen for a while, and suddenly had an idea. It was just a sliver of a thought in her mind, but she had a sudden urge to play with it and see where it went. She had nothing else to do that day.

The story begins in 1940, before America has entered World War II. Lochlan Wilder is roughly forty years old and has a fascination with old planes and collects them. He can fly anything with wings, and has spent every penny he can lay hands on to build his collection. He is passionate about flying and anything to do with aviation. He is a mechanic and a pilot, has restored many planes, and his wife, Anne, is supportive of him, although all the money he could find has gone into his planes. He inherited some money and made some, and spent it all on his collection. Their house is mortgaged to the hilt. Only Anne understands how much flying means to him. They have four children in their teens. Two of them have caught the flying bug from him. He's a handsome, sexy, wild man, and Anne is deeply in love with him. He has taught Anne to fly too, and she's a good pilot, although she doesn't love it as he does.

Anne frequently defends him to her stern

mother, Hannabel, who thinks him an irresponsible fool, and says so every chance she gets. She doesn't understand him and doesn't want to.

Their oldest son, Bill, is eighteen. His father taught him to fly and to work on the engines. Bill is solid, serious, and has his pilot's license.

But it is Maggie, their second child, who shares her father's skill for flying and love of old airplanes. She is seventeen and doesn't have her license yet, but he has taken her up with him, and she can fly everything they've got. She has her father's gift and wishes she could be a pilot one day. He has taught her to do aerobatics, and she's something of a daredevil. She has more guts than her brother in the cockpit. Bill is steady and sure. Maggie is more fiery than her brothers and more like her father.

Anne and Loch have two younger children. Greg has no interest in flying, and is constantly up to mischief in some form at fifteen. He has big dreams, none of which include planes. And their youngest child is Chrystal, a striking beauty who is boy crazy at fourteen, and also could care less about planes.

Kait was writing furiously as the story unfolded in her head.

As the war worsens in Europe, shortly after the story begins, Loch tells Anne that he wants to go to England and volunteer to fly with the Royal Air Force. They are taking American volunteers, and he knows a few other pilots who have gone. He has already made the decision and sold two of his planes to leave Anne enough money to manage without him. He feels compelled to go, and Anne knows him too well to try and stop him. Anne agrees to let him go out of love and respect for him. They tell the kids. Bill and Maggie think he's a hero. Hannabel is horrified at how he can leave his wife and family.

Loch leaves for England. Anne is left to manage without him and deal with her kids. She is a strong, quiet woman who believes in her husband, although she is afraid for him. There is a touching scene between them before he leaves. And a flood of criticism from Anne's mother once he's gone.

Loch has left them enough money to get by, although it will be tight. Anne considers getting a job for extra money, and then has an idea. They're going to put Loch's planes to good use. They can fly people short distances, like a flying taxi service. Both she and Bill are capable of it. They can also give flying lessons. Bill is determined to help his mother. She calls their business Wilder Aircraft and they put up a sign offering to charter their planes and give lessons. Maggie wants to help too but doesn't have her license yet. Hannabel, Anne's mother, is constantly furious at Loch running off to England and leaving his family. And she thinks Anne's plan to make some extra money is a crazy idea. She says Anne should sell all Loch's planes while he's gone, to give them more money to live on, and it would serve him right for going off and leaving them.

Bill tries to help his mother control his younger brother, which fifteen-year-old Greg resents. He is constantly in some form of minor trouble or other, especially in school. And Chrystal is equally hard to manage, always sneaking off to go out with some boy. Bill tries to help, but the younger two are difficult. And at seventeen all Maggie cares about are planes. She can't wait to get her license.

The business takes off slowly, but starts to work. A few people sign up for lessons. Some local businessmen charter their planes to get to meetings in other towns. And Anne manages the business well, probably better than her husband would have. She's far more practical than Loch. They're making enough money to add to what Loch left them, and it helps Anne provide for them. But when there are no lessons or charters, things are still tight. Her mother tells her again to sell some or all of Loch's planes, but she won't out of respect for him. It would break his heart. Hannabel doesn't care, and thinks he deserves it for running off. Some of the planes are very special and rare, and Maggie can fly them all. She goes up with her brother as she used to with her father. She lives to fly, just as her father does.

While Loch is flying for the British in the RAF, Anne is handling everything at home efficiently and bravely. Her little business gets solid over the next year, and does well. And then Pearl Harbor hits. The first peacetime draft in history had begun a year before, in September 1940, but Bill had not been drafted.

After Pearl Harbor, Loch comes home from England to enlist with the American flying forces. Loch spends some time with each of his children before he has to leave again, and he urges younger son Greg to behave. There is a tender parting with Anne, again, and he is proud of how she has run the business and saved his planes. Maggie is eighteen now and gets her pilot's license. Bill is drafted, and Maggie helps her mother give lessons and fly charters. Both Loch and Bill leave for war. Bill goes to flight training

in the military. Anne and Maggie run the business, while Greg and Chrystal continue to misbehave, with no male figure now to help control them. Chrystal looks older than her fifteen years and is trouble. Men are drawn to her like moths to flame and she encourages them shamelessly, and Anne tries to stop her with no success.

As she wrote the words, Kait remembered learning about the WASPs in the past, and looked them up on the internet, and was excited about what she found. She read avidly, fascinated by the history of a courageous group of women who had received little acknowledgment for their heroic acts in World War II. The Women Airforce Service Pilots program was created in 1942, after Pearl Harbor, to enlist the help of female civilian pilots. After training in Texas, they towed drones and targets with live ammunition for gunnery practice, tested and repaired aircraft, served as instructors, transported cargo to embarkation points, and ferried and delivered planes to other locations. They often flew at night and were noncombat pilots, but flew dangerous missions. They remained civilians and were used for purposes that would free up male military pilots for combat.

They flew every type of aircraft from PT-17 and AT-6 trainers, the fastest attack planes like the A-24 and A-26, and medium and heavy bombers, which were B-25s and B-17s. They were never officially part of the military, received no benefits or honors, flew when they were called upon to do so, and were paid $250 a month.

Once the WASP program was established, twenty-five thousand female pilots applied to help the war effort, and 1,830 were accepted. Other than their flying credentials, they had to be twenty-one years of age or older, and five feet and one-half inch tall. They flew their missions heroically. Thirty-eight WASP pilots were killed in the course of their assignments. And in December 1944, after nearly three years of flying, the WASPs were no longer needed and the program was disbanded. The records of their missions were sealed for more than thirty years. In 1977, Congress voted to make the surviving WASPs eligible for veterans' benefits, although they had been civilians and never enlisted in the armed forces. And at last in 2010, sixty-eight years after they had served their country, the remaining WASPs, fewer than three hundred by then, were awarded a Congressional Gold Medal in an official ceremony in Washington, D.C. It was the first time that most people had heard of the civilian women pilots who had courageously served their country in World War II.

Kait nearly stood up and cheered as she read about them with tears in her eyes, and wove what she had learned about the WASPs on the internet into her story. Anne Wilder would have been just the kind of woman to sign up for the WASPs. It was perfect. Even the story of their uniforms was terrific. The uniforms they wore initially were used airplane mechanics' overalls, the smallest size being a men's forty-four long. They were later required to buy tan slacks and white blouses for dress occasions. In 1943, a year after they started, the director of the WASPs, Jacqueline Cochran, had Bergdorf Goodman design a wool uniform in "air force blue." The new outfit was approved by two air force generals and it became the official WASP uniform. It had a skirt, a belted jacket, a white shirt, a black tie, the air force emblem, and the WASP emblem on the jacket, with a beret and black purse.

At the same time, they were issued new flying uniforms too, in the same air force Santiago blue with an Eisenhower jacket, slacks, a blue cotton shirt, and a black tie, with a baseball-style cap.

Cochran had the clothes fitted by Neiman Marcus, and the WASPs were very proud of their new uniforms. They'd come a long way from used overalls in men's sizes!

Kait went on writing the story for the bible then.

Anne is desperately worried about her husband and son in the war. And her mother is quieter than before, concerned about her grandson. She is less critical of Loch now too. But generally, Hannabel is tough as nails.

Anne and Maggie are running the business, and are doing well. Loch and Bill are flying missions in the war as fighter pilots.

A representative from the military comes to talk to Anne, and asks if she will sign up for the WASPs to ferry planes for the military across the Atlantic, without troops, which is a potentially dangerous mission. The WASP representative explains they are using women for these flights so they can spare the men for combat. She wouldn't be doing it all the time, just when they needed her. The WASPs are civilian volunteers, and paid a small fee. She agrees to sign up as her contribution to the war effort. She will do it when she is needed, and still be able to run her business.

When Anne tells her mother, Hannabel begs her daughter not to do it, and insists that she could be shot down by Germans flying over the Atlantic, but she's a good, steady pilot. Anne is determined, and finally Hannabel agrees to move in, to help her and stay with the kids when she is on missions. We see a softer side of Hannabel, who is terrified for her only daughter. Maggie wants to volunteer too, but she isn't old enough, and Anne needs her at home.

We see Anne flying ferrying missions with the WASPs and the other female pilots she meets. Anne and Maggie continue to run

the business, which makes just enough to give them much needed additional income. Anne has some close calls while ferrying, but she is never injured or shot down.

Before the war ends, Loch's plane is shot down and he is killed. And not long after, just before the war ends, their son Bill is shot down and killed too. Anne receives her last letter from Loch, telling her how much he loves her, after he is dead. Hannabel is now sympathetic and feels sorry for her daughter.

As Kait wrote the words, tears poured down her cheeks. She stopped for a minute to catch her breath and then wrote on, as the story flew out of her.

As the war ends, Maggie is twenty-two and a terrific pilot. Anne is forty-four, Greg twenty, and Chrystal nineteen, and both of the younger ones are still trouble. The family is devastated over the loss of Loch and Bill. They have two flags and two gold stars in their window.

Anne tries to figure out what to do now to support the family. Does she sell Loch's planes? Get a peacetime job? Continue trying to make ends meet with flying lessons and small charters? She comes up with an idea to use their larger, older planes to start an air freight business, and she and Maggie

will fly the planes. They need Greg and Chrystal to help in the office. And Hannabel stuns them all by telling them to put her to work too. She's on board now, and wants to do everything she can to help. She apologizes to Anne for her criticism of Loch, and says she wanted her to have an easier life, but realizes now that he was a good man and how much they loved each other.

Anne calls the freight business Wilder Express. They get a few small jobs at first and then bigger ones, and charge handsomely for them. Every job is a victory for them, as they carry cargo and are doing well. Hannabel is ornery with clients, but funny, and she works hard, and has her granddaughter Maggie give her flying lessons. Hannabel is feisty, ballsy, and tough, but also wonderful and speaks her mind. Anne is tireless and brave, and the business is holding its own. They're able to buy larger surplus planes now to carry larger cargo. They fly in tough weather conditions. Anne and Maggie have some close calls in bad weather but always make it through. They hire a terrific young male pilot, Johnny West, when they can afford to. He's a great guy, helps them immensely, and he and Maggie fall in love. (The younger two, Chrystal and Greg, continue to have misadventures.)

There is resistance from other men in aviation to two women running an air freight business that is becoming noticeably successful. They deal with threats of sabotage to one of their planes, and Johnny, their young male pilot, is beaten up. The competition is nasty and rough, and tries to drive them out of the business, but Anne hangs on. And Hannabel is bold about confronting anyone she has to, and fearless, and maybe pulls a gun on one of them, some night when they are threatened. Hannabel, Anne, and Maggie are running the business, making money at it, and become profitable. They sell some of Loch's planes to buy better ones. It's a bittersweet moment for Anne when she parts with some of Loch's beloved planes to help the business. Hannabel tells Anne one night that Loch would be proud of her, and Anne tells Hannabel he would be proud of her too.

They trade some of Loch's old planes for more war surplus aircraft they can use, but save one or two of his very favorites. Anne constantly has to deal with Greg and Chrystal's bad behavior while running the business. And Maggie and their young male pilot, Johnny West, have a strong romance.

As time goes on, they have a very, very successful business, which becomes a real money maker. Five years after the war, in 1950, it is a booming business they fought hard to build, and they still deal with constant prejudices against women. They hire more pilots, and maybe Hannabel flies a mission for them one night when they're shorthanded. She's a decent pilot now, and a feisty old woman we come to love. She has mellowed a little.

We see them running the business through the 1950s, fighting for women's rights and succeeding in a man's world. In time, it is one of the most successful air cargo companies in the country, hard earned and hard won. They hire more male pilots, some of whom they have to fire when they give them a hard time. Maybe they hire another female pilot. They hire a war-hero pilot who knew Loch and applies for the job. He and Anne spar, but respect each other. They have some battles and eventually fall in love. He is the first man in Anne's life since Loch died. It's 1953 to 1955. Their relationship is heated and passionate from the first. The business is run by three generations of strong women: Hannabel, Anne, and Maggie.

Kait sat at her computer, thinking about what she'd written, and was stunned by the story that had suddenly come to her. It was midnight, and she had been writing for fifteen hours. She called it **The Wilder Women.** It was the story of a family of women who had built an exciting business in a male-dominated industry and world.

After she read it, Kait pulled out Zack Winter's card and sent him an email to tell him she'd written a story and wondered if he'd like to see it. He responded two hours later that he would, and told her to email it to him. She hit the send button, and then wondered what she had done. What if he hated it? But even if he did, she knew she loved it. **The Wilder Women** had come to life for her. Kait was overwhelmed by pride and panic, and had no idea what Zack would think.

The next day when she woke up, the snowstorm had turned into a blizzard and her office was closed. She read the story again and was excited by it, and she sat looking out at the snow and wondered what would happen next. But one thing she did know, she hadn't had as much fun in years as she did writing about the Wilder women the day before. She dedicated it to her grandmother, and she knew in every fiber of her being that her grandmother would have been proud of her too.

Chapter 5

The blizzard took two days to clear, and when everyone went back to work, Kait said nothing about what she'd written, not even to Carmen. She was waiting to hear from Zack. And there was no word from him for three weeks. By then she had gone through various phases of embarrassment, certain that her story was terrible and he'd hated it but was too polite to tell her. So much so that he didn't even respond to her. She was trying to forget she wrote it when he called her three weeks later.

"I think my spending New Year's Eve with Sam and Jessie turned out to be fortuitous for both of us," was the first thing he said to her, and she didn't dare ask him what he meant, or if he liked what she had sent him. She could barely focus on his words and braced herself for the worst. "I'm sorry I didn't get back to you sooner, but I've been busy," he said, sounding rushed. "I'm coming to New York tomorrow for a meeting. Do you have time for a drink?" She assumed he wanted to tell her in person what was wrong with her story, and why it wasn't suitable for a bible for a show.

"Of course," she said, still embarrassed to have bothered him with it. She'd been so excited when she wrote it, but had had time to cool off and doubt herself in the three weeks since she'd sent it. She was mortified, and it must have looked like an amateurish attempt to him. She thought that now, after reading it over several times. "Where should I meet you?" He suggested the Plaza and said he was staying there.

"Six o'clock?" he offered.

"That's great."

He told her which bar to meet him at, and she sat at her desk at the magazine, staring at the computer, bracing herself for bad news the next day, and heavy criticism, despite his gracious opening when he called her. She couldn't imagine him liking the story she'd written. She was a nervous wreck that evening in anticipation of the meeting. It took three episodes of **Downton Abbey** to calm her down late at night. But all she could think of was her own story now, trying to guess what he was going to say about it. Surely nothing good.

She wore a serious black suit to work the next day, and looked like she was going to a funeral. She'd worn black stockings and high heels with it, and Carmen stared at her in surprise when she stopped in to see her that afternoon.

"Did someone die?" she said half seriously. Kait

was pale and seemed distracted, and there was terror in her eyes.

"I have a meeting after work."

"It can't be a happy one," judging by the strained expression on Kait's face.

"Probably not." Kait didn't elaborate, and then Carmen left, without prying into the nature of the meeting.

She took a cab to the Plaza after work, arrived ten minutes early, was seated at a table, and felt panicked when she saw Zack walk in. She was surprised to see him in a suit, with a pale blue shirt and a tie. There was no trace of his trendy style on New Year's Eve. He looked like any New York businessman, which set the tone for their meeting as they shook hands.

"Is everything all right? You look so serious," he said, as he sat down across from her at the table in the Oak Bar.

"So do you." She smiled at him, and he could see that she was scared. They ordered drinks before he said anything, he asked for scotch, and she for a glass of wine she was too nervous to drink. Nothing in years had frightened her as much as this meeting. She was convinced he was about to tell her how bad her story was, and had probably decided to meet with her in person out of respect for his old friend Sam.

"Did you hear what I said when I called you yesterday?" he asked her with a smirk. "I told you that our meeting was **fortuitous.** I get the feeling that you missed that word, and didn't hear me."

She looked like she was about to cry. "I thought you were just being polite," she said honestly, and he saw that her hand was shaking when she took a sip of her wine.

"I'm not that polite in business." He smiled at her, and wanted to put her out of her misery quickly. "You wrote a terrific story, Kait. It would make a fantastic bible for a series. The female characters in it are wonderful, and you could go on for years with the subplots after the backstory. I didn't want to get back to you until I had something concrete to tell you, and I think I do. I took two meetings last week about it, and another one two days ago. I didn't want to get your hopes up, but I think you may be my new good luck charm. I went to the cable networks I thought were right for it, and one of the major networks that I wanted can really use a show like this. They just had a series fall apart on them, and they canceled it. They have a gaping hole in their programming for next fall. They want to go with this, Kait. **The Wilder Women** is just what they need. It's still a little rough around the edges and it needs some work, but the right screenwriter can do it with you. They want us to develop it and get them a script as soon as we can." He beamed at her as he spoke, and Kait looked like she was in shock.

"But I can't write a script, I don't know how," she

said as she set her glass down and stared at him, trying to understand what she'd just heard. It was the last thing she had expected to hear from him.

"I don't expect you to write the script. We'll get a screenwriter for that. I already talked to the one I want. She's finishing a project right now, which is lucky too. She's young, but she's very good. You have to trust me on this, I've worked with her before. I sent your story to her, and she wants to do it. She's already written two successful shows. The network canceled one of them because they had trouble with the star, not because of the writing. I think she could do a fantastic job for you on this." He was all business as he talked to Kait and had thought of everything. He was brilliant at this.

"Okay, wait a minute. I'm trying to understand. A cable network wants the story, and you already have a screenwriter to write the script?"

"Basically, yes. We have to see what the writer gives us, and if we're happy with it, and if the network is. If we like it, we lock her in. If we get the right screenwriter, they want thirteen shows initially and nine more after that, if we get lucky." He was used to success, but Kait wasn't, this was all new to her.

"Oh my God," Kait said and closed her eyes, and then opened them and looked at him. "Are you telling me that they're going to turn my story into a series, just like that?"

"We have a few hurdles to get over first. We all

have to like the script. We've got to find the right actors for it—that's crucial, preferably some really strong female leads who can carry the show, and a director who's good with women's shows. The stars have to line up just right. If we can't get the script to work, or the right cast, we won't get the show on the air by October, which is what they need. But if everything falls into place, you could have a series on the air by next fall. And I have some ideas for a director, and someone I want to approach to play Anne Wilder. It's a long shot, but I'm going to give it all I've got. She's never done a series before, only feature films, but she'd be perfect for this if she falls in love with it. The screenwriter I have in mind can start working on it in two weeks. She wants to meet with you first."

Kait was smiling by the time he finished. It all sounded tentative and precarious, but it was actually possible that the story she'd written on New Year's Day might wind up on the air.

"We'd have to start shooting by the first of July, which doesn't give us much time. I have a lot of work to do. And you need an agent to get the contract and money side of it set up. I can recommend several to you."

She didn't want to tell him she would have done it for free, just for the thrill of it, but obviously she wanted to be paid, and had no idea what to expect financially. More than anything, she was ecstatic. The details could fall into place later. She wanted to savor the initial excitement of what was happening to her. And he was touched by how moved she was and how much it meant to her. He could see it in her eyes and the stunned look on her face.

They spent two more hours talking, and he raved about the screenwriter again. Kait trusted his judgment. He knew everything about the business and she knew nothing. He wouldn't tell her about the actors he had in mind. He wanted to do some research first about their availability before he got her excited for nothing, and he didn't want to throw out names who might not be a real possibility.

Kait thanked him profusely when they left each other in the lobby. He was going to a dinner meeting, and she wanted to go home and just enjoy the moment or run around her living room screaming. Nothing this exciting had ever happened to her before. And this was only the beginning. It was hard to imagine what would come next. He had explained it all to her, but she had forgotten half of it by the time she got home. She was feeling dazed. And she didn't want to tell her children yet, until she was sure everything was moving forward. Maybe after they knew the screenwriter would work out, and she had signed a contract. Maybe then it would feel real. For now, it felt like a dream she was having, and she was afraid she would wake up. She had forgotten to ask Zack how much time would be involved, and if she would still be able to write her column. She would have to. She wasn't going to give up her job of nineteen years for a pipe dream that might fall apart.

When she got to her apartment and took off her coat, she sat down on the couch and tried to imagine what all of it meant. She felt like she was traveling in a country where she didn't speak the language and needed everything interpreted for her. She was suddenly a stranger in her own life. But whatever came next, she knew it was going to be one of the most exciting things that had ever happened to her. She could hardly wait for it to start. She lay in bed for hours that night, wide awake, running everything Zack had said through her mind. What she could remember of it. There was so much to think about. She didn't even watch **Downton Abbey** to calm her down. She laughed to herself, thinking that soon she would have her own series. How amazing was that!

Zack called her the next morning to go over some of the details again. He wanted her to come to L.A. to meet with the screenwriter in two weeks, and spend some time going over everything with her. And he wanted to introduce her to two agents while she was in L.A. and said she would need one quickly for her contract. And by then he thought he'd have a better handle on what actors were available, and they could work on the casting together. That was an important part of the package for the network, and so was the director. He said he was planning to go top-of-the-line, which sounded great to her. It was all thrilling. She thanked him seriously again before they hung up and she left for work. They had agreed that she should take two weeks off to go to L.A. if possible, and she had to ask the magazine for the time. It shouldn't be a problem, but she had to let them know. They were always flexible about her days in the office, and she could take her work with her, and write her column and blogs on the plane or in L.A.

Her mind was racing when she got to work and filled out the forms to take two weeks off. She wasn't going to tell anyone where she was going or what she was planning to do. She didn't want to jinx it, and nothing was definite yet, nothing was formalized or signed, only a verbal agreement the network had made with Zack. But he had a golden reputation for delivering first-rate shows. She knew it was an insecure business where deals fell apart all the time and shows got canceled at the drop of a hat. She didn't want to make a fool of herself by telling people about it if that were to happen, at least until the deal was signed. And she didn't even have an agent yet. She was sure that it would all feel real to her after the contracts were in place, but that was still down the line.

"How did your meeting go yesterday?" Carmen asked when she stuck her head in Kait's office on her way to an editorial meeting. She was curious after seeing Kait dressed up the day before, and she liked knowing what was going on.

"It was fine," Kait said vaguely, feeling like a liar, but they weren't close enough for Kait to share something as confidential and important as that. She thought her children should know first, and it was too soon to tell them. It wasn't a done deal yet.

"You look a lot happier today," Carmen commented, and Kait smiled.

"I am." She didn't mention the time she was taking off to go to L.A. She couldn't without explaining why, and she hadn't come up with a good excuse yet.

"Do you want me to grab some salads on the way back?" Carmen volunteered.

"I'd love it. Mediterranean, thanks." They were good pals at work, but not best friends.

"See you at one," Carmen promised. Kait filled out the rest of the vacation form after she left, and had her assistant drop it off at HR. It was an odd feeling, wondering if she'd be working there at the end of the year, or too busy with the show. She tried not to think about it as she opened a thick file of letters on her desk, with the most recent ones she had to answer for the column. It rapidly brought her back to earth. She had a job to do here, the same one she had done for nineteen years, writing an agony column for **Woman's Life**. Hollywood could wait. It would have to for now. This was her bread and butter, and she wasn't going to forget that. But she was excited to see her story come alive, with real actors portraying the characters she had created. She wondered who they'd get, and then forced her mind back to the mundane realities of what she had to do that day.

She and Carmen had a nice time, gossiping and laughing over their salads at her desk.

"You keep getting this faraway look in your eye," Carmen accused her halfway through lunch. "What's up?" She wondered if Kait had met a man.

"I'm just tired. I didn't sleep much last night."

"You need a vacation," her friend said matter-of-factly.

"I'm going to London to see Candace when she gets back." And then she realized she had the perfect excuse for the trip to L.A. "And I thought I'd go see Stephanie in San Francisco in a couple of weeks, and maybe Tom on the way back."

"I mean a real vacation, like somewhere warm. I could use some of that myself," Carmen said wistfully.

"Yeah, me too," Kait said vaguely, and drifted off again, to her visions of L.A. and what was waiting for her there, or would be soon. "That's good advice," she said about the vacation. "Maybe I can talk Steph into a weekend in L.A. when I'm out there."

Carmen nodded and stood up to throw away the plastic cartons from their lunch. A weekend in L.A. sounded sensible to her, if Kait was going to California to see her daughter.

"Get some sleep tonight," Carmen admonished her. "You're already half asleep now." Kait laughed as the door closed behind her. But the best part was that she was wide awake, and the fantasy that was happening to her was real. She almost wanted to pinch herself to make sure it was.

Chapter 6

The two weeks before Kait was due to leave for California seemed to move at a snail's pace. Everything in her everyday life seemed tedious now, and she could hardly concentrate on the letters she was answering, on subjects she had dealt with a thousand times before. All she wanted now was to get to L.A. and find out what was happening with the project.

She felt guilty going to L.A. without seeing Stephanie in San Francisco, but she wouldn't have time. Zack had a dozen meetings lined up at the network to introduce her and to discuss aspects of the show and the direction they were heading with the story line. He was having her meet agents and the director he wanted, and she had to spend time with the screenwriter. That was essential, they needed to get her started as soon as possible, once Kait approved her, if they were going to stay on schedule. And Zack wanted Kait at their casting calls. He felt it was important for her to see the actors, since

all three women they would hire were the essence of
the show, and it was essential that they felt right to
Kait, so they didn't get off track from her concept,
although the network would inevitably demand
changes as they went along.

There was a lot to do in the time Kait was planning to spend there, she didn't see how they would
fit it all in. Zack called her three days before she was
due to leave. When she heard his voice, she was suddenly overwhelmed with panic again that the whole
project had been canceled. She still couldn't believe
it was going to happen. It still seemed so unreal to
her. But all the pieces of the machine were moving
forward in the complicated mechanism of putting
a show together. And Kait was well aware of how
much she had to learn about it. The contract alone,
conditions, and benefits to her over time sounded
so complex she could barely understand them,
which was why Zack said she needed an agent and
possibly even an entertainment lawyer, and he was
going to find them for her. They had to take care
of that immediately, while he dealt with the financial aspects with the cable network they were
working with, and the "front" and "back end" arrangements, which sounded like Chinese to her.

"There's someone I want you to meet," he said
after a minute. He sounded rushed and busy, as
he always did, juggling so many shows and trying to
develop new ones. He always had a thousand balls
in the air, and this was going to be a big one, and

would take a lot of work and meetings to get things started. They could have made a pilot themselves and sold it to the network later, which he had done many times. But getting the network involved right in the beginning was a much better way to go, and gave them a lot more money for production. This way, they already knew the network loved it and could produce a truly high-end show.

They were still debating whether to shoot it in California or New York. They needed a location with plenty of room for Loch Wilder's airplanes, their air freight enterprise and charter business, and a small airstrip. They would be using several stunt pilots in the cast, and a whole fleet of vintage airplanes. Zack already had scouts looking for planes and locations on both coasts. It would cost about the same to shoot in either place, so the network didn't care where they chose.

"She can see you tomorrow," Zack said cryptically, as Kait waited to hear the rest.

"Who am I meeting?"

There was a moment's pause before he answered, not for drama, but because he was signing checks for another show while he talked to her, with his assistant waiting next to him. "I called her last week and she said she'd think about it. She's never done TV before, and needed to adjust her thinking to what television is now. It's not like the old days when there was a stigma attached to doing TV. Now some of the biggest names in the business are in series. She gets that, and she just called me back. She wants to meet you to understand the character better, and make sure it's right for her."

Everything he said made sense to Kait, but she could hardly stand the suspense. He had hinted at this before.

"We want her for the part of Anne Wilder, obviously. She's not old enough for the grandmother. I think she's perfect for us, if we can grab her. She'd have to be able to do work in features during the hiatus, she's not going to give that up for us. She's already won two Oscars, and a Golden Globe. I promised her another Golden Globe for this one," he said, laughing, as Kait waited to hear who it was, but was already vastly impressed. "I worked on a film with her a long time ago. I was a lowly assistant then, and she doesn't remember me. She's an amazing woman. You'll love her, Kait. Maeve O'Hara," he said, as though mentioning some ordinary person he had met on the street.

"**Maeve O'Hara?**" Kait asked with reverence and awe. "For our show? Are you serious?"

"I'd like to be. Let's see if she is. She's not making any promises. She said she wants to meet you before she goes any further. I think you're going to love each other." In Zack's mind, Kait had some of the same qualities as Maeve, a mix of talent and humility, with her feet on the ground. "She said she can see you at four tomorrow. She suggested a deli in her neighborhood. You can share a pastrami sandwich," he said, teasing Kait. "She's a very down-to-earth person, she has two daughters who are trying to be actresses. I'm not sure they have her talent, few people do, and they're very young. If we can sign Maeve for this, we have a sure shot at a major hit show. This story, and the part of Anne, are made for her. I want you to meet her before you leave New York and come out here. If we have Maeve attached to the project, we can get anyone we want. Other actors will kill to work with her. Knock her dead, Kait. I know you will."

For an instant, Kait didn't know what to say. She was overwhelmed. "I'll try," she said, hoping not to seem starstruck or ridiculous, but she was about to meet Maeve O'Hara, one of the biggest female stars in the business, at a deli the next day. "I'm not used to this, Zack. I don't want to blow it."

"You will be used to it by the time we get going. And something tells me that you two will wind up friends. Just be yourself, and tell her about Anne Wilder. I think she'll see how right it is for her. I sent her the bible last week, that's why she called me back. That's going to be tough for her to resist, if it fits in with her plans. She's always working on something, although she said she's taking a break at the moment, for personal reasons, and not starting any new projects. But that never lasts long with talent like hers. She's a workaholic like the rest of us.

She'll be doing something again soon, and I want it to be this. I'll shoot her an email and tell her you can make it."

He told Kait the name and location of the deli, and she jotted it down. It was on West Seventy-second Street. Maeve lived at the Dakota on Central Park West, where lots of famous actors, producers, writers, and arty and intellectual people lived. It was a well-known building of enormous old apartments with views of the park. She wondered what Maeve's apartment was like and if she'd ever see it.

"Call me after the meeting," he told her, and they hung up. She had all day and night to think about it, and worry. She was way out of her comfort zone and normal life, meeting movie stars of Maeve O'Hara's stature, but everything about what she was doing now was exciting. Whatever happened, meeting her for coffee in a deli was going to be a high point in Kait's life.

Kait left work early the next day, and took the subway from work to the stop closest to where she was going. It was north of Lincoln Center. It was a cold day, but crisp and clear, and her nose was red, her eyes watering, and her hands frozen by the time she got to the deli, Fine and Schapiro, and walked in. She saw Maeve O'Hara immediately, sitting discreetly at a back table in a parka with a wool cap on. People had already recognized her but no one had bothered her. Kait approached her with her heart pounding, and Maeve smiled at her and seemed to know who she was. She was sipping a steaming cup of tea and looked just as cold as Kait.

"I should have had you to the apartment," Maeve said apologetically, "but my husband isn't well, and I try to keep traffic to a minimum for him. Our kids live with us, and that's hectic enough."

"It's fine, and I envy you that," Kait said as she sat down across from her, feeling like she was meeting an old friend. "Mine have all flown the coop," Kait volunteered.

"Where do they live?" Maeve asked with interest as she studied Kait carefully, and liked what she saw. Maeve was a few years younger, but not by much. She hadn't worn makeup, and rarely did when she wasn't working. She had worn jeans and an old pair of riding boots, and a heavy sweater under her parka.

"San Francisco, Dallas, and wherever the BBC sends my middle daughter, if there's a war on there. She's based in London."

"That must be hard on you," Maeve said sympathetically, and Kait nodded. "My oldest daughter's at Tisch at NYU and wants to be an actress. The youngest one is still trying to find herself. She dropped out of college last year as a freshman, and is doing Off Broadway, and so far she has gotten some really awful parts."

The two women exchanged a smile as Kait sipped her coffee and felt instantly at ease with her. They had their kids in common, and she could sense that despite being a star, Maeve was an involved mother.

"I keep trying to brace myself for the empty nest, but so far no one's going anywhere, thank God. They drive me crazy, and keep me grounded," Maeve said, and they both laughed. "I'm going to be lost without them, when they finally move out. I keep waiting on them hand and foot, so they don't want to leave. Food service, laundry, their friends drop by at midnight. Until Ian got sick, we had an open house. It's more complicated now."

Kait didn't want to pry and ask what her husband was sick with. She got the feeling it was serious from the look in Maeve's eyes when she said it. She knew that Maeve was married to Ian Miller, a famous actor who had become a director many years ago.

"I've read your column, by the way. I love it. I used to read it whenever Ian and I had a fight, to figure out whether to call a divorce lawyer or forgive him. I think you've kept our marriage together." She laughed and Kait grinned, pleased that she read it. "You've helped me a lot with the girls too. Contrary to common belief, nineteen and twenty-one are not easy ages. One minute they're grown women, attacking you, and the next minute they're babies and you want to send them to their room and can't. How old are yours?"

"Twenty-six to thirty-two, a son and two daughters. My son, Tom, lives in Dallas, and has become a Texan, married to a girl from Dallas. My daughter Candace is in London, and Stephanie, my youngest, works for Google in San Francisco, she's a computer geek and went to MIT. They're all different. I had them when I was barely more than a kid myself. Their father left when they were very young, and the kids and I are very close."

"I'm very close to Tamra and Thalia too, my two girls. How do you manage without them now?" Maeve looked worried as she asked. It was the universal fear of many women.

"I stay very busy. As my grandmother used to say whenever things changed, 'That was then, this is now.' It's not an easy concept, but you're better off if you accept it and don't look back at what used to be."

Maeve was trying to do that with her husband, and a cloud passed over her eyes for an instant as Kait said it. The two women seemed to understand each other instinctively.

"So tell me about Anne Wilder. Who is she really?" Maeve asked, moving on to the bible she had read and fallen in love with.

"I'm not sure how she happened. I just sat down to write a story, and she sprang to life. In a modified version, at a different time, I think I was channeling my grandmother, who was a brave and fascinating woman, totally gutsy, real, and incredibly brave. And she had an amazing optimism and philosophy of life. She had some really hard times and never complained. She just did whatever she had to do to fix it. To be honest, thanks to her, I've always had a safety net under me to some degree. It was hard raising three kids alone, and we've faced all the same problems everyone else does. But my grandmother didn't have that net under her, she had to weave the net herself. She was smart and resourceful. She convinced me that I could face anything I had to."

She told her grandmother's story then, and Maeve listened with fascination and respect for Constance Whittier and her granddaughter, who was so much like Constance but didn't know it or take credit for it. Maeve thought that Kait was brave too, just as Maeve was trying to be, as the sands were shifting under her, and she had no map to chart her course yet. She was flying by the seat of her pants, as brave women did. Men were more methodical, and women more intuitive.

"Anne Wilder is like that in the story I wrote. I love stories where women succeed against the odds in a man's world. It's ten times harder for us than it is for guys, and it certainly was then, in aviation during and after the war, and for my grandmother in 1930, building a business and selling cakes and cookies to restaurants and grocery stores with four kids to feed. I can't even imagine how she did it."

Maeve could see the tie between the fictional character and the grandmother Kait described. "I love women like that," Maeve said quietly, watching Kait's eyes and deciding to confide in her.

"We're keeping it quiet, to avoid the press, but Ian was diagnosed with ALS last year. It's been rough. He did all right until recently, but it's a degenerative disease and it's getting worse. We have nurses for him now. He's still mobile, but he's getting weaker, and his breathing is a problem. It could go on for a long time, but it's only going to head in one direction.

"He's very strong, and he wants me to go on working. I've slowed down and I've been turning down projects, but when I read your story, Anne Wilder is who I want to be when I grow up. I'd love to do the project, but I'm not sure what I'd do if Ian gets worse quickly. I think we still have a few decent years left, but you can't predict that. One thing I do know, if I do it, we'd have to shoot it in New York. I won't move him to California. We have a good setup here and fantastic doctors, and I don't want to be away from him. If I'm working here, at least I'll come home every night, and they can shoot around me if he has a crisis."

Kait was bowled over by what she told her, and deeply touched by her confidence. She knew that ALS was progressive, which would eventually weaken all his muscles and paralyze him and ultimately it was fatal, though sometimes not for many years. The only person she knew of who had survived it was Stephen Hawking, but no one else had. And maybe Ian would survive it too. She hoped so for them, although it was a terrible blow of fate to be stricken with such a terrifying illness. There were tears in Maeve's eyes when she told her.

"I think you're already as brave as my grandmother, or more so," Kait said quietly. It always amazed her the challenges that people faced in their daily lives. So much of it wasn't fair, and some people had such enormous courage. Maeve was clearly one of them, watching the man she loved waste away and die before her eyes, and she was still listening to details about Kait's project. "Only you can decide what's right, given what you're dealing with," Kait said as she would have to someone who wrote in to her column. "No one can make that decision for you, or has the right to. Obviously, I would love to have you play Anne Wilder, it would be a dream come true for me, but it's just a TV series. This is your life, and that's more important. No one has the right to mess with that or try to influence you," she reminded her, and Maeve smiled gratefully.

"Thank you, Kait. Ian wants me to do it. He read it and loved it too, he says the role is pure me, and in some ways it is. I just don't know if I should work that hard right now on a long-term project, one that could last for years."

Kait smiled at what she said. "Thank you for your faith in me! It might give you some structure, or it might be too much pressure on you."

"I don't want to screw it up for you."

"Think of yourself, and do what's best for you and Ian," Kait said generously, and meant it. It was just a TV show, Maeve and her husband were dealing with far bigger issues.

"I'll give it some more thought. I'd love to do it. And part of me wants to go on with normal life, which is what Ian wants. He doesn't want me sitting around and staring at him. And I'm intrigued with all these series. They're really working. The fans like them better than movies now."

Kait sheepishly admitted to her then that she was addicted to **Downton Abbey,** and Maeve burst out laughing.

"Me too! I watch an episode of it every night on my iPad after I put Ian to bed. On bad days, I watch two," which was precisely what Kait did. They chatted for a few minutes about how much they loved the show, and how sad they were that it had ended, and then Maeve got serious again.

"**The Wilder Women** could be even better, you know. It's such a strong message to women, to be resourceful and not let life do you in. Who are you considering for Hannabel, Anne's mother?"

"I'm not sure. Zack is a lot more knowledgeable than I am, and I know he has some ideas. I don't know who yet."

"What about Agnes White? She's fantastic. I've worked with her a couple of times and she's an incredible actress. She'd be perfect for the part."

"Is she still alive?" Kait looked surprised. "I haven't seen her in anything in years. And she must be ancient."

"Not as old as people think. I think she's in her early seventies, which is about right for this. She had some tragedies in her life, and became reclusive and stopped working. If you want her number, Ian knows her. He was a big admirer of the man she lived with, Roberto Leone, who was his mentor. They lived together for about fifty years but never married. I have a feeling he was married to someone else and never got divorced. We had them to dinner once, they were an amazing couple. He was one of the great directors of our time, and convinced Ian to stop acting and switch to directing. And Agnes is the best actress I know. She's my idol." She said it so warmly that Kait was moved, and realized that she would be perfect for the part, if she was still working, or willing to come out of retirement and do the show.

"I'll talk to Zack about it. I never thought about her."

"I'd love to work with her again, if you can talk her into it. She's always been very quixotic and unpredictable about the parts she played. She was beautiful when she was young, but she always loved the challenging roles and wasn't afraid of them. She's a true actress. I've tried to follow her example, but I have to admit, I'd rather look good on screen than have them age me forty years to play Queen Victoria on her deathbed. I've always thought you could be a good actress and still look halfway decent. I guess I'm vainer than Agnes."

They both laughed at that and Kait didn't blame her, and she was impressed to see that Maeve didn't look as though she'd had any cosmetic "work" done on her face, not even Botox. She was beautiful for her age and she looked real, unlike most actresses their age, who were unrecognizable after too many face-lifts.

Maeve glanced at her watch regretfully then. They had been there for two hours and the time had flown. The foundations of a friendship had been laid, even if she didn't take the part. And given what she was facing, Kait could understand if she didn't. Her husband was infinitely more important.

Kait could sense that Maeve was torn between living a normal life and becoming a nurse, which would depress them both even more. She shared with Kait that Ian had said he wanted to see her coming and going, working, and leading a full, healthy life, and he would live vicariously through her, since he could no longer work himself and missed it fiercely. Maeve said he had fallen in love with Kait's story and wished he could direct it.

"I should get back. I try not to stay out for too long if I don't have to, and the nursing shift changes in half an hour. I should check on what's going on," she said with a sigh and a smile at Kait. "You have no idea how wonderful this has been. Whatever happens, I'd love to see you again. Besides, I need your advice about my girls."

They both laughed at that, and Kait grabbed the check when it came. They squabbled over it briefly, and Maeve said it was just one more reason to meet again. "And don't forget about Agnes White for Hannabel. Talk to Zack about it. He seems to have an eye on some big names, and she should be on the list, whatever it takes to convince her. I'll email you her home number. She may not have an agent anymore, if she's not working." They exchanged information, and promised each other to stay in contact and meet again. "She always preferred working on projects where her great love Roberto Leone was the director, but if she likes your director, she might do it. Has Zack made a deal with anyone to direct yet?" That would be an important factor for Maeve too.

"I don't think so, he's talking to a few. He wants a woman."

"I agree, although Ian wouldn't. He always likes male directors better."

The two women hugged when they left the deli. It had been a wonderful two hours. And it had gotten colder. It was six o'clock by then, and Maeve pulled her hood up and headed toward Central Park with a wave, as Kait hailed a cab to go home, thinking about her. She was a remarkable woman, and everything Kait had thought she'd be and more.

She took her coat off when she got back to her apartment, as her cellphone rang. It was Zack, and he sounded stunned.

"What did you do to her?" he asked in a tense voice.

"Nothing," Kait answered, sounding baffled. "I thought we had a great time. Did I do something to offend her?"

"I don't think so, Ms. Whittier," he said, his voice switching from shock to jubilation. "I just got an email from her about ten minutes ago. Four words. 'I'm in. Maeve O'Hara.' Kait, you did it!" Kait was as floored as he was, and just as thrilled. Even more so, she was deeply impressed by the woman she had just spent two hours with, and knew she would make the show a huge success, and would bring Anne Wilder to life.

"We have to shoot it in New York for her, or the vicinity," Kait said. "That's the only condition she told me about." She didn't explain why to him out of respect for Maeve and Ian, since they wanted it kept quiet about his grave illness.

"I know, her agent told me. I don't care. I would shoot it in Botswana if that means we get her. The network is going to go insane. We can't go wrong with Maeve O'Hara playing Anne Wilder." He was over the moon about it, and so was Kait. It would make the show a sure success, if they had a good script for her.

"She suggested Agnes White for the part of

Hannabel, by the way. She said she'd be fantastic," Kait said matter-of-factly.

"We can't, she's dead," he said smugly. And he had someone else in mind, who was good with comedy and might lighten the part, particularly if some of the dialogue was funny.

"I thought so too. Maeve says she's alive. She's in retirement, or a recluse or something."

"I'll check it out," but he liked his pick better, although the actress was being difficult and laying out a lot of conditions and benefits he didn't want to give her, and had a very tough lawyer negotiating for her.

When they hung up, Kait saw that she had an email on her iPhone from Maeve too. It said, "Thank you for everything! Here's to a great show! Love, Maeve." Kait stared at her phone and grinned broadly. The Fates had smiled on them again. She wondered if this was how her grandmother had felt when she sold her first batch of cookies to the neighborhood restaurants. Maeve was going to be a huge part of the package, and attract the other talent they wanted. They were on their way.

Chapter 7

The two weeks Kait spent in Los Angeles were crammed full. She met with two agents on the first day, and selected one of Zack's recommendations. They were nothing like what she'd expected. She thought they'd be very Hollywood, in jeans, T-shirts, and gold chains. Both greeted her in enormous offices, at the two most important agencies in L.A. The walls were covered with expensive art by Damien Hirst, de Kooning, and Jackson Pollock. The men themselves looked like New York ad men, or bankers, in impeccable custom-made suits, crisp white shirts, expensive ties, and serious John Lobb shoes. They were the epitome of conservatism, with short hair, clean shaves, and perfect tailoring. And their conversations with Kait were as serious as they were.

She would have been satisfied to be represented by either one, but the second one, Robert Talbot, was slightly warmer, easier to talk to, and answered more of her questions, so she decided to go with him, and called to tell him an hour after their meeting. He sounded delighted, and assured her he'd start going over the contracts immediately and get back to her. When she saw Zack, she thanked him again.

She looked at film clips of all the actors Zack was considering for the other parts. The actress he wanted for Hannabel was still being difficult, and hadn't signed yet. The actress they all liked best for the part of Maggie was an unknown, but she was perfect in the role, though Zack still wanted to attach another big name to the show to balance Maeve. The fact that Maeve had committed to the show made other important talent want to join them.

They had a popular, sexy young actress named Charlotte Manning to play Chrystal, the bad-girl younger daughter. She had the reputation of being difficult and unreliable, but she was exquisitely beautiful, was twenty-two years old but could play fourteen in the beginning, and had been in enough movies and series with short-term roles to have a face and name people would recognize. Younger audiences would love her, especially men. She had the right look for the role. She had dated every bad-boy young actor in Hollywood, and rock stars who got arrested. She was so right for the part, and so hot at the moment, that the network loved her and was pleased. And they had a possible big star to play Loch, since he only appeared in the first few shows and then he died, so it wasn't a long-term commitment for a busy actor in feature films.

On her third day in L.A., Kait was scheduled to meet Becca Roberts, the screenwriter that Zack had raved about. He had set up the meeting in his office, at nine A.M., and she showed up two hours late. Kait was there on time, and Zack kept assuring her that Becca was young and a little flaky but she was great. When she finally arrived, she was wearing dark glasses and looked like she'd put on whatever clothes she'd found on the floor, with a pixie haircut that seemed like it had never seen a brush. She groaned as she walked into the conference room and saw Zack conferring quietly with Kait.

"Oh God, you're here," Becca said, melting into a chair at the enormous table, like a kid sliding into the back row in school, and asked his assistant for black coffee. She slouched in her chair, and looked about fifteen years old. She was twenty-four, but Zack continued to swear she was the best and one of the hot young talents in L.A. "I'm really sorry. Yesterday was my birthday, and I got a little crazy last night. I came home at five A.M., my phone died and I couldn't find the charger, so I had no alarm. Thank God my dog woke me up half an hour ago. I got here as fast as I could. The traffic sucked. I live in the Valley," she said to Kait as though that explained everything.

They were off to a bad start, Kait was trying to be patient but thought her excuses were pathetic. She couldn't imagine this disorderly hungover waif writing a hit show, or even a bad one. She was waiting for her to say "The dog ate my homework" next.

"I love the bible," Becca said to Kait. "I've actually been working on the first episode for the last week, and trying out some different directions on it. I'm not sure about the grandmother, though. I don't think we need her, she's such a bitch. I have an aunt like that, I can't stand her. I think we'll alienate the viewers. I think we should cut her out." Kait could almost feel the hair rise up on the back of her neck as Becca said it.

"The whole point is that she's tough on Anne in the beginning, but when the going gets rough, she comes around, and even learns to fly to help the business. She's a good balance for the others," Kait explained, and Becca shook her head.

"I don't buy it, and Bill, the oldest son who gets killed, reads like he's gay. He's such a wimp." Zack looked like he was going to cry, and Kait glared at him meaningfully as though telling him they were wasting their time. She was not going to agree to anything the young screenwriter had suggested. The only thing she had in her favor so far was that Zack said she was fast, and could have a script ready to shoot by July first. Anyone else could stall them for a year. And the network wanted them shooting by July and on air in October. Maybe Becca could do it, but what would she write? Nothing Kait wanted associated with her show, not from what she was hearing. The only thing keeping Kait in her chair was Zack, and not wanting to be rude to him.

"Why don't you show us what you've got," Zack said calmly, "and we can work from that, and see where it goes."

"Can you print it for me here? Mine is broken," she said, pulling her laptop out of her backpack. She sent the file to Zack's assistant, who came back with three copies five minutes later and handed a set to each of them. It was Becca's preliminary work on the script for the first few scenes.

Kait only got three pages into it, set it down, and looked directly at Becca when she spoke.

"This has absolutely nothing to do with the story I wrote. If you don't like the bible, you don't have to do it, but you can't rewrite the whole thing on your own. The premise of this is all wrong. And the dialogue is too modern for the time. This isn't a punk rock musical, it's a family drama, and starts in 1940."

"We could speed it up," Becca suggested, "and start it later. It's so old-fashioned the way it is," she complained.

"It's supposed to be," Kait said tersely. "That's the whole point. Anne Wilder succeeds and builds her business at a time when that was nearly impossible to do, in a field that was almost exclusively open to men, and closed to women."

"I get that, and I really like Maggie. She's kind of a tomboy. It would make more sense if we do her as a lesbian. This could be about fighting for gay rights in the 1940s."

"It's about fighting for **women's** rights, gay or straight," Kait said bluntly, wanting to end the meeting as soon as possible.

"I can take another crack at it," Becca said, glancing at Zack to rescue her, as Kait looked daggers at him, and wanted out. Becca was wasting everyone's time and clearly wasn't capable of giving them the script they needed. But much to her dismay, Zack refused to give up. Becca was available, she wrote quickly, and he was convinced she could do the job.

"Becca, **focus,**" he said to her quietly. "Do you remember when you wrote **Devil's Daughter** and you were completely off the mark at first, and turned yourself around? You handed in the best damn script I've ever seen, and you wrote a hit show. You need to do that now. You're off point on this one so far, but that can change. This show could run five or ten seasons, which would be great for you. But not the way you've interpreted it. You have to wipe the slate, clear your head, and try again."

She looked sobered when he said it, and both disappointed and confused. "You want a script like **Devil's Daughter**?" She seemed surprised.

"No, I don't. But I want you to do what you did then. You turned it from the worst script I've ever seen to the best one. I need you to do that again." He was adamant and sounded strong. He wanted **The Wilder Women** to work, and they needed a script right away. A great one, or the network would postpone it, or back out and shelve it forever.

"You don't like this one, huh?"

Kait and Zack both shook their heads.

"Let me tell you something," Zack said bluntly. "We have Maeve O'Hara to play Anne Wilder. She won't do a script like this. We've got Charlotte Manning to play Chrystal, you can go crazy with that. But we're not doing an LGBT manifesto here. This takes place in the 1940s and '50s. It's about women in aviation, not gay rights," Zack explained.

"I'm afraid to fly," she said mournfully, and Kait almost laughed.

"Becca, do you want to do this or not?" Zack asked her directly, almost as he would a child, and she nodded.

"Yes, I do," she said in a small voice.

"Then go home, work your ass off, respect the bible we gave you, and come back when you have something to show us."

"How long have I got?" she asked nervously.

"As little time as possible, because if this doesn't work, we have to attach someone else to the project, and the writer is key."

"I get it. I'll be back," she said, stood up, stuffed her laptop into her backpack, saluted both of them, and left the room with the laces of her Dr. Martens trailing behind her.

Kait stared at Zack in dismay. "You **can't** let her write this script," she said anxiously. The meeting had been a disaster, and Becca appeared to be completely incapable of relating to the story or writing the screenplay for the show.

"Trust me, she does this. She's a complete mess in the beginning, and just when you're about to give up on her, she pulls the rabbit out of the hat. I've seen her do it several times."

"We're wasting time. And she acts like a spoiled teenager. How is she going to write the kind of emotional content we need? And I'm not writing out Hannabel because she reminds Becca of the aunt she hates."

"Of course not. Just give her a chance. I know she'll be back in two days with something we like better. Maybe not the final script yet, but if she gets a grip, she can do it." He sounded sure.

Kait thought he was crazy, and wondered if he was in love with her or sleeping with her. She couldn't think of any other reason to put up with Becca. In Kait's opinion, she was unprofessional and a mess. "She looks like she needs a month in rehab and a bath." Kait had no patience for girls like her, who partied and couldn't do their jobs. And she was convinced Zack was overestimating her, whatever his reasons.

"Just wait," Zack said, and they went to lunch together to go over the casting again. They were having trouble casting the two boys. They had one strong possibility for Bill, the oldest son, and he was a big name, but he had a terrible reputation on set and was known to screw anything that moved and cause dramas and jealous scenes among his costars, a headache they didn't want. With him and Charlotte Manning on the same set, Zack was afraid their bad behavior would slow them down. And the best option they had for Maggie was still the total unknown, and he wanted a name for that part, but the girl was very, very good. They had watched her screen test several times, and she impressed them each time they did.

True to Zack's prediction, Becca was back two days later, with a totally different take on the script. This one didn't work either, but she was closer to the concept and had stopped trying to get rid of the grandmother and turn it into a show about gay rights. But this time, the script was dull, and Kait was bored out of her wits by page five.

"We're getting there," Zack encouraged Becca, not wanting to beat her up. "You need to try to relate to the characters more, and we need some fire in it. It's too flat." He gave her examples of the scenes that didn't work and those that were better, and she loped off again, promising him a third version after the weekend. Kait had been there for almost a week by then, and she'd had a nice email from Maeve wanting to know how the casting was going, and if they were considering Agnes White.

They had live casting calls over the weekend, and none of them could deny that Dan Delaney, Hollywood's latest Casanova, was the best man for the role of Bill. They agreed to give him the job, with severe warnings to his agent that he couldn't misbehave on set. It was a great opportunity for him, and his agent swore he would tell him to be good and hold him to it. He would die during the first season, so they only had to get through one season with him and didn't have to worry about him long term. And they picked Brad Evers, a young actor who had done a few good shows, to play Greg.

They didn't have an actor to play Anne Wilder's war hero lover, but they didn't need him till late in the first season, possibly not till the Christmas special, so there was no rush to choose an actor for the part. The role of Maggie was still up for grabs and that of her boyfriend, Johnny West, but at least the roles of Bill and Chrystal had been filled with young talent with big names, and the actor to play Greg was solid too. They had gotten nowhere with an actress to play Hannabel. Their negotiations with the actress Zack wanted kept falling apart.

On Saturday night, Zack and Kait had dinner with the director he was hoping for, Nancy Haskell, who had done two successful series and many important feature films, and had an Oscar to her credit. Maeve knew they were talking to her and said she'd be thrilled to work with her. She had no objection so far to the young talent they had hired. They had also signed Phillip Green, a big film star, to play Loch, and had been pleased to find he would be

free between films he was doing for the four episodes they needed him in. Nancy had worked with
him before and liked him. He was professional and
reliable and another big name associated with the
show.

They met Nancy Haskell at Giorgio Baldi in
Santa Monica, near Malibu, where she lived. The
food was fabulous, and the conversation lively.
She was a talented, experienced, serious director in
her sixties, and was excited about the show. She and
Kait had a long conversation over dinner about the
characters, and then Nancy talked about her recent
travels in Asia, her passion for art, and her latest
film. She was a fascinating woman, had never married and had no children, and had an insatiable
curiosity about the world and people. She was currently studying Mandarin before her next trip, and
planned to spend a month in India before the show
started. She liked all their casting choices so far,
particularly Maeve, who was almost certain to carry
the show and make it a success. She wasn't as sure
about Becca as the screenwriter, and Kait shot a dark
look at Zack. And then Kait brought up Maeve's
suggestion of Agnes White in the role of Hannabel.

"If you can get her," Nancy said skeptically. "I
don't think she's done anything for at least ten
years, since Roberto died. That hit her very hard,
and Agnes hated getting older. I don't have the feeling she wants to work anymore, or to play some-

one that old, although she's got the character for the part. She's a brilliant actress, she can play anything. But she's never done TV."

Zack told her who else they were talking to for the part, and said she'd been difficult and their negotiations with her had stalled. Nancy promised to think about it, and then at the end of dinner, she brought up Agnes White again. "You know, I think Maeve's idea isn't so crazy after all. But I doubt Agnes will do it. It would take a lot to drag her out of her cave. She had some pretty tough breaks for a while."

Nancy didn't go into specifics, but whatever the reason, Agnes White had gone into retirement, and most of her old fans, and they were legion, thought she was dead by now. She was one of the old greats of Hollywood films. "She never won an Oscar, but she should have. She must have been nominated a dozen times. Her best films were the ones Roberto directed. I'm not sure she'd even be willing to work without him. He was a staunch Italian Catholic, so he never got divorced and married her. They had a child at some point, which they never talked about. She's a very private person and always was, now she's more of a recluse."

"How does she look?" Zack asked with mild interest.

"I have no idea," Nancy said honestly. "I haven't seen her myself in twelve or fourteen years. That's a long time. But she can act like no one else I know, even Maeve. I'd love to work with her, if you can talk her into it. I'm sure she hasn't lost her touch. Talent like that doesn't fade. It just gets better with time." Her words weren't lost on Zack, and he brought it up with Kait on their way back to Beverly Hills, after they agreed on how amazing Nancy was. Kait wanted her to direct the show, and so did Zack, more than ever.

"Do you think she'll take the job?" Kait asked, loving her new universe and the people she had met, Nancy Haskell at the top of that list, after Maeve.

"I think so," Zack said confidently. "And she's got me intrigued about Agnes White. Maybe you should try to see her when you go back to New York. I looked her up and she has no current agent, and you said Maeve has an in to her through Ian. It might be worth a shot. You certainly worked your magic with Maeve better than I could have. Maybe you can convince Agnes White to take the part." He was tired of their battles with the actress they'd been talking to, he was ready to give up on her.

"I'll try," Kait said with enthusiasm, and when they got back to the hotel, Zack suggested a drink to sum things up. Kait was tired but enjoying every minute of what they were doing, putting the show together. He consulted her about everything, and they were spending almost every waking minute working side by side, although he had additional meetings as well for other projects. And his respect for Kait was obvious. He kept their relationship on a professional level, but he enjoyed her company too. In other circumstances, if they weren't involved in a project, Kait had the feeling he would have asked her out. But the show was so important to both of them that neither of them wanted to muddy the waters with a casual romance, and a serious one would have been even harder. Without even discussing it, they both had opted to be friends and working partners, and stay clear of any emotional involvement. He was an attractive man, but Kait was relieved. She didn't want to spoil what they had, and neither did he. They had a drink at the bar, and half an hour later he was on his way home, and she was in her room at the hotel.

The next day, she and Zack agreed that the best woman for the part of Maggie, Anne Wilder's oldest daughter, was their unknown, Abaya Jones. Maeve had seen Abaya Jones's screen test and thought she was fabulous, and predicted Abaya would become a big star. And Zack was sure she would. The network endorsed it on Monday morning, and an hour later, Nancy Haskell's agent called Zack and told him that Nancy had agreed to accept their offer to direct their show, and was excited about it.

"We're on a roll," he told Kait, grinning broadly as they walked into his conference room to meet with Becca for the third time. They got along perfectly, except where Becca was concerned. Kait wasn't hopeful, but Zack stubbornly insisted that she wouldn't let them down. She was everything

Kait didn't want: unreliable, scattered, disorganized, immature, and off the mark.

She seemed more serious this time as she handed them each a short script for most of the first episode.

"I got my printer working," she said proudly, "but this is still pretty rough. I did it over the weekend. I worked all night Saturday and last night, and I think I'm in the right place with it now. I read the bible about ten more times."

Kait glanced at the first few pages, prepared to hate it again, and was surprised to find that what Becca had written this time closely reflected what Kait had tried to convey, and showed a deep understanding of the characters. The elfin screenwriter was terrified.

"This is good, Becca," Kait said, stunned, and then relaxed into a smile.

"Thank you. I just had to clear my head and get into it. I did a juice cleanse this weekend, that always helps me think. I can't write when I eat a lot of crap," she said seriously, and Kait refrained from comment. But whatever it took, the script was infinitely better than what Becca had done before. "I'm working on the second episode. I like that one better. I can email it to you both tomorrow. I think I've got it now. And the grandmother is a bitch we wind up liking, and love to hate. It took me a while to get that, and the 1940s thing, and women's rights. And what they do with the old planes is very cool, and three women running the business. I like it a lot."

Zack shot an I-told-you-so look at Kait as they continued to read through it, and there was no denying the script was good. It was still in a rough state, but Becca had clearly understood the issues in the story now, and done a good job.

"Give me two or three finished scripts by the end of the week, and if Kait approves them, I'll send them to the network and see what they think." Becca was the only screenwriter he knew who could write that fast. No one else would have done it, but he knew she could, if she stayed with it and worked hard.

"I did what you said. I focused. And I think I channeled some of it. I really want this show, Zack." The possibility of five or ten seasons had gotten her attention and woken her up.

"Then write me the best scripts you've ever given me," he told her with a serious expression.

"I will," she promised, and left a few minutes later as Zack smiled at Kait victoriously.

"I think she'll do it," Zack said. She'd had him worried for a while, and his faith had been hard to justify to Kait.

"I'm beginning to think you're right," Kait said, smiling. Zack had an amazing knack for assembling talent, and people who complemented each other. He was a master at what he did, and Kait had deep respect for him.

"Let's see how it looks when the scripts come in. I won't hire her if they're not good, I promise," he said and Kait nodded, impressed all over again with what they were accomplishing and how far they had come in a short time. She loved working with him and his direct, no-nonsense style, but he was kind too, as he had been to Becca, and brought out the best in everyone. They wanted to do a great job for him.

There were still more people to hire—a costume designer, production assistants, all the technical advisers, and a historical adviser—but they had come a long way on the talent. The only big pieces of the puzzle still missing were the young pilot who would become Maggie's boyfriend, Johnny West; Anne Wilder's lover; and Hannabel, the grandmother. All three were important parts.

By the time Kait was ready to leave L.A., Becca had delivered three scripts, and they were great. Kait had promised to try to make contact with Agnes White when she got back to New York. It had been an incredibly productive two weeks. She and Zack had a last conversation before she left on Saturday, and they were both pleased with how everything had gone. He was involved in the money aspects now, their deal with the cable network, insurance for the show, and all the parts of the project that didn't involve talent but took a huge amount of organizing and time. He thanked Kait for her input while she was there. She had loved all of it, and everything had fallen into place as they hoped.

Kait sat quietly on the plane on the way back to

New York, thinking about all the meetings and the people she had met. It was still hard to believe this was happening to her and she was part of it. But it was beginning to seem real. Her new agent was negotiating her deal with the cable network, as creator of the series and co-executive producer, and so far all was going well. Step by step, it was all falling into place. She'd been planning to watch a movie on the flight, and instead she read Becca's rough scripts again for the first three episodes. With a satisfied smile, she closed her eyes for a minute, fell into a deep, peaceful sleep, and woke up when they landed in New York.

She felt like Cinderella after the ball as she pulled her rolling cart behind her and headed for baggage claim to get her suitcase and try to find a taxi. She had to be at work at the magazine in the morning for a meeting, and was happy she had kept up with her column while she was gone.

The reality of her quiet, solitary New York life hit her when she walked into her dark, empty apartment. It made her long for L.A., and all the discussions and adventures she'd had there. She had entered a whole new world.

Chapter 8

The office was hectic the next day after being gone for two weeks. She was up to date with her column, blog, Facebook, and Twitter feeds, but she had a stack of mail, and countless memos waiting for her by email, about editorial meetings she had to attend. Carmen stopped by to tell her how happy she was to see her back. She said she had missed her. But being at the magazine felt strange now after her meetings in L.A. The magazine no longer felt like her life, but someone else's. She still hadn't told anyone about the show yet, although she planned to tell her children about it soon. And at the right time, she would have to tell the magazine. She didn't want to tell them prematurely in case it fell apart. But that didn't seem likely now.

Once they started shooting in July, she would no longer have time to come into the office. She planned to continue writing her column, and updating her blogs and social media, if the magazine let her, but she'd have to do it in her spare time off-site. She hadn't decided yet if she wanted to ask for a leave of absence for three or four months, while they shot the first season of **The Wilder Women,** or if she wanted to leave her time away open-ended. If the ratings were good, they'd start shooting again in late January after a four-month hiatus, and it might not even make sense, in that case, to continue writing her column. But she didn't want to assume anything yet. The show might be an enormous bomb and get canceled, although with Maeve O'Hara in it, that seemed unlikely. Kait needed some time to figure out her plans. And until she did, she wanted to keep quiet about it.

True to her word, Maeve had sent her Agnes White's phone number and address. Kait had promised Zack she'd call her, but it was Wednesday night before she had a chance to do so. She had so much work on her desk, a stack of letters to read and respond to, and the column to work on at night, and she didn't want to talk to her when she felt rushed or frazzled. She had a feeling that calling the old, reclusive actress was a delicate mission, and she didn't want to blow it.

Kait tried her phone number when she got home from the office, and she was just about to hang up after no one answered for a long time, when the famous actress picked up the phone, was silent for an instant, and then said "Yes?" in barely more than a whisper. It was more of a hoarse croak, as though she hadn't talked to anyone in months, and didn't want to. Kait felt her heart beat faster as she got ready to tell her about the series, and ask for an appointment with her.

"Hello, Miss White," Kait began in a bright, polite voice, not sure of the best approach. "My name is Kait Whittier, and Maeve O'Hara was kind enough to give me your number. She and I are going to be working on a television series together, about women in aviation in the 1940s. And there's a part in it we both felt is perfect for you. Nancy Haskell is going to direct it, and she thought so too." She threw in all the names she could, hoping that one of them would be the "open sesame" she needed into Agnes White's private world, and to gain her trust, or arouse her curiosity about the project.

"I'm not an actress anymore, I'm out of the business," she said firmly, her voice sounding stronger and very definite about it.

"Could I send you a copy of the bible for the show, or come to talk to you about it?" Kait said cautiously, not wanting to offend her, but hoping to entice her and get a good foot in the door, literally.

"If Maeve is involved in it, I'm sure it's a good show," she said generously. "I'm just not interested in working anymore. . . . I haven't been in many years. I don't want to come out of retirement. We all have an expiration date, and I reached mine ten years ago. We can't force these things, and I've never done television, and don't want to."

"It would be a great honor to meet you," Kait

said, trying another tack, and it was true, just as it had been to meet Maeve, and Kait couldn't wait to work with her. And casting Agnes White as Hannabel would be another major coup. There was a long silence at the other end of the phone, and for a moment she thought they'd been disconnected or that Agnes had hung up.

"Why would you want to meet me?" she said finally, sounding baffled. "I'm just an old woman."

"You're my idol, and so is Maeve. You're the two greatest actresses of my lifetime," Kait said with reverence and meant it.

"All of that's in the past now," she said, her voice drifting off. She slurred on the last words, and Kait wondered if she'd been drinking. "You won't talk me into it. Are you writing the screenplay?"

"No, just the bible."

"It sounds like an interesting subject." And then after another pause, she startled Kait. "I suppose you could come to see me. We don't have to talk about your show. I won't do it anyway. You can tell me what Maeve has been up to. How are her children?" She seemed lonely and a little disconnected, and Kait was concerned that she might have the early stages of dementia, and wondered if that was why she had retired.

"I haven't met them, but I think they're fine. Her husband isn't well, though."

"I'm sorry to hear it. Ian is a wonderful man," she said and Kait agreed without telling her how sick he was, which might upset her unduly and betray a confidence.

"Come tomorrow then, at five o'clock. Do you know where I live?"

"Maeve gave me your address," Kait assured her.

"You can't stay long. I get tired easily," she said, seeming older than she was, and as though she wasn't used to visitors. Kait wondered how long it had been since she left her house. She had a feeling that the visit was going to be depressing, and not achieve the desired result. Agnes really did sound too old and frail, and even confused, to resume her career. But at least she could tell Zack and Maeve she tried.

They hung up a moment later, and the next day Kait left the office early to get to Agnes's house on time. She lived in an old brownstone in the East Seventies, near the East River, that looked as though it had been handsome when it was kept up. The paint was peeling off the black shutters, one was hanging at an awkward angle on a broken hinge, and two were missing. The black paint on the front door was chipping in several places, and the brass knocker was tarnished. And there was a big chunk missing out of one of the stone steps that looked like it would be dangerous for an old person.

Kait walked up the steps, avoiding the broken one, and rang the doorbell. Just like the phone, for a long time no one answered. And then finally it opened, and a small, thin, wizened woman who looked a hundred years old stood in the doorway, squinting in the daylight. The hallway was dark behind her. Kait realized that she would never have recognized Agnes if she saw her on the street. She was painfully thin, and her white hair hung long and straight to her shoulders. Her famously exquisite features were still beautiful, but her eyes seemed vacant. She was wearing a black skirt, flat shoes, and a sagging gray sweater. Observing her, it was hard to believe that she had once been a great beauty, as she stood aside and gestured Kait in. The droop of her shoulders exuded despair and defeat.

"Mrs. Whittier?" she asked formally and Kait nodded, and handed her a small bouquet of flowers she had brought with her, which made the old woman smile.

"That was nice of you. But I still won't do your series." She sounded feisty as she said it and motioned Kait to follow her. They walked the length of the house, down a dark hall into the kitchen. There were cooking pots in the sink, and dirty dishes, stacks of newspapers and old magazines everywhere. A single frayed place mat lay on the table, with a linen napkin in a silver ring. The room had a pretty view into a garden, which was overgrown. Kait noticed a half-empty bottle of bourbon standing next to the sink, and pretended not to see it. She glimpsed a back balcony with a rusted table on it, which led down to the garden. Kait could easily imagine that the house had been lovely once, but not in a long time. Through the open door to the dining room she caught a peek of handsome antiques, and the table was piled high with newspapers too.

"Do you want something to drink?" Agnes asked Kait, as she glanced longingly at the bourbon herself.

"No, I'm fine, thank you," Kait said, and Agnes nodded.

"Come into the library," she said, leading the way and when they got there, Agnes sat down on a dark red velvet couch with a gray cashmere throw blanket on it. The walls were lined with books, there was a beautiful English partners desk piled high with papers and what looked like unopened mail, and a television set up on a low table, with stacks of DVDs and old envelopes from Netflix on it. With a single glance, Kait realized that they were Agnes's movies, and seeing them made Kait instantly sad for her, as she got a glimpse into the great actress's life. She was spending what was left of it alone in a dark room, watching her films and drinking bourbon. Kait couldn't imagine a sadder fate than that. She seemed to have given up on the world and shut everyone out, but at least she had let Kait come to see her.

"Some of my pictures," Agnes said, waving a still graceful hand at the stack of movies. "They're all on DVD now."

"I think I've seen most of them. I don't think you realize how many fans you have in every generation, or how thrilled they would be to see you again, and on TV in their living room every week. You could have a whole new career," Kait said, not even for the sake of her series, but for this poor, lonely woman who had locked herself away from the world.

"I don't want a new career. I liked my old one, and I'm too old for all that now. And television isn't a medium I understand, nor do I want to."

"It's very exciting these days, and some major actors are doing TV series, like Maeve."

"She's young enough to do that, I'm not. I've had all the great roles I could ever want. There's nothing left I want to play. I've worked with all the great actors and directors. I'm not interested in taking part in some kind of new wave or new movement as an experiment."

"Even to work with Maeve?" Kait asked, and Agnes smiled at that. Looking at her more closely, Kait recognized the face she'd seen on screen. But she seemed a great deal older, and there was something desperately unhappy and tormented about her eyes. Kait wondered if anyone came to cook for her. The house didn't appear as though it had been cleaned or tidied in ages. Agnes saw Kait glancing around and was quick to explain.

"My maid died last year. I haven't replaced her yet, and I live alone here anyway. I can take care of it myself." But it didn't look as though she had. She was clean and neatly dressed, but the house was a disaster and made Kait want to take off her coat and put it in order for her.

"I can't work anymore," Agnes said, without explaining why. She didn't appear to be suffering from any illness, she was just old and frail beyond her years. She was alert and intelligent but now and then she lost the thread of the conversation or lost interest and stopped paying attention as though none of it mattered. Kait thought she might be tired, or had a shot of the bourbon before her guest arrived. She suspected that was the case, and was curious if Agnes had become an alcoholic as well as a recluse.

"You're cheating the world of your talent," Kait said quietly, and Agnes didn't answer for a long moment. Kait noticed that her hands shook as she fiddled with the edge of the cashmere blanket.

"No one wants to see an old woman on the screen. There is nothing more unattractive than people who don't know when to take a final bow, fold the show, and leave," she said firmly.

"You weren't old when you did that," Kait persisted, afraid Agnes might tell her to go, but daring to say it anyway.

"No, I wasn't, but I had my reasons. And I still do." And then, without explanation, she got up and left the room for a few minutes. Kait could hear her doing something in the kitchen, but felt too awkward to follow her. And in a moment, Agnes was back with a bourbon on the rocks in her hand. She turned to Kait before she sat down on the couch again. And she made no apology for her drink. "Do you want to watch one of my movies?" she suddenly offered.

Kait was taken aback and didn't know what to say, and silently nodded.

"I like this one very much," Agnes said, setting the drink down, taking a DVD out of its case, and putting it in the machine. It was the film **Queen Victoria,** for which she had been nominated for an Oscar. "I think it's my best." She had portrayed the queen from her youth to her deathbed. Kait had seen it before, and it was a remarkable performance. It would be an extraordinary experience watching it with the great actress herself. No one would have believed it.

They sat silently together for two and a half hours in the dimly lit room. Kait was mesmerized by the extraordinary performance, one of the finest in movie history. Agnes went back to the kitchen and helped herself to another bourbon halfway through, and after that, she dozed from time to time, and then would wake up and continue watching the movie. She seemed a little drunk when it was over and unsteady on her feet when she took the movie out and placed it back in its box. It felt tragic for her to be watching herself as a young woman and clinging to the past, shut away in her house and forgotten by the world. There was something heartbreaking about it.

"I doubt that your show on TV will compare to that," she said bluntly, and Kait was equally so when she answered.

"No, it won't, but if I have anything to do with it, it will be a damn good show. I'm sure Maeve will be wonderful, and so would you if you did it." The more Kait looked at her, the more beautiful she seemed, and would be, if she gained a little weight and stopped drinking. She had the matchstick legs, bloated belly, and sallow complexion of an alcoholic, which seemed like such a terrible waste, considering what she had been. And then Kait dared to ask her a question Agnes didn't expect. "Would you stop drinking if you came back to work?"

Agnes looked shocked as their eyes met, and Kait could see that there was still fire in the old woman's eyes.

"I might," she said tartly, "but I didn't say I'd do the series, did I?"

"No, you didn't. But maybe you should. You have too much talent to sit here drinking and watching your old movies. Maybe it's time to make new ones," Kait said, feeling very daring.

"Television isn't movies," she said harshly. "Not by any stretch of the imagination. Not like the film you just saw." Her lover had directed it, and had won the Oscar for best director. And she got a nomination for her performance.

"No, but TV is very good these days," Kait said

staunchly. "You can't waste your talent, hiding in your house." It suddenly made Kait angry, thinking about it.

"I'm not hiding. And I could stop drinking whenever I want. I have nothing else to do," she said stubbornly. She was surprised when Kait stood up and took a thick envelope out of her handbag and put it on the coffee table in front of her hostess.

"I'm leaving you a copy of the bible, Miss White. You don't have to do it, or even read it, but I hope you will. I believe in the project, and so does Maeve. So does Ian. He convinced her to do it, and it would mean the world to all of us if you would take the part of Hannabel, or at least consider it. I won't be angry if you don't do it, but I'll be disappointed and sad. And so will Maeve. She suggested you for the part, which was an inspired idea. You would be brilliant in it." Kait put on her coat then and smiled at Agnes White. "Thank you for letting me come to see you. It was a huge honor, and I loved watching **Queen Victoria** with you. I'll remember it forever."

Agnes didn't know what to say to her, and then she stood up too, and nearly stumbled as she walked around the coffee table to see her out. She didn't say a word until they got to the front door, and then she looked at Kait, and seemed more sober again.

"Thank you," Agnes said with dignity. "I enjoyed watching it with you too. And I'll read the bible when I have time," which Kait suspected would be never. She would let it sit there in the manila envelope and ignore it. And the worst part of it was that she needed them even more than they needed her. Someone had to save her from herself and the destructive path she was on, and probably had been for a long time.

"Take good care of yourself," Kait said gently, and then made her way gingerly down the front steps to avoid the broken one. She heard the door close firmly behind her, and suspected that the old actress would head straight to the bourbon bottle, now that her visitor was gone and she could drink freely.

Kait thought about her visit and was profoundly depressed all the way home. It was like watching someone drown and not being able to save them.

She had just walked into her apartment when Maeve called her.

"How did it go?" she asked, obviously anxious. Kait had emailed her that she was going to see Agnes White that afternoon.

"I just got home," Kait said with a sigh. "I was with her for three hours. We watched **Queen Victoria** together. She must have every movie she ever made, on DVD, and I get the feeling she spends her days alone, watching them. It's really very sad, and she doesn't want to do the series."

"I figured she wouldn't, but it was worth a try," Maeve said, disappointed too. "Other than that, how was she? Does she look all right? Is she in good health?"

"At first glance she looks a hundred and two, but when you talk to her for a while, you see the same face emerge, just a lot older. She's very thin. And," Kait hesitated, not sure how much to tell her, "I urged her to come back to work, but she'd have some things to work out if she did."

"She's drinking?" Maeve asked, worried.

"You know about that?" She hadn't told Kait about it.

"More or less. I guessed. Her life fell apart pretty brutally when Roberto died, and some other things happened. She drank a lot then. I hoped it was only temporary."

"Her hands shake pretty badly, and I suspect she drinks all the time. She had a couple of stiff bourbons while I was there. She says she can stop whenever she wants to. She probably could, but it wouldn't be easy, especially if she's been drinking for a long time. I left the bible with her, but I doubt she'll read it. In fact, I'm sure she won't."

"She's stubborn, but she's a tough old bird, and she's far from stupid. It all depends if she wants to come back into the world or not."

"My guess would be 'not.' And aside from wanting her to play Hannabel, it's just such a terrible waste, to see her locked up in that house, drinking and watching her old movies. It was pretty depressing."

"I can imagine it would be," Maeve said sympathetically. "I'm sorry if I sent you on a wild-goose chase."

"It's all right. It was an honor to meet her. It was surreal, sitting there with her and watching the movie." Kait laughed at the memory of it. "How's Ian?" she asked.

"He's all right, about the same. He's in good spirits. Well, let's see if you hear from her."

"I don't think I will," Kait said and they hung up. She went to make a salad, and then she worked late at her desk on the column. She wanted to do a special one for Mother's Day, which took a lot of thought, given the complexity of mother-daughter relationships. She called Stephanie, but she was out. And she didn't want to bother Tom, they were always busy.

From time to time as she worked, she thought of the afternoon she had spent with Agnes White, and then went back to her work. It made her want to write about adult substance abuse. Many of her readers wrote to her about their alcoholic or drug-addicted spouses, or young people about their parents.

She went to bed late that night and got up early the next morning to get a jump-start on her desk at the office. It was Friday and she was looking forward to the weekend. She'd been going at full speed for weeks. It was seven when she got home that night, too tired to eat, feeling totally drained and longing for her bed. And she saw on her email that Becca had sent her a second draft of the latest script, but she was too tired to read it. She decided to look at it over the weekend with a fresh eye.

Kait was running a hot bath when she heard her phone ring, and rushed to pick it up, hoping it was one of her kids. She was still waiting to hear from Candace about dates when she could come to London, and she answered the phone as she turned off the bath.

"Mrs. Whittier?" a shaking voice asked her, and Kait knew instantly it was Agnes White.

"Yes," she said, wondering if Agnes was sober or drunk. She was almost too tired to deal with her, but didn't want to put her off.

"I read your bible," she said, and Kait was surprised. She'd obviously been curious about it. "It's a handsome piece of work and a good story. I can see why Maeve is doing it." She sounded sober, and Kait hoped she was, for her own sake if nothing else. After her visit the day before, Kait imagined her blind drunk, asleep on the couch every night, with one of her movies on TV. "I don't know why you want me in it, and I'm not sure it's the right part for me, but I thought about it all day today. I'd like to do it. I like the idea of working with Maeve. And I want to assure you," she said cautiously, "that I'll do what I need to do before we start shooting." Kait knew exactly what she meant and couldn't believe what she was hearing. Agnes was telling her that she was going to stop drinking. "When do you start?"

"July first," Kait said, utterly amazed.

"I'll be fine by then," Agnes assured her. "In fact,

long before that. I start tomorrow." Kait didn't want
to ask her where or how, but figured she could take
care of that herself, and maybe had before. And
if she didn't want to go to rehab, she could go to
AA, which worked too. She had four months to get
sober and ready to work.

"You're sure you want to do it?" Kait asked in disbelief.

"Do you still want me?" Agnes sounded worried
that Kait had changed her mind.

"Yes, I do," she said clearly. "We all do. Your being
on the show will make it a guaranteed success."

"Don't be so sure," Agnes said modestly. "Maeve
will do that for you."

"With both of you, it will be a sure hit. Should we
contact your agent?" she asked, although she hadn't
been able to find one listed for her.

"I think he's dead. I'll have my attorney handle it.
I don't need an agent anymore." She hadn't worked
in over ten years.

"The network is going to go crazy when we tell
them," Kait said, smiling, although she was nervous
about Agnes getting sober, and hoped she could
do it. But she seemed confident she could. "We'll
be in touch. I'll have the executive producer, Zack
Winter, contact you. Should I tell Maeve or do you
want to?"

"You can tell her. Tell her I'm doing it because of
her. And because of you," she said and startled Kait.

"What did I do?" Kait was surprised.

"You watched my movie with me. You're a good woman. It was a kind thing to do. And you wrote a good part for me. I wouldn't do it otherwise. I like playing cantankerous. I'll have some fun with it. Do I have to learn to fly?"

She seemed concerned about it, and Kait laughed. She was almost giddy at the news that Agnes White had accepted to play the role of Hannabel. What a victory for them! "We have stuntmen for that. All you have to do is learn your lines and show up on your shooting days."

"That's never been a problem."

"And we'll be filming in the New York area. That was one of Maeve's conditions."

"Thank you," Agnes said simply, and they both knew why. Kait had walked into her house the day before and saved her life. If no one had stopped her, she would have just sat there and drunk herself to death, and Agnes knew it too. "I won't let you down."

"I know you won't," Kait said solemnly, and prayed that she was right. She couldn't wait to tell Zack and Maeve as soon as they hung up.

Chapter 9

With Agnes White agreeing to play Hannabel, they almost had their full cast, and with some
very important names. Agnes White and Maeve
O'Hara would knock everyone's socks off on a TV
series. Dan Delaney was the handsome young heart-
throb they needed as a draw for younger women,
no matter how slutty his reputation was, they ate it
up. And Charlotte Manning was more of the same.
Abaya Jones was their hot new ingénue, a fresh face
on the scene, and Brad Evers, in the role of the bad-
ass younger brother, was a promising young actor
people liked. He was only twenty-one, and teen-
age viewers would adore him. And they had found
the perfect actor to play Johnny West, Maggie's
big romance. He had been on two very successful
soaps and had a number of devoted fans. His name
was Malcolm Bennett. He had played mostly vil-
lains and was excited about playing a good guy for
a change. There had already been some meetings
with the cast, and they all seemed pleased with their

roles, although no one was enthused about working with Charlotte Manning, who was said to be a diva, and never got along with the other women on the set. But there was no question her name was a big draw, which was what mattered to them all. It was going to be a fantastic cast.

The one missing link was Anne Wilder's lover late in the show. They were talking to Nick Brooke, a huge film star, but hadn't convinced him yet. He was afraid to get locked into a long-term show if it was a success. His entire career had been spent in feature films, and it would be a big change for him if he took the part. Phillip Green, the big star slated to play Anne's husband, Loch, was delighted to sign for four episodes. They had their cast.

As soon as Kait signed her own contract the following week, she knew she had to tell the magazine, particularly before it leaked out. She had no idea if the editor in chief of **Woman's Life** would want her to give up the column, or try to juggle it while she was working on the set. It was still possible that the show would fail in the ratings and get canceled, but with the lineup they had, it seemed unlikely. Kait was willing to do whatever the magazine wanted, at least until they knew how the show was doing in its early episodes. If they were green-lighted for a second season, Kait was thinking that that might be the right time to end her column, or pass it on to someone else if they preferred. It would be a big change for her after twenty years, and for her readers, who would be heartbroken to lose her.

Paula Stein, the editor in chief, cried when Kait met with her later in the week, but she was enormously impressed by what Kait had undertaken, which was essentially starting a new career, and not an easy one.

"It's all happened very fast. I wrote the story three months ago, and it's just been a series of lucky breaks. I never thought this would happen. We go on the air in six months, and start shooting the show in three. I just signed my contract a few days ago, so I thought I should talk to you. I'll do whatever you want. Quit, work on the column at night. We'll be shooting for about three and a half months. I think I can manage it for that long. And we should have a sense of how the show will do after the first few episodes. We're shooting thirteen episodes, and if the network is happy, they'll have us do another nine."

"I'd love to have you keep writing the column for as long as you can," Paula said hopefully. "I don't see how we can continue it once you quit. The readers love you, and no one can do what you do." It was flattering to hear, but not necessarily true.

"I grew into it. Someone else can too."

"You have a magic touch."

"I just hope the magic works on TV," Kait said cautiously.

"I'm sure it will." Paula hugged Kait when the

meeting ended, and Kait agreed to write the column until the end of the year. It gave them time to groom someone else, or hire a new writer just for that. They had time to figure it out.

By that afternoon the rumor mill was buzzing, and Carmen slipped into her office with a worried frown, and closed the door.

"There's an ugly rumor out there that you're leaving. Tell me it isn't true." She looked bereft at the thought.

"I'm not leaving," Kait said, sorry she hadn't told her first, but she had felt obligated to tell her editor in chief before she told anyone else and let her make the announcement. Paula Stein was a good woman and deserved the courtesy. She had always been fair to Kait, although Kait had been there ten years longer than she had. "I'm taking on a second job for now. We'll see how it works out. I may come crawling back in no time. I'll be here till sometime in June, and then I'll be writing the column off-site."

"Why?" Carmen looked shocked. All she'd heard was that Kait was quitting, or might be, she had no idea about the rest. Kait had asked Paula not to disclose it until the show was announced, and clearly she hadn't.

"It sounds crazy, but I'm doing a TV show. I wrote the bible for it, and I'm co-executive producing. It's a big job. I'll do the column for as long as I can."

"A TV show? Are you kidding? How did that happen?"

"It just did. I sat next to a TV producer on New Year's Eve, and the next thing I knew, I wrote a story, and it all fell into place like lightning after that. I'm still in shock myself."

"That's crazy," Carmen said, as she slipped into a chair and stared at her friend. "Who's in it?"

"You can't tell anyone," but she trusted her not to talk, and reeled off some of the names. Carmen stared at her in disbelief.

"You're lying. Dan Delaney? Oh my God, give me one night with him and I'll die a happy woman."

"Maybe not," Kait said, laughing. "Apparently he'd sleep with a yak and cheats on everyone, and all his ex-girlfriends hate him. We're scared to death of what he'll do on the set, but everyone has the same reaction to him you do. So he's good for the show, if he doesn't drive everyone nuts."

"What's Maeve O'Hara like?"

"Wonderful. The nicest person you've ever met and a real pro. I can't wait to watch her work."

"I can't believe this. It just fell out of the sky?"

"Pretty much."

"What's the producer like? Is he cute? Are you having an affair with him?" She was dying to know.

"Yes, he's cute, and no, I'm not having an affair with him. We work really well together, but I think we both want to keep it that way and not screw it up.

This is business. And the serious people in it don't play around. I'm learning a lot from him."

"Can I come watch on the set?"

Kait nodded, and realized that she was going to miss seeing Carmen every day.

"I'm happy for you, Kait," Carmen said. "You deserve this. I would never have said it, but you were stuck in a rut here. You're too talented for this, and too good a writer. I hope this turns out really well for you." She sounded totally sincere.

"I hope so too," she said, and got up to give Carmen a hug.

"And I don't care if Dan Delaney is a slut. I want to meet him."

"You will, I promise."

"I can't wait to watch the show." She left Kait's office a few minutes later, and the magazine was buzzing with the news that Kait was leaving. That night, Kait called Stephanie in San Francisco. She had friends over and they were watching a basketball game.

"You're doing **what**?" Stephanie thought she'd heard wrong. "What kind of show? And you're selling bibles? Have you lost your mind, Mom?" She knew her mother went to church occasionally, but that sounded extreme to her. "Did you just become Mormon or something?"

"No. I said I wrote a bible for a TV series, and one of the cable networks picked it up. We're shooting it in July, and it goes on the air in October."

"You did? When did that happen? Who's in it?" Stephanie sounded dubious, and her mother told her the major names. "Holy shit, do you mean it? This sounds like a big deal."

"It could be, if people like the show."

"What's it about?"

"Women in aviation in the 1940s and '50s."

"That sounds a little weird. Why did you write about that?"

"I used my grandmother for inspiration. Even you will have to watch it at least once," Kait said, teasing. She knew that Stephanie and Frank never watched TV, except sports. They were baseball fanatics, and loved football and basketball as well.

"Well, I'm proud of you, Mom. I never expected you to do something like that."

"Neither did I," Kait said, and laughed.

"Can I tell people about it?"

"Not yet. The network will make an announcement once we have all the contracts signed, all the deals set. That takes a while."

"Can I tell Frank?"

"Of course." They talked for a few more minutes and then Stephanie went back to the game and their friends. But before she did, she told her mother again how proud of her she was.

Kait called Tommy after that. They had just finished dinner, and Maribeth was putting the girls to bed. Tommy was even more startled than his sister, and asked Kait various questions about the deal she'd made. He was impressed by the contract she'd gotten and that she would be co-executive producer with Zack, making many of the decisions with him.

"What are you going to do about the column?" he asked her.

"I agreed to do it till the end of the year, but it's going to be a juggling act once we start shooting. I'll stay at the magazine till June, after that I have to be on the set." She didn't go to the magazine every day anyway, and worked from home a lot of the time.

"Did you tell the girls yet?"

"I just called Stephanie, and I'm going to call Candace in a few hours, and try to get her in her morning. I'm not even sure where she is. I haven't talked to her in weeks. Have you?"

"Not since we Skyped with her on Christmas at your house. I never know how to reach her."

"Neither do I," Kait admitted. "I want to go over and see her when she has a break, but I don't think she's had one in months. She goes straight from one story to another."

He knew that about his sister too. "Give her my love when you find her. And, Mom, I'm really proud of you," he said it with real emotion in his voice, and she was touched.

"Thank you, sweetheart. And give Maribeth my love."

"She's going to be blown away. She has the hots for Dan Delaney." It seemed like every female in America did, which confirmed to Kait that they had made the right decision when they chose him for the part. "And she loves Maeve O'Hara. She's a very big deal."

"Yes, she is, she's great," Kait confirmed. "But don't say anything until it's announced."

"Thanks for calling to tell me the news," he said, and one minute later, they hung up. All Kait had to do was tell Candace now, if she could reach her. She stayed up till two A.M. to call her at seven A.M. in London, but the call went straight to voicemail, and Kait had a feeling she wasn't back yet from wherever she was. She could have sent her a text or an email, but wasn't sure she'd get them, and she wanted to tell her on the phone. It had been too long since they'd talked, at least several weeks, before Kait went to L.A. But she was pleased that she'd told Stephanie and Tom, and their reaction had been warm and loving. It was definitely a new chapter in her life, and she wanted to share it with her children.

She was amused by all the women's reactions to Dan Delaney, and had to remember to tell Zack. As Zack had predicted, Becca's scripts were improving day by day, as she hit her stride and got comfortable with the characters she was writing. She sent scripts to Kait by email, and she read them at night after work. Becca had done some really great writing for the first episodes and despite her youthful looks, she had talent and depth to her writing when she worked at it. Kait made suggestions whenever she thought it was necessary, and Becca took the comments and added additional material to the scripts without resistance. And the distance between them didn't seem to be a problem.

Everything was going smoothly. Agnes had called her to say she had gone to AA and was looking for a sponsor. She admitted that she had been to meetings before and knew how it worked.

"Do you need to worry about someone talking to the press?" Kait asked her with concern, and Agnes sounded incensed.

"I should hope not. That's the whole point of AA. What you hear and who you see there stays there. I've seen people at meetings who have a lot more at risk than I do. No one ever breaks that code. I'm going to two meetings a day."

"Is it hard?" Kait asked gently, touched that Agnes had called to check in and reassure her.

"Of course it's hard. It's a bitch. But I'd rather be working than watching myself on DVDs all day. I got in a bad spot. You jolted me out of it. I don't know if the show will be any good, or me in it, but I needed to do this anyway. I hired a maid yesterday. It was either that or burn my house down. I had ten years of magazines stacked up in every room. I told her to throw them all away." What was happening to Agnes was a miracle. She was finding her way back to the human race.

"Let me know if I can do anything to help," Kait offered.

"I'll be fine," Agnes promised again. "I didn't

want you to worry." And then she sounded serious. "I called Maeve. She told me about Ian. That's
a tragedy. He's incredibly talented and a wonderful man. I don't know what she's going to do
after . . . when . . ." She couldn't bring herself to say
the words, but Kait understood, and was worried
about it too. They had been married for twenty-five
years. "At least the show will keep her busy, and her
girls. We'll have to be there for her when things get
rough." It dawned on Kait as she listened that the
show was going to be more than just a workplace
and a lucky break for all of them, and an opportunity for the lesser-known actors in the group. It
would be a family of sorts and a support system too.
And if the show ran for a long time, they would
face life's challenges together, its joys and tragedies
and the important moments in their lives, for several years. It was comforting in a way, and she was
looking forward to it. The people on the show were
going to fill her life.

Zack emailed her that day to tell her that they
had hired a very talented young British costume designer, Lally Bristol. She was fantastic with historical work, was already starting to research the time
period of the series, and was very excited to be on
board. He had sent Kait a photograph of her with
his email. She was a beautiful young woman, about
six feet tall, with a shapely figure and long blond
hair. Kait just hoped that Dan Delaney didn't go
after her, but she was probably used to men like

him and dealt with them all the time. It was going to be her first series too. She had done most of her work in feature films, as many of the actors had.

Agnes had promised to call her again, and Kait tried to reach Candace several times in the next few days. Her calls continued to go to voicemail immediately, without ringing first, which usually meant she was out of the country. Kait had no idea where she was, and that always made her uneasy.

She was working on Becca's most recent script, making notes one night, when the phone rang. An unfamiliar voice with a British accent asked for her by name. She had no idea who it was, and her caller ID just showed that the call was from the BBC with a London number, but it was the middle of the night for them, and nine P.M. in New York.

"Yes, this is she," she said, putting the script down, with a sudden anxious feeling. "Is something wrong?"

"I'm calling about your daughter Candace. She's all right," he said immediately, to reassure her. "There's been an incident."

"What kind of incident? Where is she?" Kait said immediately, as panic seized her in a viselike grip.

"She's actually in Mombasa. She was doing a story on a refugee camp a hundred miles out of the city, and there was an attack on the road. A mine, she's been injured, but she's all right, minor burns to her arms and chest." He didn't tell Kait that the driver and photographer with her had been killed.

All Kait needed to be told was that her daughter was alive. "We're airlifting her to London tonight. She's in stable condition, and we wanted to get her medical care here at home." Kait was on her feet immediately, pacing the room, thinking of Candace injured, and her heart was in her mouth.

"How bad are the burns?"

"Second and third degree, I'm told. Mostly second, with a third-degree burn on one hand. It just seemed the wisest course to get her out. We will keep you fully informed, Ms. Whittier, I can assure you. Her plane should land in a few hours. She's coming in by medevac and she'll go straight to the hospital when she arrives. I'll call you with an update then."

"What hospital is she going to?"

"The adult burns unit at Chelsea and Westminster Hospital. They have one of the best burn centers in England."

"I'm going to try to catch a flight tonight," Kait said, suddenly distracted, trying to think of everything she had to do. "Please tell me your name and how to reach you."

"You really don't need to rush over. I was told that her condition is stable, and she is not at any life-threatening risk."

"I'm her mother. I'm not going to sit in New York while she goes to a hospital in London with third-degree burns."

"I understand," he said coolly.

"Please call me or leave me a message when she

arrives. I'll contact you as soon as I land, or go straight to the hospital. Thank you for calling me." She was listed as Candace's next of kin, and she lived in dread of something like this happening. She called Tommy in Texas as soon as she hung up and told him the situation, that she was going to try to catch a flight that night and wanted him to know where she was. He said he'd call the hospital himself in a few hours to see what he could find out about his sister's condition, and try to reach her when she was admitted. He was worried about her too.

And then Kait hung up and called British Airways. They had a one o'clock flight to London that night. She had to check in at eleven, and leave her apartment by ten to get to the airport, which left her forty minutes to pack, dress, and go. She started racing around the apartment as soon as she paid for her ticket and booked a seat.

She was out the door at five to ten, and had called for an Uber car, which was waiting downstairs. She had thrown whatever clothes she thought she'd need into a small rolling suitcase she could take as carry-on, and threw Becca's script, a file of letters for her column, and whatever else she could think of into a tote bag, and she got to the airport on time to check in for the flight. Her phone rang as she was boarding the plane. It was the same man in London, who said that the medevac flight had arrived, Candace was en route to the hospital at that moment, and was reported to be in good condition. Kait called her cellphone as soon as they hung up, and for the first time in weeks, Candace answered, in a groggy voice.

"Are you okay, baby?" Kait asked her, feeling tears fill her eyes.

"I'm fine, Mom. We ran over a land mine."

"Thank God you weren't killed."

"I wasn't, but other people were. It was a mess."

"How bad are the burns?"

"They don't hurt," Candace said vaguely and Kait knew that wasn't a good sign. "I can't see them, they're covered up."

"I'm getting on a flight now. I'll be there at one P.M. your time and I'll come straight to the hospital." Kait was talking to her on her cell as she took her seat on the plane.

"You don't have to do that, Mom. I'm fine."

"Well, I'm not. You scared the hell out of me. I'm coming over to be with you and see for myself."

Candace smiled as she listened to her. "Don't you have something better to do?" she asked. She knew her mother, and had suspected she would come as soon as she heard. Her first priority had always been her children, and nothing had changed since they'd grown up.

"Actually, no, I don't. See you in a few hours," she said, and had to turn off her phone. She had sent a text to her editor in chief, and another one to Zack to tell them where she was going, and promised to be in touch. And she'd sent her flight details to Stephanie and Tom.

She was awake for most of the flight, worrying about her daughter, and nodded off just before they landed. She woke up as soon as the wheels hit the runway. All she wanted to do was get to the hospital to see Candace. She had no luggage to get at baggage claim, and raced through customs after explaining to them it was an emergency, and then ran to the curb to find a cab. She was at the hospital forty minutes later, and a nurse directed her to her daughter's room. She found Candace sedated and half asleep with heavy bandages on her arms, and another one on her chest. She woke up and smiled when she saw her mother, and Kait leaned down kissed her forehead, relieved to be with her.

"You couldn't go to beauty school like a normal person?" It was an old joke between them about the kinds of dangerous jobs Candace had always been drawn to. This was the first time she had been seriously injured. A doctor assured them a little while later that the burns weren't as bad as they had feared. There might be some scarring, but she wouldn't need skin grafts, and they thought she could go home in about a week, after they checked her out more thoroughly and observed her for a while.

"I was supposed to start another story tomorrow," Candace complained. She was the image of her mother, with the same green eyes and red hair.

"I don't want to hear a word about another story, or I'm taking you home to New York with me," she said sternly, and her daughter smiled again.

"Tell that to my bosses," she said groggily.

"I'll be happy to. I wish to hell you'd get another job," Kait said and settled into a chair in the room, and they both took a nap. Doctors had told Candace she'd have to wear the dressings for about a month, but she didn't seem to mind. She was far more upset about her colleagues who had been injured, and the two who had died. The others had been too badly wounded to be moved.

Kait dropped her bag off at a hotel the next day, and checked her messages. Zack had emailed her several times, and she called him as soon as she got to her room.

"Are you okay? How's your daughter?" He was seriously concerned about both of them.

"She's okay. She got some nasty burns on her arms and chest, nothing on her face, and she won't need grafts, although there may be some scarring, but thank God, she's alive." Kait still sounded badly shaken by what had happened. "She's the only one they shipped back. They were making a documentary at a refugee camp, and hit a land mine on the road to Mombasa. I hate her fucking job," she said with feeling, and he laughed at how she said it.

"So would I in your shoes. Let's find her something else to do," he said quietly.

"I've tried. She loves what she does, and thinks she's going to change the world. She might, but she'll give me a stroke in the meantime."

"Let me know if there's anything I can do. And get some rest, Kait. It sounds like she's going to be okay. This is hard on you too." She was touched by the concern in his voice, and she called Tommy and Stephanie after that. They had both spoken to their sister after Kait left the hospital, and were worried about her.

"I asked her if her face is messed up and she said it's not," Stephanie told her mother. She was brilliant with computers but had no filter with humans, and Kait could just imagine her saying it to Candace.

"She's going to be okay," Kait told them both, but it was a harsh reminder of the dangers Candace faced constantly. And she had a serious talk with her daughter about it the next day. Candace wasn't as groggy, and insisted to her mother that she was fine, she loved her job, and she didn't want to move back to New York.

"Can't you make documentaries in England or Europe? Why do you have to be in every war zone in the world?"

"Because that's where the interesting stories are, Mom," Candace insisted. Kait could see she wasn't getting anywhere, and told her about the series then, and just as her siblings had been, Candace was enormously impressed. "That's fantastic, Mom."

Kait told her who was in it, what the story was,

and everything she'd been doing for the past three months. And then she went back to the hotel while Candace took a nap. She had the hotel print out the latest script Becca had sent her, and she made notes on it, and then went back to the hospital. Candace had just woken up and was talking to her boss at the BBC. She was upset that they had given her next assignment to someone else, and they were insisting that she take several weeks off. Kait knew that it was a losing battle and she'd be back in the field as soon as she could.

She stayed in London until Candace was released a week later, and settled her at home. Candace was determined to at least go to the office then, bandages and all, and once she did, Kait knew it was time to go home. Candace was doing well, and Kait had nothing to do now that she was back at work. She had been in London for ten days, and she'd enjoyed being with her despite the circumstances. She hated to leave, but she could sense that she was getting on Candace's nerves by being around. She didn't want anyone fussing over her, she just wanted to be in the office. Kait was worried, sure that she would talk them into sending her somewhere too soon. She didn't want her going anywhere dangerous again, but Candace had a mind of her own.

Kait was sad to leave. They went out to dinner the night before, and the next morning before Candace left for work, Kait gave her a long hug. And then Kait took off for the airport.

Maeve called her as soon as she got back. She had heard about Candace's accident from Zack and had texted several times with Kait while she was away.

"How is she?" Maeve asked her.

"She's all right, all she wanted was to go back to work."

"Can't you talk her into doing something less dangerous?" Maeve felt sorry for Kait. She could hear the fatigue and worry in her voice.

"It's an argument I never win with her. She thinks she's wasting her life unless she's risking it to make it a better world. Her sister is perfectly happy going to basketball games, and her brother is selling fast food in Texas. Meanwhile, Candace has been on some mission or other since she was twelve years old. I have no idea how three children with the same parents can be so different. She's been giving me heart failure for twenty years. She could have been killed."

"Thank God she wasn't," Maeve said with deep compassion for Kait.

"What have I missed since I've been gone?" Kait sounded bone tired after a week at the hospital with Candace and the flight home. She missed her already, but it felt good to be back to more mundane pursuits. Nothing worried her more than her children when one of them had a problem or was hurt.

"I think Nick Brooke agreed to take the part of my big love interest in the final episode of season one, which means that he'll be back in season two as a main character, if we last," Maeve filled her in. "I'm looking forward to working with him. He's a terrific actor, and a serious guy. He lives in Wyoming when he's not working. He's a real man's man, and kind of a cowboy. He's perfect for the part, as an ex–fighter pilot and war hero. Ian knows him better than I do." He was a huge name, which would be a big draw for season two, if they got that far, which they all hoped they would. "We have a passionate relationship. We have a huge fight and it ends in a big love scene at the end of the first episode I do with him. That ought to be fun. He's a good actor. Let's have lunch when you have time," Maeve suggested. They could both hardly wait to start the show. And she said that Ian was doing well. Nothing had changed or gotten worse, which was a victory for now.

Kait checked in with Zack too, and he brought her up to speed on everything. He had sent her flowers in London to cheer her up, and she'd been very touched. He told her about Nick Brooke too, and she congratulated him for talking him into it.

"I don't think I deserve the credit for it. He wanted to work with Maeve. The prospect of a weekly show with her was too appealing to resist, although he was disappointed we don't have any horses in the show. He flies his own plane too. He's definitely the right man for the job. He wanted to do his own stunts, but the insurance company won't let him. He knows a lot about planes and aviation in the early days."

"He sounds like an intriguing guy," Kait said.

"He is. Now get some rest. I'll talk to you in a few days."

Kait climbed into her bed after calling to check on Candace in London, and Agnes called just as she was falling asleep. It took her a minute to figure out who it was. Agnes's voice sounded rough.

"Is something wrong?" Kait could barely keep her eyes open, and forced herself to wake up.

"I can't do this. I can't do the show."

"Why not?" Kait asked her, suddenly wide awake.

"I just can't. It's too hard. I went to three meetings today."

"Yes, you can," Kait told her in a stern voice. "You know you can. And you want to do the show. You've done this before, and you can do it again."

"I'm powerless over alcohol," she said, repeating the first step in AA.

"No, you're not. You're stronger than that."

"I want a drink," she said miserably.

"Go to a meeting, call your sponsor. Go for a walk. Take a shower."

"It's not worth it."

"Yes, it is," Kait insisted. "Just take it one day at a time. Go to bed. And go to a meeting in the morning." There was a long silence at the other end, and then a sigh as Agnes exhaled.

"All right. I'm sorry I called you. You sound exhausted. I just had a bad moment. I was sitting here staring at a bottle of bourbon, and I wanted to drink so badly, I could taste it."

"I thought you got rid of all your booze." She had told Kait that the last time she called.

"I found the bottle under the bed, literally," Agnes said.

"Pour it out, and throw the bottle away."

"What a waste," she said, sounding despondent. "Okay, I'll do it. Get some sleep," she said, seeming better, and Kait fell back against her pillows with a groan after she hung up and realized what had happened. She had just adopted an entire cast of children, to worry about along with her own. She was going to have to be concerned about who Dan was sleeping with, if Charlotte was fighting with someone, if Agnes was staying sober, if Maeve's husband was still alive, if Abaya could remember her lines, and if Becca could write the show. She had taken all of them under her wing, with their problems, their fears, their quirks, their tragedies, their needs and desires. The thought of it was overwhelming as she closed her eyes for a minute, and within seconds, she was asleep.

Chapter 10

Life seemed to calm down for Kait in May. Zack called her every few days to report progress on the preparations for the show. All the contracts had been signed, the actors lined up. Lally Bristol was working on the costumes. And the scouts had found two perfect locations for them. One was a small airstrip on Long Island where the owner had an extensive collection of antique planes he was happy to rent to them, and he was excited to be involved in the show. And they had found the perfect family "home" for the Wilders in upstate New York. They were going to shoot it to look like the airstrip and house were on the same property, which wasn't hard to do with computers in postproduction. Becca was writing dynamite scripts. Agnes called Kait from time to time and was still going to AA. Candace reported that her burns were healing and she was chafing to be off and running again. And Maeve and Kait had lunch at the deli where they had met originally, and Maeve said Ian was responding well to some medications they were giving him to slow the progression of the disease slightly, and there had been no recent change. And Kait was keeping up with her column.

She realized that this was the quiet before the storm, and that from July on she'd be running like a madwoman to attend their shooting schedule, work on the scripts with Becca, help solve problems on the set, and write her column and blog whenever and wherever she could. And it occurred to her that Carmen's original suggestion had been a good one. She wanted to take a vacation with her children, while she still had the time to do it and before her schedule got away from her.

She called and asked each of them to set aside a week in June. They had to wait until Merrie and Lucie Anne got out of school, and she researched places online that would be fun for all of them and easy to get to. The BBC had decided not to send Candace on heavy assignments for a while, much to her chagrin, so she said she could make it too. The location Kait homed in on was a ranch in Wyoming, outside Jackson Hole, which sounded ideal. She checked back with all of them, set the date, and booked rooms at the ranch for the second week in June, which suited her too, since she and Paula had agreed that she would start her "work at home" arrangement with the magazine on June first. She didn't have to go to the office, and she had agreed to continue to respond to letters and write

her column till the end of the year. They would re-
visit the subject again then, depending on plans for
the show.

She couldn't wait to go to the ranch with her
kids, and they were excited too. And so were the
girls. She sent her granddaughters pink cowboy
boots in the sizes Maribeth gave her, and Tommy
emailed her pictures of them wearing them with
little denim skirts and cowboy hats. They were all
set for their big adventure, and the date came faster
than expected.

There was a lunch for Kait at the magazine on her
last official day of work onsite. She was turning
her office over to one of the senior editors, and Carmen looked mournful at not having Kait to visit
anymore during their workday. She whispered to
Kait during lunch that she was trying to get a column now too.

Everyone was thrilled for Kait and excited about
the show. The network had made a big announcement on May first, with posters everywhere with
teasers, and photographs of Dan, Charlotte, and
Abaya to appeal to younger viewers, and others
with Maeve, Agnes, and Phillip Green, the actor
who would play Loch, and some that showed the
entire cast. TV commercials for the show would
begin in September, from scenes they'd have shot by
then. They were spending a fortune on advertising,
and people were talking about **The Wilder Women**
with anticipation. It gave Kait a rush every time she

saw one of the posters, and Zack said there were billboards up on Sunset Boulevard in L.A.

Her colleagues at the magazine were sad to see her go, but everyone wished her well.

And when Kait left for Wyoming, she couldn't wait to spend a week with her kids. Zack mentioned to her on the phone the night before she left that Nick Brooke's ranch was an hour outside Jackson Hole. He said he had a big spread with lots of horses.

"Maybe you should call him and say hi," Zack suggested. They were keeping him a dark secret until the last episode of the show, a teaser for season two. A hot romance between Maeve O'Hara and Nick Brooke would be a tremendous draw, and bring everyone back for sure. So his joining the show was very hush-hush, but he had signed his contract for the final episode, and a provisional one for the second season, provided the show was still running. They had paid him a fortune, but Zack and Kait agreed that it was worth it for the viewers it would attract. Women of every age went crazy over Nick.

They had Dan to appeal to the younger women, and Nick was a powerful draw. He was fifty-two, but didn't look it, and had the kind of rugged, masculine image that made women swoon. And their male viewers could lust over Charlotte or Abaya, or Maeve. Their older audience would be ecstatic to see Agnes again. There was something for everyone on the show. And some great flying scenes during the war with the vintage planes they'd be using. The show had everything it needed to be a huge success. And Nick would be an important part of it. He had a big movie coming out that summer, which would be a great prelude to his appearing as a surprise on the show.

"Won't he think I'm weird, just calling him to say hello out of the blue?" Kait had responded to Zack when he told her to call him. They were shooting him in late August or early September for the last segment on a closed set, and everyone had to sign confidentiality agreements not to reveal that he'd be on the show.

"Of course not," Zack answered her question. "You're the co-executive producer. He might have questions about the character, and it would be nice to get to know him." Zack and Kait had met him in a meeting with his lawyer, and Kait had shaken his hand, and was struck by how handsome he was. He was a quiet, retiring person, and Kait knew he never went to L.A. unless he was working. He was originally from a small town in Texas, and had bought an enormous ranch in Wyoming when he started to do well. He was supposed to be very professional, no problem to work with, and kept to himself. And whatever he did with his personal life, he managed to keep out of the press. He had said he was reluctant to do interviews about the show, even once he was officially part of the cast. "You don't have to spend the week with him, just make contact. I want him to feel like he's part of it, even if he's only appearing once this season. Meeting him there might be an easy way to break the ice."

Zack had discovered that Nick had started his career as a country music singer in Nashville but wouldn't sing on their show. Nick said that was past history, but Zack had found an old CD of his, and said he had a great voice.

Nick's personal life was a mystery to everyone except a few close friends, and his agent had informed them that he intended to keep it that way. No one knew if he had a girlfriend, who he dated, or what he did when he wasn't working, other than run his ranch, where he bred horses. He was occasionally seen at high-end auctions, buying champions to breed. They were his passion, and the horses he sold were said to be among the finest in the state. Zack texted Kait his number, but Kait wasn't sure if she would call him or not. She wanted to concentrate on her kids, and didn't want to steal time from them with business meetings for the show.

They were each flying to Wyoming separately. Candace was flying from London to Chicago and from there to Jackson Hole, Stephanie and Frank had a direct flight from San Francisco, and Tommy and his family would be using his father-in-law's plane. Kait was flying to Denver from New York, and from there to Jackson Hole, and they would all meet up at the ranch within a few hours of one another. The only caution was that Candace couldn't expose her recently burned arms to the sun. But they were all planning to ride, and Kait had already arranged for mountaintop picnics, a fishing expedition for Tommy and Frank with a guide, and she wanted to take them all to the rodeo. There was apparently a great one on Wednesday nights that all the locals went to and the tourists loved. She'd asked the ranch to organize it for them.

Kait finished her next column on the flight from New York. She knew she'd have to be artful now to find the time to do it, once she was spending her days and nights on the set. She watched a movie during lunch, and when they landed in Jackson Hole, she noticed how many private jets were sitting in a designated space. It was a beautiful place, a watering hole for the rich and famous who didn't want to go to the more obvious locations like Sun Valley or Aspen. The Teton mountains looked majestic as she got off the plane.

She claimed her baggage and found the driver the ranch had sent for her. He told her on the way to it that Tommy and his group had already arrived about an hour before, and were settling in. She knew there was a pool for the children, and they would be in a cluster of cabins, with specific horses assigned to them for their stay, according to their equestrian ability. Tommy's girls had their own ponies at home, which their grandfather had given them, and Maribeth was an expert rider. Kait's children knew how to ride, but had never spent much time doing so, since they had grown up in New York, but they were proficient enough to enjoy it at the ranch. She had booked a sunset ride for all of them that night.

Tommy and Maribeth and the children were in the lobby waiting for Kait when she arrived, and Merrie put her arms around her and gave her a big hug, while Lucie Anne explained that she was going to ride a horse that was bigger than her pony, and this horse was named Rosie and she was very nice.

"Are you going to ride with us too?" she asked her grandmother. She was wearing the pink cowboy boots Kait had sent them, and pink shorts and a pink T-shirt with the map of Texas on it. Tommy thanked his mother and said their cabin was great. Kait was just as pleased with her own when she saw it. They were comfortable and luxurious and simply decorated. An hour later, Stephanie and Frank showed up, in their usual hiking gear, which was their uniform for all occasions, including work. They were holding hands when Kait saw them, and Stephanie whispered to her a little later that Frank was afraid of horses but wanted to be a good sport.

"I'm sure they'll put him on a nice, tame horse, they must deal with all kinds of people who aren't great riders here. Just be sure you tell them at the stable, and he doesn't have to ride with us if he doesn't want to." Kait wanted everyone to have a good time, and didn't want anyone to be forced to do things they didn't want. She told Frank and

Tommy about the fishing trip she'd arranged for them the next day. Tommy loved to fish, and he went deep-sea fishing with his father-in-law in the Gulf of Mexico every chance he got. He knew this would be less exciting, but fun too, and he liked Frank and was happy to spend time with him.

It was four in the afternoon when Candace arrived looking pale and tired, but delighted to see them all. She had on a long-sleeved blouse so you couldn't see the dressings she still had to wear on her recent burns. Her mother noticed that she'd lost weight but didn't comment. The vacation would do her good after what she'd been through. They were all thrilled to be there, and loved the idea of the sunset ride, and they turned up at the main barn promptly at six in jeans and boots. They were given helmets and introduced to their horses. The two little girls looked adorable astride their very sedate horses, and Frank was assigned an equally quiet one. They had a female guide who was a senior at the University of Wyoming and said she worked at the ranch every summer. She led them out on a path into the hills, between fields of wildflowers, and pointed out landmarks of interest. She was from Cheyenne and told them about the Indians who had lived in the area long ago, and encouraged them to make sure they went to the rodeo on Wednesday night.

"And we have our own rodeo here at the ranch on Friday nights. You just missed it, but you can sign up if you want to be in it next week. And you can even win a ribbon," she said to the girls, and they begged their mother to let them do it.

They were back from their ride in time for dinner in the main ranch house, and had their own table, and the girls were happy playing with their two aunts.

"My daddy said you got blown up and hurt your arms," Merrie said seriously to Candace, and she smiled.

"Yes, I did, sort of, but I'm fine now," Candace said, and Merrie showed her some of the games on her iPad, and they helped themselves from the buffet. There was a barbecue every night, and a campfire afterward where two of the stable hands played guitar and sang familiar songs, and everyone chimed in and sang along. It was exactly what Kait had hoped for, and she sat back, watching them with a peaceful smile on her face.

"You look happy, Mom," Tommy said when he noticed, and she nodded.

"I always am when I'm with all of you." This was a rare treat for her, and a longer time than she had spent with them in years. She was grateful they had each made the effort to spend a week as a family with her.

Stephanie and Frank were the first to leave the campfire and go to bed, and Maribeth and Tommy took the girls back to their cabin when Merrie started to yawn. Lucie Anne was already asleep on her father's lap, and he carried her easily to bed. Candace and her mother sat enjoying the songs for longer, and had a glass of wine at the bar afterward. Candace teased her that several of the old cowboys had been watching Kait. She had noticed it too, but didn't pay any attention. She assumed they were just curious and not attracted to her.

"You're a beautiful woman, Mom. You should get out more. Your new venture in TV will do you good."

"I'm going to be busy on the set with the cast and the scripts, not picking up men," she brushed off Candace's comments.

"They'll be picking you up." Candace smiled at her. She didn't admit it, but she had missed her mother after she left London. As much as it annoyed her at times when Kait fussed over her, it was nice to know that someone cared.

"Are you feeling all right?" her mother asked her. "You looked tired when you arrived."

"It's a long flight for me. And it's been boring stuck in London. I miss being out in the field, working on the documentaries. A desk job just isn't my style. I think they'll send me somewhere next month. Dealing with the dressings on my arms has been a drag. I have a nurse come in to do it now. They're almost healed. It took longer than I thought it would."

"I was hoping you'd stay around London for a while, and rethink what you're doing. Driving over a land mine, as a normal occurrence in your line of work, is not what I want for you," Kait said quietly, it had been haunting her since it happened. "You could have been one of the unlucky ones who got killed," she reminded her. She had thought of it a thousand times.

"It doesn't happen often, Mom," Candace said and sipped her wine.

"You only have to get killed once." Kait looked at her sternly, and Candace laughed.

"I get the point. I'm always careful. I don't know what happened this time. We had a lousy guide."

"Which can happen. Just do me a favor and think about it before you go running off again to some godforsaken place."

Candace nodded but didn't promise. "I guess I don't know what I want to be yet when I grow up. Stephanie has always been exactly what she is now, a total geek, and she's good at it. And Tommy seems so sure of his Texas life and being the fast food king one day when Maribeth's father retires. And I can't see myself coming back to New York to sit at a desk. I've always wanted to make the world a better place and right injustice. I'm just not sure how anymore. We see so many terrible things when we're on the road. And there's so little we can do to change them. What we do with the documentaries feels like a drop in the bucket sometimes. And too often the women who cooperate with us and let me interview them are severely punished afterward, which makes things even worse."

She had always been the idealist who wanted to stop man's cruelty to his fellow man, and was discovering that it was not easily done. It was a bitter pill for her to swallow. "I feel so guilty when I'm sitting around London or New York, leading an easy life in my comfortable apartment, or even here. You've made it so nice for all of us, but while we're sitting here, eating barbecue and riding horses and singing songs, children are starving in Africa, and dying in the streets of India, and people are killing each other for a variety of reasons we can't change and maybe never will." It had been a depressing discovery for her, and she felt helpless at times.

"Maybe part of growing up is accepting that, Candy." Her mother hadn't called her that since she was a little girl, and Candace smiled. "What you're doing is noble, but if you get killed, it won't do anything to help them. You'll just be another casualty of their wars, and it would break my heart," she added in a whisper, as Candace reached out and touched her hand. They had a special bond. "Please be careful, I love you."

"I love you too. But I have to do what I think is right. I can't do it forever. Someday I'll settle down," but Kait wondered if she ever would. Her middle child had a restless soul and always had. Candace was a seeker, and she hadn't found what she was looking for yet, nor felt she had done all that she was put on earth to do. And Kait knew that until she came to peace with it, she would continue roaming around the world, trying to do whatever she could to help.

"I wish you were more selfish, and didn't feel you should be curing the ills of the entire world."

"Maybe that was what I was born to do, Mom. We each have our own path."

"And mine is to do a TV show?" Kait smiled at her ruefully.

"You've helped a lot of people with your column, and you've been wonderful to us. You have a right to some fun."

Kait nodded, thinking about it, but she also knew that Candace wasn't ready to give up her dangerous job yet. They finished their wine and walked back to their respective cabins, which were luxurious and beautifully decorated in the lush, natural setting, and the mountains loomed over them, looking mysterious in the night sky filled with stars.

"I'm glad we came here," Candace said as she kissed her mother good night.

"So am I," Kait said, smiling at her in the moonlight. "I love you." And then they left each other and went to bed, each with their own thoughts.

Except for Tom and Frank who had gone fishing, the others met at breakfast in the morning, and were startled by the enormous buffet with a station for pancakes, waffles, and eggs any style. The ranch offered a hearty breakfast before the activities of the day, and by the time they finished Tom and Frank were back from their fishing expedition, and the kitchen was going to clean their fish for them, so they could have it for dinner if they liked.

The girls had a riding lesson in the corral, and afterward the women went into Jackson Hole to look around, and Tom and Frank kept an eye on the girls at the pool, and they all met up again for an enormous lunch.

"I'm going to gain ten pounds while we're here," Maribeth commented while helping herself to a slice of apple pie at the end of lunch, and Candace picked at a salad. She hadn't had much appetite since the accident, but was trying to make an effort to please her mother, and had cheesecake for dessert. The food was fabulous, and all the adults went for a hike that afternoon to counter the effects of lunch, and the girls took a crafts class with other children their age, and emerged with baskets and bracelets they had woven and a key chain for their grandmother, which she promised to use forever. She loved spending time with them and getting to know them better, and she offered to have them sleep in her cabin with her that night, which would give their parents a break too.

The days sped by too quickly for all of them, and on Wednesday, they got ready for the rodeo with great anticipation, and drove into Jackson Hole late that afternoon. It was a big deal, even though it happened once a week. There was steer roping and bronco riding, and clowns to distract the bulls from attacking the riders when they fell off. There were prizes, country music, and people of all ages watching the event. They took their seats right before "The Star-Spangled Banner" was sung, and Kait was startled when she heard Nick Brooke's name announced as the person about to sing the national anthem. He had a powerful and moving voice, and it reminded her that she hadn't called him, although she had promised Zack she would. She was having too much fun with her kids. After he sang, she got up, and told her family she'd be back in a minute. This would be an easy way to see him, if she could catch up with him. But she didn't have far to go. He was standing near one of the bull pens, with his horse tied to a rail, chatting with some of the other men he knew. He looked like a real cowboy, in a blue shirt and a battered cowboy hat, wearing chaps. She stood to one side, waiting to talk to him when he was free, and he noticed her after a few minutes and looked at her quizzically as she approached him.

"I didn't want to bother you. I'm sure you don't remember me. I'm Kait Whittier. I'm the co-executive producer of **The Wilder Women,** we met with Zack Winter in L.A." He smiled broadly as she said it, and held out a hand to shake hers.

"Of course I remember you. I don't forget beautiful women. I'm not dead yet. How's the show going?" He had a wide smile and brilliant blue eyes, and a casual, warm style. He was much friendlier than he had been in L.A., and more at ease on home turf. He had seemed tense to her at their meeting, but he didn't now.

"We start shooting in two weeks. Everyone's very excited about it, and the media welcome has been strong. We have some great talent in the cast. And we're all very excited about your joining us. Season two will be a knockout thanks to you."

"I doubt that. It's going to be a new experience for me. I've never done TV before, but it seems to be the hot ticket now. My agent didn't think I should miss the chance." She just hoped they would have a second season, so he could be part of it. Nothing in life was sure, nor on TV, if their ratings weren't strong. Shows as good as theirs had died an early death for no reason anyone could figure out, but she wanted the show to be lucky and have a long run. "I'd rather be here," he confessed to her. "I spent ten years in L.A., but I'm a cowboy at heart." Someone signaled him as he said it, and he nodded. "Now you'll have a chance to watch me make a fool of myself." His smile grew even wider as he pushed his hat down securely and climbed the railing of the pen next to them.

"What are you going to do?" She looked surprised as he laughed.

"I try my hand at the broncos every week. It keeps me humble," he said, as he smiled down at her from the upper rail where he was sitting, as she remembered the clause in their leading actors' contracts which forbade them to skydive, parachute, or do dangerous sports, but bucking broncos weren't on the list, and suddenly she smiled too. "Keep this to yourself," he said in a sheepish tone.

"I won't tell. I have a daughter who isn't happy unless she's risking her life."

"I'm not shooting till August or September," he reminded her. "That'll give me time for the broken ribs to heal."

"You're crazy," she said, and he laughed again. But she knew he wasn't, nor stupid. He just liked doing what he wanted, and the life he led suited him. "I was going to call you, by the way, but I didn't want to intrude."

"Come for dinner at my ranch," he said, and then hopped off the railing, went down a narrow passage and then up a short ladder to where he would mount the bronco he was riding that day. She watched him, fascinated, and felt as though she knew him even after such a short conversation. She hoped he wouldn't get hurt. A moment later, they announced his name, and he and the horse exploded out of the stall. He managed to stay on the rocketing horse for several seconds, and then got tossed, as three clowns danced around and men helped him up and led him out of the ring. He was unfazed by the rough ride, and came back to see her with a lopsided smile as he put his hat back on.

"See what I mean? There's nothing in L.A. to compare to this." He looked happy as can be as she shook her head in wonder, and two women rushed over to ask for an autograph, having realized that he was **the** Nick Brooke, not just any rider.

"Are you okay?" she asked, after he'd signed his name and was pleasant to the two women, and posed for a picture with them.

"Of course. I do this all the time."

"Maybe you could skip this while you're shooting," she suggested and laughed.

"I didn't see any rodeos in the bible."

"That's true," she admitted.

"Will you come to dinner?" He looked her straight in the eye with his piercing gaze and waited for her answer while she hesitated.

"I'd love to, but there are too many of us. I have my kids with me, their significant others, and my son's two little girls."

"You don't look like you'd have grandchildren," he commented, admiring her from his considerable height.

"If that's a compliment, thank you. Anyway, I'll spare you feeding all of us, but you're welcome to come to the ranch."

"I think I can rustle up enough food for your whole group," he said casually. "Tomorrow at seven?" She didn't want to seem rude by declining, so she nodded. "Circle Four Ranch. Your ranch will know where it is. Where are you staying?"

"The Grand Teton Ranch," she answered quickly.

"That's a nice one," he said, approving. "See you tomorrow. Nothing fancy, just come in jeans. The kids can swim while we have dinner if they want. The grown-ups too."

"Are you sure?" She was embarrassed to impose on him.

"Do I look like a man who doesn't know his mind, or is afraid of a few kids?" He was teasing her, and she laughed.

"No, you don't. And thank you," she said, as he waved and walked away, and glanced back at her once. He was painfully handsome, and had a kind of innate charm that turned her legs to mush, and she scolded herself for it on the way back to their seats. He was a movie star, for God's sake, she reminded herself, of course he was charming. And the last thing she needed was to make an ass of herself flirting with him, or being bowled over by him, just because he rode a bucking horse and looked cute in a hat.

She was apologetic when she got back to the others. "I'm sorry. I needed to talk to the guy who sang the anthem."

Tommy laughed at her. "You think I don't know who he is, Mom? That's Nick Brooke, the actor. Do you know him?" He was surprised. She had a whole life that was unfamiliar to him now.

"He's the leading man in our second season, if we last that long. I was supposed to call him this week, and didn't. He invited us all to dinner tomorrow night, and I didn't know how to get out of it."

"Get out of it?" Tommy said. "I want to meet him!"

"Meet who?" Maribeth leaned over to ask. The girls were covered in cotton candy and having a great time.

"My mother knows Nick Brooke. We're having dinner at his house tomorrow."

"Oh my God, I didn't bring anything fancy," Maribeth said, panicked, and Candace leaned toward them too.

"Neither did I. Where are we going?"

"To have dinner with a movie star," Tommy said, enchanted with the idea. Nick was his favorite actor.

"I'll lend you both something," Stephanie volunteered and everyone laughed. She was wearing jeans with holes in them, with high-top sneakers that were in shreds, just as she had every night.

"I think I'll borrow something from Mom," Candace said diplomatically.

"He said to come in jeans, and the kids can swim during dinner, and so can we. That was him on the last bucking bronco, by the way," she told them, and Tommy was visibly impressed.

"Now, that's a real guy," he said admiringly.

"He must be insane," Frank commented. "I felt sick watching it."

"So did I," Kait said ruefully. "If he kills himself, we have no male lead for season two."

They chatted animatedly and watched the rest of the rodeo, and talked about dinner with Nick on the way back to the ranch. They were all excited to meet him, and still startled that Kait knew him.

"Your life has definitely gotten interesting, Mom," Tommy said, and she laughed.

"I guess it has," she admitted. She hadn't really had time to think about it, but she had met a lot of important actors in the past four months, and she and Maeve had become good friends. She didn't really know Nick Brooke except to shake hands with him. And now they were all going to dinner at his ranch. It didn't mean anything, she knew, but at least it impressed her kids. That was something.

The clerk at the desk gave them the directions to Nick's ranch, and Kait didn't know what to expect as they drove there. They had worn shirts and jeans, and those who had them wore cowboy boots. The Texas part of the clan was properly equipped, and she and Candace had bought some boots a few days before in Jackson Hole. Stephanie and Frank were wearing their holey Converse high-tops, but they all looked respectable as they reached the ranch, spoke into an intercom, and the gate swung open to let them in. They drove what seemed like miles to the main house, past horses grazing in pastures. The place had a peaceful feel to it, and the land around it seemed vast. The house was a big, rambling ranch house on top of a hill with an immense patio and a huge barn nearby, where he kept his best horses.

Nick was waiting, and offered them drinks and beer, and sodas for the girls, and from the patio they had a sweeping view of his land as far as the eye could see. Kait could imagine sitting for hours, just admiring the view. And there was an immense pool, with tables with chairs and umbrellas around it. It looked like a small hotel more than a house.

"I spend a lot of time here," he explained. "This is my home." He chatted easily with Frank and Tom, joked with the children, and invited everyone to sit down. There was a chef working at the barbe-cue, and a young man in jeans and a checked shirt served hors d'oeuvres, grilled cheese sandwiches cut up in tiny bites. Nick asked if there were any vege-tarians in the group, and Stephanie raised her hand. They had a special meal for her. And they chatted comfortably for an hour while he talked about his horses, and they watched a spectacular sunset. He took them to his main barn at Tom's request. Every-thing was high-tech precision there, and the horses he bred were obviously thoroughbreds.

"My father-in-law has racehorses," Tom said quietly, "but I don't know anything about them." He started asking questions and Nick politely an-swered everything he wanted to know. Then they wandered back to the house, and dinner was wait-ing for them. It was all easygoing food that most people loved to eat, Southern fried chicken, barbe-cued ribs, corn on the cob, mashed potatoes, string beans, a huge salad, and a veggie plate for Stephanie. And for dessert, there was peach pie Nick said he had made himself from their own peaches. He had seated Kait next to him and chatted with her, and made sure he talked to the others as well. He and Tom particularly hit it off, and of course Nick knew who Maribeth's father was when Tom said he worked for him. Nick was originally from Texas, and everyone in the state knew who Hank Starr was.

"And which one of you is the one who likes to live on the edge of danger?" he asked amiably, and his eyes went straight to Candace, and she laughed.

"I guess you could say that, or that's how my mother sees it. I'm just doing my job," she said benignly, with an embarrassed glance at her mother for outing her.

"Which is?" Nick asked with interest, and Kait suspected that he was attracted to her, although he was more than twenty years older, but there was nothing lascivious in his look. He just admired pretty women, which Candace was. But he seemed more interested in Kait, and spoke quietly to her whenever he got the chance, as though they knew each other better than they did.

"I produce documentaries for the BBC," Candace answered. "Sometimes we go to out-of-the-way places."

"She got blown up by a land mine near Mombasa three months ago." Tom dotted the i's for him, and Nick nodded.

"Yeah, that's definitely out of the way. And you're okay now?" He was sympathetic.

"Her arms caught on fire, she still has to wear

bandages," Merrie explained, and Candace shot her a quelling glance.

"I'm fine. Mom came to London and took care of me." She smiled at her mother as though it was an ordinary occurrence.

"And you can't wait to go back for more?" he challenged her, and she laughed and nodded, while Kait said nothing.

"You're as crazy as I am," Nick said. "I ride the broncos every week. I've given up the bulls. No land mines in the ring, though. You're playing against some heavy odds there." He told it like it was and she shrugged, and he didn't say more. He was a straight shooter and straight talker, and more than just a cowboy. He was very scientific and knowledgeable about his horses and his breeding operation. "We've sired some of the finest horses in the country here," he said proudly.

After dinner, the others went swimming, and Nick and Kait sat on the patio and talked quietly while she enjoyed the view. He smiled at her.

"I like your family, Kait. Your son's a good man. It's not easy bringing up kids like that these days. You must spend a lot of time with them."

"I used to, when they were growing up. Now we're all spread out and don't see much of each other. Never enough for me." She tried not to sound melancholy about it, and she was loving the vacation with them. The evening with Nick was an added bonus, getting to know him a little before he did the show. "Do you have children?" she asked cautiously. Sometimes that was an intrusive question, but he didn't seem like a man of secrets. He had a natural reserve, but she didn't have the sense that there was anything hidden about him.

"No, I don't. I'm not sure I'd have been good at it. When I was young, I didn't want them. Now I wish I had, but I feel too old for them. I like my life the way it is and doing what I want. You have to be unselfish to have kids, and I'm not. Acting is a demanding profession, if you do it right. I paid attention to it for a lot of years when I was younger. Now I pick and choose what I want to do. There's not a lot of room for kids in that, or there wouldn't have been then, when it counted. There's nothing worse than lousy parents. I didn't want to be one. I had my own.

"I grew up on a ranch until I was twelve. I was state raised after that for four years when my father died in a bar fight. I never knew my mom. I went to Nashville at sixteen and thought I wanted to be a country singer, and figured out I didn't want that life. It was all seedy guys backstage trying to take advantage of the new kids. I didn't see daylight for a year. I wound up in L.A., and got a lucky part. The rest is history. I studied acting, went to college at night, worked hard, made some money, and moved back to the real world when I got the chance. Now here I am, happy at last. If I'd dragged a kid through that, I would have made a mess of it. You pay a price for success. I gave up children. I'm not sorry."

"It's not too late," she said, smiling at him. He was still young, two years younger than she was.

"I'm not that guy," he said simply. "I don't want to be some old guy with a twenty-year-old wife and a baby. It took me a long time to grow up, now I'm here. I don't need to prove anything to anyone anymore, or show off with a girl young enough to be my granddaughter, who'll run off on me in a few years and leave me crying. I like my life the way it is. A good part in a picture now and then, good people, good friends, and I have a great life here. The L.A. scene is not my thing. It never was."

"Have you ever been married?"

"Once. A long time ago. It was one of those country music deals, about cheating hearts and broken dreams." He smiled as he said it. "I was very young and naïve, and she was a lot smarter than I was. She took my heart, my credit cards, emptied my bank account, and ran off with my best friend. That was when I left Nashville and went to L.A. I concentrated on my career after that, and I did okay."

She laughed at the way he said it. "You certainly did."

"Not in the way you think," he said very specifically, looking her in the eye again. "It feels great getting an Oscar as a reward for hard work. The okay part is here," he said, waving at the hills around them, and the mountains beyond. "This is where I live, and who I am." He was an honest man with no artifice and no pretensions, who knew what he wanted and who he was, and had worked hard to get there. And now he was enjoying it to the fullest. "Are you married, Kait?" He was curious about her too.

"I was. Twice. Two mistakes. The first time I was young too. He didn't steal my credit cards, he just never grew up, and took off. So the kids grew up with me, and he was out of their lives. The second time I was older and should have known better. There was a misunderstanding about who we were. It ended pretty quickly when he made it clear."

He nodded, wondering about it. "Another woman?" he asked her directly.

"Another man," she said simply, without anger or bitterness, and sounded matter-of-fact. "I was stupid not to see it."

"We're all stupid sometimes. Sometimes you need to be, to get by. You can't face yourself all the time. It's hard work," he said with considerable wisdom, and she nodded. He was right.

The others had finished swimming by then, and came to thank him for a wonderful evening. And they left a little while later.

"Would you like to join us for dinner at the ranch tomorrow?" Kait asked him before she got in the car with the others.

"I'd have loved it," he said and looked as though

he meant it, "but I'm going to Laramie to buy some horses. There's an auction there. I'll be back on Sunday."

"We're leaving then," she said regretfully. She had really enjoyed getting to know him. "We had a wonderful evening."

"So did I." He smiled at her. "I'll come to New York to see how the shooting's going. I want to get a feel for it before I step into it at the end, as the teaser for next year."

She smiled at what he said. "See you then."

"Good luck with the show," he said warmly as she got into the car. He waved as they drove away, and they watched him walk back into his house.

"What a great guy!" Tommy said as they headed back to the ranch.

"He likes you, Mom," Stephanie said with rare insight. She and Frank had been impressed with the sophisticated computer setup in his office, the others with the art he collected. Candace looked knowingly at her mother.

"Steph's right."

"I like him too. He's nice. We're going to work together, he just wanted to get to know the co-executive producer," she said blithely, and they all hooted at her.

"He'd be great for you, Mom," Tommy said happily.

"Don't be silly. He's a movie star. He can go out with anyone he wants to, and I'll bet he dates women half his age," although he had indicated otherwise to her. But she knew she couldn't go there. If she started falling for him, she'd be in big trouble on her show. This was work, and that's all it ever could be. She wasn't going to start having fantasies or falling for superstars like Nick Brooke and make a fool of herself.

"You have our full approval, unanimously, if you want to marry him, Mom," Candace teased her, and Kait ignored her and looked out the window, trying not to think of Nick. He was way, way, way out of her reach, and she knew it. But it had been a terrific evening anyway. She didn't say another word about him when they got back to the ranch, and they all kissed good night and went to bed.

Chapter 11

The end of the vacation came too quickly, and it was painful saying goodbye. The girls and Kait had flights within an hour of each other, and waited together at the airport, and Tom and Maribeth and the children had left that morning on Hank's plane. It had been everything Kait had hoped for and wanted to share with her family. There were tears in her eyes as she hugged each of them, and Tom's daughters had cried when they left too.

Candace was the last to leave, and Kait held her tight and told her to be careful when she said good-bye, and the two women looked at each other for a moment.

"Please don't do anything foolish," Kait begged her and pulled her close again before leaving her.

"I won't. I promise," Candace whispered, and didn't tell her she'd received a text that morning. They were sending her to the Middle East, to a remote area where there had been a slaughter of local women who had not followed their religious leader's orders, as a warning to the other women in the town. Their murders had been brutal, and the segment was going to be part of a larger documentary she had been working on for months, and she wanted to go. "I love you, Mom," she said seriously. "Thank you for a great vacation," and then to lighten the moment she added, "I think you should go after Nick Brooke."

"Don't be ridiculous." Kait laughed at her, and waved at her daughter as she ran to catch her flight to New York. It had been a vacation none of them would ever forget. She wanted to do it more often, and had suggested it before they left, and they all agreed. It was the benefit of their growing up. They could spend good times together, even if it was hard to find the time and arrange. It had been a magical week, and had strengthened the bonds between them.

She was sad alone in her apartment that night, and missed them fiercely. Tommy had texted her when they got back to Dallas, and she knew Candace was on her flight to London by then. And Stephanie called to thank her again.

And the next morning, life became real again. Maeve called her at seven-thirty and sounded somber as soon as Kait answered the phone and heard her voice.

"Ian has a bad cold. He can't clear his own lungs. It could kill him," she said, crying as she reported it to Kait. "If he gets pneumonia, it could be the end."

"What can I do to help?" Kait offered.

"Nothing," Maeve said. "I can't start shooting in two weeks if he's this sick."

"Let's wait and see what happens. We can shoot around you for a while. Becca has those scripts ready if we need them." But the truth was that Maeve was in almost every scene for most of the show, except for the war scenes, where Loch was on his own. But if they had to, they'd shoot those first.

"I'm really sorry. But I wanted to warn you. We're going to hospitalize him today."

"Are the girls okay?"

"Tamra and Thalia are holding up. They worry about him too. How was your vacation? I hate to hit you with this the first day you're back."

"Let's see how it goes," she repeated, and Maeve promised to keep her posted.

Kait called to let Zack know after they hung up. He had the same reaction Kait did, not to panic until they had no other choice. But they had known they would be facing challenges with Maeve, since her husband was so sick and would get worse.

"Did you ever call Nick Brooke, by the way?" he asked her.

"I didn't have to. We met him at the rodeo. He sang the anthem and I went to say hello. He invited us all to dinner at his house. He's a terrific person. I think he'll bring a lot to the role."

"Yeah, good looks, talent, and a big name. That never hurts," Zack said, being flippant about it, and

Kait said no more. But she was looking forward to seeing Nick again, and felt stupid having a crush on a movie star at her age. But she was sure that once they worked together, it would pass. She could have fallen for Zack at one point, and now they were good friends. It was all she wanted with Nick Brooke. She wasn't about to turn their workplace into a hotbed of romance, or use it as an opportunity to meet men, particularly movie stars who were way out of her league. They would have enough headaches with that with Dan Delaney and Charlotte Manning, who turned their movie sets into giant bedrooms and slept with anything that moved.

For the next three days Maeve's reports about Ian weren't encouraging, but by the end of the week, miraculously it turned around and got better. A week after they'd hospitalized him, he went home, and returned to the condition he'd been in before. They were no longer on red alert. And Maeve's daughters were staying close in case she needed help. She said they were good about that.

Kait had called to check on Agnes too, who was in fighting form and had added a yoga class and a Pilates class to her routine of daily AA meetings, to get in shape. She couldn't wait to start the show. She was miles away from where she'd been when Kait had met her as a drunken recluse months before. Now she was a talented, famous actress, ready and waiting to start work. She fully attributed the change to Kait, who reminded her, whenever she did, that she had found the strength in herself to do it, and no one had done it for her.

In the last days before they started shooting, Kait worked closely with Becca on the scripts, and was happy with how tight they were and true to the bible Kait had written. The material was strong and beautifully developed. Zack had been a hundred percent right about her, which Kait admitted freely, especially to Becca.

The costume designer had everything ready, and the entire cast had had fittings, and hair and makeup tryouts, especially to get all the wigs and hairpieces right since it was a period piece. And as always, Maeve and Agnes had shown up to every appointment on time, and so had Abaya Jones. Only Charlotte Manning wanted them to come to her apartment with the wigs, canceled meetings, and missed lines in rehearsals, which drove everybody crazy. She was a big name and a gorgeous woman and a huge pain in everyone's ass. And Dan Delaney was no better. He had already put the make on the costumer during his fittings, which had amused her to no end.

"Just to spare you a lot of time and trouble," Lally explained to him, "I'm gay, my partner is fabulous and twice the man you are, and she's pregnant with our baby. So cool your jets, hot guy, and let's get your costumes right. How does that jacket feel? Too tight under the arms? Can you move in it?"

"Sorry, I didn't know," he said, referring to the pass

he'd made, which she took in stride. She had dealt with men like him before. And everyone laughed when he left the room, after she'd marked the jacket to release it under the arms and across the chest. He was a big man with a small brain and a huge ego, as she commented to her assistant.

"Good one, Lally," one of the soundmen said to her, and she laughed too.

They were planning their first scene at the airstrip they had rented on Long Island with the vintage planes, and to film all the scenes they needed to before moving their location to the house in upstate New York.

Everyone was ready the day they started rolling. Kait sat on the sidelines with Becca, watching the script carefully as the actors said their lines. Maeve was in the first scene with Dan Delaney and Phillip Green, the actor playing her husband, Loch. Phillip was flawless while Dan wasted everyone's time, looked gorgeous, and fluffed his lines. And as expected, Maeve stole the scene as Nancy Haskell directed her and wrung every ounce of emotion out of her. Kait had tears in her eyes when Nancy signaled to the camera to cut at the end of the scene.

It was a hot day, and the commissary trucks were pouring gallons of water and handing out cold sodas and iced tea and lemonade. Nancy seemed pleased when they stopped for lunch. They had gotten two scenes in the can that morning, once Dan finally got his lines right.

Kait went to visit Maeve in her trailer and told her what a great job she'd done. Agnes was in her own trailer, watching daytime soaps and waiting to go on that afternoon. Kait dropped by to see her too, and Agnes was happy in a satin dressing gown with a wig on. She looked every inch a star. And there was no question that Maeve and Agnes raised the caliber of the show to another level. Kait was grateful they were in it, and so were they. And there was a strong bond between them, the director, and Kait. They understood the material in their gut as well as their lines. The characters were part of them by now after weeks of rehearsing and months of reading the scripts.

The shooting went without a hitch for three days, and then came to a grinding halt when Charlotte had a raging fit because she didn't like her wig, threw it to the ground, and refused to do the next scene until it was changed. Nancy Haskell handled it with the utmost calm and switched the call sheet to a scene between Maeve and Agnes, and both were willing. They got it with two takes, and after that, Nancy went to see Charlotte in her trailer. The young actress was still pouting over the wig, while two of the hairdressers worked frantically, and one of them was in tears after Charlotte had thrown a Coke can at her. The hairdresser had a bruise on her arm and was threatening to quit. It was classic Charlotte and why she was always hated on set.

The director walked in and quietly closed the door.

Charlotte looked up in surprise as Nancy stood in front of her, a daunting figure with a frighteningly soft voice.

"You're in the next scene, and, frankly, I don't care if you go on bald. But you'd better get your butt out there, and if you throw **anything** at **anyone** on this set again, I'm calling legal. It's not too late to write you out of the show. Is that clear?"

Charlotte nodded, speechless. No one had ever spoken to her that way before. And everyone was amazed to see her come out of her trailer ten minutes later, wearing the wig and meek as a lamb. She did the scene without missing a line. Nancy winked at Kait as they moved on to the next scene with Agnes and Maeve, which was a pleasure to behold. And that night they watched what they had shot that day, and everyone was pleased. Zack was in L.A. closing another deal, and Kait reported to him that everything was going well in New York. Maeve's husband seemed to be back on even keel again and out of imminent danger for now. It was the best they could hope for with him, and for Maeve.

Abaya was even better than they had believed she would be as Maggie. And she worked brilliantly with Maeve, who taught her some tricks. She was flawlessly professional, a very good actress although she was new in the business, and she was proving that taking a chance on her had been the right call. The only one trying to distract her was Dan Delaney, who kept asking her out. He showed up in her trailer without knocking while she was getting out of the shower, and she covered herself with a towel as she told him to leave.

"That would be hard," he said evilly. "If you get my drift," he continued, pointing to his crotch.

"What are you, in high school? Whoever told you lines like that were cute?" Abaya found him insulting and rude, and turned down every invitation to go out with him. He just moved on to the next one, and was soon after one of the hairdressers and an extra who thought he was hot. The extra had sex with him in his trailer one day during lunch, and he told everyone on the set about it.

"He's either a sex addict, or he has no dick and he's trying to prove something," Abaya said to Maeve in disgust. She was dreading her upcoming scenes with him, but since they were supposed to be brother and sister, he had no opportunity to get his hands on her, much to her relief. He was actually a decent actor, though not as talented as she was, he was just a sleazy guy in real life, and she couldn't stand him. Conflicts like that were standard on any set, Maeve explained to Kait. Someone always hated someone, and half the cast were having sex.

The big excitement for all of them was when they finished the Long Island scenes for the opening show. It was turning out exactly as Kait had hoped it would. Maeve was fabulous, Agnes was brilliant as the grandmother, Phillip Green was perfect in the role of Loch. Dan Delaney actually pulled it together and kept his pants up long enough to give believable performances, and in the final scene, flying with her father, Abaya stole the show. Everyone applauded with the last shot, and Kait almost cried, she was so happy. Charlotte and Brad, as the bad younger children, made only brief appearances in the first episode, so they didn't have a chance to screw anything up, and Brad had been no problem so far. From what Kait could see, it was going to be an absolutely perfect first night for the show, especially once they added the scenes in upstate New York.

Kait was on a high when she got home that night, and smiled to herself every time she thought about it, but her elation ended quickly when Candace called her from London to say she was flying out that night on another dangerous assignment. It was the first Kait had heard of it, and her heart sank.

"How many times are you going to do this? You're tempting fate. Wasn't last time enough?"

"I won't do it forever, Mom. I promise. I have to get it out of my system. And these documentaries open people's eyes to what's going on in the world."

"That's great," Kait said angrily. "Let someone else do them. I don't want to lose you. Don't you understand that?"

"Yes, I do. But I'm twenty-nine years old. I have to live my life in a meaningful way for me. I can't just take some job that bores me to death because you want me to be safe. Nothing's going to happen to me." She was as adamant as her mother, who had tears running down her cheeks.

"You don't know that. There are no guarantees in life. You put yourself at risk on every one of these assignments."

"Stop worrying about me so much. It puts too much pressure on me. Just let me do my job."

Kait didn't know what else to say to convince her, and knew she couldn't anyway. It was a battle she would never win with Candace. "Just take care of yourself," Kait said unhappily, "and call me when you can. I love you. That's all I have to say."

"I love you too, Mom. Take care of yourself too." They both hung up frustrated and unhappy. Kait sat crying for a minute and then called Maeve.

"She's leaving again, to some shithole where someone can try to kill her. She's an accident waiting to happen and she doesn't know it. Sometimes I hate my children, because I love them so much."

Maeve understood what she was saying and felt sorry for Kait. "I'm sure she'll be all right. I think there's a special guardian angel for stupid kids," she said warmly.

"Not always," Kait said, with despair in her voice. "She just doesn't listen. She's so busy trying to save the world."

"She'll get tired of it eventually." Maeve encouraged her, and could only imagine how hard it was to accept, after Candace had been injured so recently and could easily have been killed.

"I hope you're right, and she lives that long."

"She will," Maeve said firmly, and then they talked about how great the scenes had been that day, and how terrific the first episode was going to be once it was complete. They had sent it to Zack digitally, and he called her late that night and raved. She was thinking about Candace when she answered his call.

"What are you sounding so down at the mouth about? The first episode is great."

"Sorry. Nothing. Family stuff. Sometimes my kids drive me insane."

"Something serious?" He worried about her, which touched her.

"Not yet, and never, I hope."

"Not to change the subject, but what did you do to Nick Brooke, by the way? He called me today and couldn't stop talking about you and how fabulous you are. I think you've cast a spell on him."

"Not likely. He can have anyone he wants," she said, flattered, but she didn't take it seriously. "We had a nice evening at his house. He's a really great guy."

"Well, he thinks the same of you. He said he was going to come early and watch the shooting, to see how the dynamics are. But, frankly, I think he's coming to see you."

"Don't be silly," she said blithely.

"I think I'm jealous."

But she didn't believe that either. She had heard

rumors recently that Zack was quietly dating a major actress, and she was happy for him.

They talked about the first episode again, and he congratulated her on having the makings of a fantastic opening show. He told her the network would go nuts when they saw it. But it was hard to go wrong with two major actresses like Agnes and Maeve. The others were the icing on the cake. And Nancy knew just how to weave their performances together and create magic.

Kait tried to keep her mind on their first episode when she went to bed that night, but all she could think of was Candace, winging her way toward danger again. The thought of it was unbearable, and yet there was nothing she could do to stop it. It was at times like that, feeling totally powerless to turn the tides, that she realized again how hard it was being a mother, especially of adults, but at the same time it was also what she loved most.

Chapter 12

The scenes they shot at their airstrip on Long Island went remarkably well, and the atmosphere on the set was positive, enthusiastic, and productive. And in the third week of shooting they moved to upstate New York, to shoot scenes in the house, and were hit by a terrible heat wave that made everyone uncomfortable, crabby, and short-tempered, even Maeve, who was the consummate professional, and Abaya, who was usually an angel. Everyone was hot and miserable. And Charlotte started throwing up as soon as they got there. She kept blaming it on the food trucks, and poor refrigeration in the trailer that had been set up as a commissary. She called her agent to complain, and insist they call a doctor. She said she had salmonella.

"What's her problem now?" Zack asked when he called Kait.

"She thinks we're poisoning her," Kait said, sounding tired. The heat was getting to her too. "It must be a hundred and ten degrees up here, and the house isn't air-conditioned." Everyone was sitting in their air-conditioned trailers until they were called to the set.

"I'd like to poison her," Zack said, exasperated. "Is anyone else getting sick?"

"Not a soul," Kait confirmed. She was letting the production assistants deal with Charlotte as much as possible, but occasionally she felt she should step in.

"So what do you think this is about?" Zack asked her. He had come to respect Kait's judgment more and more. She had great instincts about people.

"I have no idea. More money, time off, a better trailer, top billing. Who knows with her?" Kait was rapidly becoming experienced with the antics that went on while filming a show.

"Do you think she's really sick?" He was worried. She was in a lot of scenes and could really slow them down.

Kait thought about it for a minute. "I'm not sure. She looks okay, but she could have some kind of stomach bug or bacteria she picked up. I don't think it's food poisoning, or we'd all have it. It could be the heat. We called a doctor for her, I think he's coming later. She's not running a fever, I checked."

He laughed when she said it. "You sound like you're running a camp for wayward girls."

"I feel like it, except she's the only bad girl on the set."

"It's a good thing you have kids. Call me after she sees the doctor. I just hope he doesn't tell her to take two weeks off. We've been right on schedule so far. I'd hate to see her screw that up."

"So would I," Kait said seriously. She went back to see Charlotte then. She was lying in her trailer with a damp cloth on her head and said she had thrown up again.

"What do you think it is?" Kait asked her, sitting next to her and stroking her hand gently, as Charlotte suddenly looked up at her with enormous eyes and dissolved in tears. She was obviously frightened, and Kait felt sorry for her, despite what a pest she was at times. "Maybe it's just the heat."

Charlotte shook her head, and went to throw up again. Things were not looking good. She was still crying when she came back five minutes later and sat down facing Kait.

"I don't know how it happened . . ." she said miserably. "I think I'm pregnant," she whispered. She started sobbing and dissolved in Kait's arms, as Kait stared straight ahead of her, not wanting to believe what she had heard, but it sounded all too true.

"Are you sure?" she asked her, trying to get her to calm down.

Charlotte nodded and blew her nose on the tissue Kait handed her. "I'm positive."

"The father?" Kait asked in a choked voice, and the beautiful starlet looked at her.

"The drummer in a band I hang out with some-times."

"Are you sure?"

"Almost. I think he's the only one I've slept with in the last three months, but I can't remember. I fool around a lot, but I only go all the way with a few guys I know, and two of them have been working in L.A. recently." Kait hardly found that reassuring, but at least Charlotte thought she knew who the father was. "Almost."

"Do you know what you'd want to do about it?"

"I don't know. I think I'd have it. It wouldn't be right to get rid of it, would it?" Kait almost groaned. And what about her part on the show? It was the least of Charlotte's problems, but foremost on Kait's mind, and Zack would have a fit.

"You have to make that decision yourself," Kait said quietly, the doctor arrived then, and Kait left them alone. She went back to the trailer she was using as an office and put her head in her hands on her desk. She didn't hear Agnes walk in behind her.

"That doesn't look good," Agnes said in a strong voice, Kait jumped and grinned at her.

"It's not."

"Anything I can help with?"

"No, but thank you. I'll work it out." Charlotte's assistant came to get Kait then, and she left Agnes in a hurry. The doctor had come and gone by then. He'd confirmed Charlotte's own diagnosis since she had taken a pregnancy test that morning, after she'd sent an assistant to a nearby drugstore to get it, and she looked at Kait with big, innocent eyes.

"I'm going to have it, Kait. I don't want another abortion."

"What do you want to do about the show?" The rest was Charlotte's problem to work out. Kait only had to deal with the show.

"I want to stay on. Can I?" Her eyes filled with tears as she asked. "It's such a great part for me." Kait nodded and knew it was true. But what would they do with Chrystal in the story?

"How pregnant are you?"

"About three months, I think. It won't show for a while. I didn't show last time till I was five months pregnant."

"You have kids?" Kait looked shocked.

"I got pregnant in high school when I was fifteen and gave it up for adoption. I've had two abortions since, and I don't think I should do that again. I'm twenty-three now, that's old enough to have a baby, don't you think?"

"That depends on if you're prepared to take on the responsibility," Kait said seriously.

"I think my mom would help me."

It all sounded like a mess to Kait, with a possible drummer father who wasn't even her full-time boy-friend but just a guy she hung out with, and not even the father with any certainty. She was "almost" sure, but not totally. "I have to talk to Zack," Kait said, looking stressed. She left the trailer a minute later, headed straight for her office, and called him.

She got him at his office, about to leave for lunch. "We have a problem," she said bluntly.

"She's really been poisoned?"

"She's pregnant. Three months. She wants to keep it, and stay on the show." She did a rapid calculation. "That means she'll have it in January. We're on hiatus then, so she could come back to work after the baby, if she's willing, or we could even film her having the baby. She says you won't be able to see it for another two months, which gets us till the end of September. We'll be finished shooting by then. We could move all her scenes up front and shoot them now, so by the time she looks pregnant, we won't need her, and we can bring her back right afterward, if you still want her. Or we fire her now and replace her." She was thinking on her feet, trying to save the show.

"Oh, for Christ's sake, are you shitting me? Who's the father? Does she know?"

"I don't know, maybe some guy she sleeps with, among others. She's not sure. We could write the baby into the script if you want to keep her. Since she's the bad girl in it, it could work. We're talking about 1940 here. She could decide to keep it, which would be very brave for those days, but kind of works with the theme of the show. We'd have to hire a guy for her," Kait said, her mind racing.

"No, we don't. She doesn't know who the father

is, but keeps it anyway. That would be brave, and they might love a baby and an unwed mother on the show. If we're stuck with it, we can make it work. I'd rather do that than fire her. She's a big name, even if she drives us nuts. And for God's sake, get Becca on it right away. Let's shoot all her scenes from before the pregnancy in the next month, and then we can shoot her again when she starts to show."

They were thinking in sync about it and Kait agreed with him.

"I just want to warn you, I may kill her the next time I see her. And I have to tell the insurers that we have a pregnant woman on the set now."

"What do I tell Charlotte?"

"That she is the luckiest woman on TV, and we'll keep her on. It actually might work in our favor, though I sure as hell wouldn't have hired her if I knew she was pregnant. It's kind of a fitting plot twist for a promiscuous bad girl. And she can have some kind of bad boyfriend, who runs away and we never have to see him, if that works better for you and Becca."

"We'll figure it out."

"Good. I'm late for lunch at the network. I'll call you later. And she has to do her job, she can't lie around whining over this. She's young and healthy, tell her to get back to work."

"Terrific. I'll let her know." Kait went back to Charlotte's trailer then. She was looking better and had color back in her face.

"What did he say?" Charlotte asked, terrified. She was sure they were going to fire her.

"We're going to write it into the show, if you want to stay."

"I really do, and I promise I won't be a problem. I wasn't sick last time. It must be the heat. I just called my agent and told him."

"We'll make it work," Kait reassured her. "We're going to shoot all your non-pregnant scenes up front as soon as we can. And once you start to show, we'll write it into the scripts. Becca and I can work on that. How do you feel now? Are you ready to go back on set?"

Charlotte nodded meekly, and was grateful to her and Zack. "Thank you for not firing me," she said, as docile as a lamb.

"No more tantrums today, okay?"

"I promise. I'll do whatever you tell me."

"Go see them in hair and makeup and be ready to roll in half an hour." They'd have to adjust wardrobe for her eventually too. Kait felt as though her mind was exploding as she went to find Becca and warn her of what was coming. They were going to be spending some long, hot nights together adjusting the script and adding Chrystal's illegitimate baby to the story. She ran into Maeve along the way.

"How's the princess?" she asked with a disgusted look in the direction of Charlotte's trailer. She was more trouble than she was worth, in Maeve's opinion.

"I have bad news for you," Kait said, straight-faced.

"Shit, now what? She wants a pedicure before she goes back on set?"

"Mrs. Wilder, I regret to inform you that your fourteen-year-old daughter, Chrystal, is pregnant. She's going to give birth at the beginning of season two. She's keeping it. And she may not be sure who the father is." It took a minute for it to register, but suddenly Maeve got it and stared at her.

"Are you **kidding**? She's knocked up? Holy shit! What did Zack say?"

"He agreed to keep her and write it into the show. We can have her give birth on set. Or at least do a whole delivery scene with you and Agnes delivering the baby."

Maeve burst out laughing at the thought of it. "Well, that should be interesting. I can't wait till you tell Agnes. I don't think she pictures herself as a midwife."

"We have to move up some of her early scenes, while she's not showing, so the schedule is going to get a little scrambled, but I think we can pull it off, without running late. Becca and I have work to do," Kait said as she saw Becca in the distance and waved to her. "Sorry about the bad news about your slut of a daughter, Mrs. Wilder."

Maeve laughed again then, and went to find Agnes to let her know about Charlotte.

The news was all over the set by the next day.

Charlotte looked faintly embarrassed, and a few people congratulated her, and the costume designer told her that her own baby was due in September.

They got back to work in earnest shortly after Charlotte had told Kait the news. They were resilient, and Becca was already working on the adjustments to the scripts in the scenes that involved Charlotte, and writing a new script for the episode where she would tell her mother she was pregnant. Kait was just grateful she'd never had to face that problem, and even more so that Charlotte was not her daughter. Neither of Kait's daughters had ever gotten pregnant, whereas this was the fourth pregnancy for Charlotte at twenty-three, with a guy she wasn't even sure was the father.

But all Kait had to worry about now were the scripts they were changing. As she explained, it actually provided a new wrinkle to the story, and Chrystal Wilder deciding to keep the baby, and her mother letting her, made her a brave woman in 1940. Having the baby and fessing up to it was a bold move in those days, and almost unheard of. And Hannabel would have plenty to say about it. Agnes could hardly wait, and had some ideas of her own on the subject. Anne and her mother would have a couple of major arguments over it. Loch didn't need to know until he came home from England, and he'd be shocked by his wife's decision to let their daughter keep the baby. No decent man would ever want to marry her in the circumstances back then. Kait had already figured out that they'd need a baby on the show in season two, but that was easy enough to cast. Kait had thought of everything.

Charlotte's behavior was exemplary on the set from then on. There was no more complaining about her wig, her dress, or her makeup. She didn't say a word. She threw up only once, and came right back to the set after she did.

"This could be the best thing that ever happened to us working with her, if it calms her down," Maeve whispered to Kait. Charlotte was so grateful she was still on the show that she didn't cause any problems for at least a week, which was better than she had been so far. And the scripts Becca came up with, incorporating the pregnancy, were among the best Kait had read. It was beginning to seem like a blessing in disguise for all of them, and hopefully for Charlotte most of all.

The news of Charlotte's pregnancy was instantly eclipsed by a call from Zack with major news. He had met with the head of the network. And based on the dailies they were watching carefully, and the powerful cast they had on board, they had agreed to greenlight them for the additional nine episodes. They would have to work harder and faster and come up with nine more scripts, but it was fantastic news. The entire cast cheered when they were told.

* * *

Kait was so busy dealing with Charlotte and the script changes to accommodate her pregnancy and the additional nine scripts she and Becca were working on that she was the last one to notice Dan going in and out of Abaya's trailer every day. Agnes pointed it out to her with a look of amusement. Kait was worried as soon as she heard about it, and went to visit Abaya during a break the next day. She knew how much Abaya had disliked him until then and how he had harassed her, pressing her to go out with him.

"Is something going on with you two? Is he bothering you?" she asked, trying to sound casual about it.

"Not really," Abaya said at first. "Well, maybe something's going on." She blushed. "Actually, sort of. We had dinner a couple of times this week."

"What happened to your thinking he was a sex addict and a pervert? How did that change so quickly?" Kait was worried.

"He says he's never met anyone like me, and he's crazy about me, Kait. He keeps bringing me flowers, and he had a really difficult childhood." Abaya's beautiful face was full of trust and innocence, and Kait's heart sank as she listened to her.

"Dan is a pretty busy guy," she said, referring to the half dozen women he had already slept with on the set. Kait didn't want her to be next and get hurt. She tried to say that as gently as she could.

"This is different, I can tell. He respects me."

Kait almost groaned out loud and wanted to shake her, but she had no right to interfere. She warned her again to be careful, and crossed paths with him on the way to Abaya's trailer after she left. She looked at Dan fiercely.

"If you screw her over, I will personally kill you," she said in a low voice so only he could hear her. "She's a lovely girl, and a decent human being, if that means anything to you."

"I'm falling in love with her," he said, looking righteous. Kait didn't believe a word of it. Working on the show was an education for her too.

"I mean it, Dan. Don't play with her. You can have anyone you want. Don't screw around with her for the hell of it."

"Why don't you mind your own business, Kait?" he said roughly, and shoved past her into Abaya's trailer. Kait was steaming by the time she got to Maeve, who was having an iced tea with Agnes, waiting to get her hair and makeup done before their next scene.

"I hate that guy," Kait said as she sat down. The three of them had become fast friends.

"Who?" Maeve looked startled at the uncharacteristic vehemence in Kait's voice.

"Dan. He's going to break Abaya's heart. He doesn't give a damn about her. He just wanted to win her over because she didn't want him."

"Hell hath no fury like a narcissistic actor who's been spurned," Agnes said wisely, and Maeve agreed.

They'd both seen it happen hundreds of times over the years.

"She thinks he's falling in love with her and he 'respects' her," Kait said, worried about Abaya. Kait was sure he'd be cheating on her within days, or already was.

But despite the personalities involved, Charlotte's pregnancy, and Dan's budding romance with Abaya, due to the professionalism of the cast, the actual filming was going smoothly, and much to Zack's delight, they were ahead of schedule, which would give them the time they needed to shoot the nine additional episodes.

Maeve's and Agnes's performances had been astoundingly powerful. Becca's scripts were working well. They were still saving Nick Brooke for the final episode of the season, and fitting the additional nine episodes in before that. Kait and Becca were working on them.

And by mid-August, they had finished the scenes they needed to with Charlotte before the pregnancy, and she looked great. And Abaya absolutely glowed, she and Dan had become inseparable on set and off. They were going back to Long Island in two weeks to shoot at the airstrip again, and everyone was pleased. The heat had been blistering in upstate New York.

* * *

Kait was surprised one morning when Agnes didn't show up for her call. She went to find her in her trailer and she wasn't there, and hair and makeup said she hadn't come in yet. It was the first time she'd been late, and Kait was concerned that something might have happened to her, so she drove the few miles to her motel. It was a dismal place. There was no answer when she knocked on Agnes's door, and she borrowed a key to let herself in. She found Agnes blind drunk on the floor with a bottle of bourbon next to her. She tried to sit up when she saw Kait and couldn't. Kait pulled her up onto the bed, as Agnes rambled incoherently. She kept talking about Johnny as though Kait knew who he was. She thought she meant the young pilot on the show, but her ramblings made no sense. Kait texted Maeve, who showed up twenty minutes later, and they got Agnes in the shower together, with her clothes on. She was only slightly more sober when they laid her back down on the bed and got her into dry clothes. She sat up on the bed then, and stared at both of them.

"Go back to the set," she said sternly. "I'm taking a day off today," and then started groping around the floor, looking for her bottle, which Kait had taken away. It was almost empty, and Kait assumed she had drunk almost all of it the night before.

"Let's get you some air," Maeve said, and the two women half-dragged her outside, but the heat was so oppressive, it didn't help.

"You know what today is, don't you? He was out on the boat with Roberto. It wasn't Roberto's fault. They got caught in a storm on the way home." The two women exchanged a look but didn't comment, and helped Agnes into bed. "Leave me alone," she said to both of them, with an authoritative tone, and they went outside to confer for a minute.

"What's going on?" Kait whispered to Maeve. "Who's Johnny?" It no longer sounded like she meant the pilot on the show, but someone else.

"She and Roberto had a son," Maeve said in a conspiratorial tone. "They kept it very quiet. In those days having a child out of wedlock would have been a huge scandal and hurt her career. I don't know all the details, but Roberto had him out on their sailboat. They got caught in a squall on the way back, the boat overturned, and the boy drowned. He was eight. Today must be the anniversary of his death. She may have started drinking then. I know she took a couple of years off. According to Ian, Roberto blamed himself forever. She was never quite the same after that. She has never admitted to having a son, or that he died. I heard it all from Ian. It was one of the great tragedies of her life. The other was losing Roberto."

Kait's heart ached for Agnes at the story, and she was sorry she hadn't known about it sooner. Maeve went back into the room where Agnes was sleeping, and Kait went to the desk to inquire about a local

AA meeting. They said there was one at the church down the street every night. It was about a mile away. She thanked them and went to find Maeve.

"You have to go back," Kait told her. "You have a scene with Abaya this morning. I'll stay with Agnes. They can manage without me for the day."

Maeve nodded. "I'll come back when we finish shooting. We should probably just let her sleep it off," Maeve said sadly, and Kait agreed.

"I'll take her to an AA meeting tonight. There's one down the street."

"She may not want to go," Maeve said, glancing at her.

"I'm not giving her the choice. She can sleep it off now, and I'll try to get some food into her when she wakes up. Tell Nancy to do her scene tomorrow. She can work with you and Abaya all day today. Dan can spend the day learning his lines for tomorrow."

"Don't worry about it," Maeve said as the two women exchanged a look of understanding, and a minute later, Maeve went back to the set.

Agnes didn't wake up until five o'clock, and when she did, she saw Kait sitting quietly in a chair in the corner of the room, watching her.

"I'm sorry I fell off the wagon," she said in a hoarse croak, she looked old and beaten, as she had when they first met. Kait didn't ask her why it had happened, she knew enough from Maeve.

"It happens. You'll get back on it." Kait came and sat on the edge of the bed. "Do you want something to eat?"

"Maybe later. Thank you, Kait, for not telling me what a loser I am."

"You're not a loser, I'm sure you had your reasons," she said quietly, not judging her.

Agnes lay on the bed for a long time, staring at the ceiling, remembering. "Roberto and I had a son. He drowned in a boating accident with Roberto when he was eight years old. Today is the anniversary of when it happened." Kait didn't tell her she already knew, she just gently patted her hand.

"I'm sorry. I can't imagine anything worse than losing a child. It must have been terrible for both of you."

"I thought Roberto was going to try to kill himself. He was so dramatic anyway. He'd been trying to get a divorce before that, so we could get married. His wife wouldn't agree to it, and there was no divorce in Italy then. So he tried to get an annulment. But he gave up on it after that. He gave up on a lot of things. He was never the same again. It was good for his work, but not so good for us. We got drunk a lot together, it was the only way we could get through it. He stopped drinking eventually and went to AA. I never really did. I'd stop for a while and then I'd start drinking again. Today is always a hard day. The worst day of the year for me."

"You should have told me."

"Why? Nothing you could do would change it," she said with a deep well of despair in her voice. "And now they're both gone."

"I could have spent the night with you."

Agnes shook her head, and a little while later she got off the bed and walked around the room.

"Let's go get something to eat," Kait said. There were a coffee shop and a grocery store across the street. Kait was starving. She hadn't wanted to leave her and hadn't eaten all day.

"Let's go get a drink instead," Agnes said, only half-joking.

"We're going to an AA meeting at seven," Kait said firmly.

"They have one here?" She looked surprised when Kait nodded.

"I'll go with you, but I need something to eat before we do."

Agnes went to comb her hair and wash her face, and she still appeared ragged when she came out of the bathroom wearing black slacks and a white blouse and sandals.

They went across the street to the restaurant. Kait had a salad and Agnes ordered scrambled eggs, hash browns, and black coffee. She seemed better but still desperately sad, and she said very little. At a quarter to seven, Kait walked Agnes to her car and they got in.

The meeting was in the basement of a church. Agnes asked Kait to go in with her, and it was very moving. She shared about her son's death, and the fact that she had just blown five months of sobriety, but by the end of the meeting she looked better, and they stayed to chat with the others for a few minutes. They all expressed their sympathy, since during her share, no one was allowed to speak. And she had cried when she told the story.

Kait drove her back to the motel then and followed her into the room. Maeve joined them a few minutes later. The three women talked for a while, and Agnes turned on the TV. She told them she'd be fine now, but Kait knew she only had to cross the street to buy a bottle at the 7-Eleven, and she wasn't going to let that happen.

"Like it or not," Kait told her, "I'm spending the night with you."

"I'll be fine tomorrow. I'll be back on the set."

"I'm staying anyway," she said, and Agnes smiled at her.

"You don't trust me."

"You're right, I don't," she said, and all three women laughed.

"Fine, if you want to be that way," but she was secretly grateful. Half an hour later, Maeve left to go back to the hotel where she and Kait were staying. There hadn't been enough room for all of them at any one hotel, so they'd booked rooms all over the area in small, ugly motels.

Kait walked Maeve to her car, and they both turned when they heard voices coming out of another room, as the door opened and two people came out. They glanced instinctively, and there was no mistaking who it was. It was Dan, with one of the hairdressers he'd been sleeping with before Abaya. He was shocked when he recognized the two women, and he stared at Kait with defiance and terror. He was already cheating on Abaya. Kait turned away as he hurried to his car, like the rat he was, and she and Maeve exchanged a long look.

"I was afraid of that. I knew he'd cheat on her," Maeve said sadly.

"So did I. I loathe the guy. She doesn't deserve this," Kait said angrily.

"Are you going to tell her?" Maeve asked, and Kait didn't answer.

"Are you?" Kait wondered, not sure what to do.

Maeve shook her head. "She'll find out soon enough. Someone will tell her, or she'll catch him. He didn't have any scenes today. He's probably been here all afternoon."

"I hate him for what he's going to do to her," Kait said with feeling. Maeve nodded, got in her car, and drove away, and Kait walked back into Agnes's room, feeling sick. Dan didn't deserve their silence to protect him, but Kait knew that telling Abaya would be even worse. He was a lowlife, and Kait was sorry they'd hired him for the show. But whatever they did now, Abaya was going to be wounded, and it would hurt like hell.

Chapter 13

With the help of nightly AA meetings after her slip, Agnes got back on track pretty quickly. She was a strong woman. She didn't talk about her son anymore, but she thanked Kait for saving her, again.

They were all anxious to get back to the city. The heat was oppressive, the town was boring, and the cast was starting to get on each other's nerves, which wasn't surprising. They needed a break. Nancy had been driving them hard, and they wanted to return to New York and their significant others, and start shooting again on Long Island. At least there'd be an ocean breeze there, and some of them could be at home and commute from the city.

A week before they were due to leave, Maeve got a call from Ian's doctor. The medicine wasn't working as well, and he thought Ian was slipping. The situation wasn't at crisis level yet, but they knew his condition could change very quickly. Her daughters were taking turns watching him with the nurses, which gave Maeve enough relief to continue working. She was ready to leave at a moment's notice, if she got a call. It added an additional layer of tension to the atmosphere, although nothing showed in Maeve's performance. She was a total pro, and had adjusted to the new scripts where her daughter Chrystal told her she was pregnant, and the sixteen-year-old boy who had gotten her that way had run away. She had to admit to her mother that she wasn't even sure if he was the one who had gotten her pregnant. There was a heart-wrenching scene where she decided to keep the baby and Anne promised to support her. It wasn't what she wanted for her daughter, but she was willing to face it with her. And there was a brilliant scene between grandmother, mother, and daughter, where Agnes delivered an unforgettable performance, begging her daughter not to let Chrystal destroy them, and to send her away to have the baby, and Anne refused.

The new script Becca had written for the scene had brought out the talent of each one, and they delivered their best performances. And Nancy had directed them like an orchestra of finely tuned instruments. Kait had cried as she watched them do the scene.

And ever since she had seen Dan at the motel, he had avoided her assiduously. He was sure she would tell Abaya. But she didn't have the heart to. She had decided to let her find out for herself. It was only a matter of time before she would, and Maeve had agreed. He wouldn't be on the show much longer anyway, since he died in the first season.

Kait was going over one of the new scripts again with Becca, refining it and discussing it with her, when one of the production assistants came to tell her that her son was trying to get through to her and hadn't been able to reach her. She had forgotten her phone in Maeve's trailer earlier that afternoon. She was surprised that he had called. They'd spoken two days before, and she'd talked to Maribeth and the children too. She'd been meaning to call Stephanie, but she'd been busy. And she hadn't heard from Candace in a week, but knew she would be back in London soon. She used the landline in her trailer to call Tom.

"Hi, what's up?" she said when she got him on the line at his office. "I'm sorry, I forgot my phone in someone's trailer." For a moment, he didn't answer her, and when he did, she could hear that he was crying. "Tommy? What's wrong?" Her heart nearly stopped, thinking that something had happened to one of his children. "Is it the girls?"

"No," he said, trying to pull himself together, for his mother's sake. It had taken him an hour to get up the courage to call her. "It's Candy," he said, using her childhood name. "Mom, I don't know how to tell you this. . . . She was killed last night in a bombing. . . . They bombed a restaurant she was in. Thirty people were killed, and she was one of them. I just got a call from her boss at the BBC.

They tried to call you on your cell and couldn't get you, so they called me. I'm next on Candy's list to call in an emergency. It was a freak thing. They were coming back today."

Kait felt like she'd been shot as she listened to him, and Maeve walked into the trailer with her phone and saw her face. She wasn't sure whether to leave the room or stay.

"I don't . . . are you sure? She wasn't just injured?" she said, clutching at straws, her face contorted in pain, as Maeve went to her and held her shoulders. She couldn't leave her like this.

"No, Mom, she's dead. They're sending her body back to England. I'm going over in Hank's plane and I'll bring her home." For a moment, Kait was bereft of speech as the pain of it sliced through her, and then she sobbed uncontrollably as Maeve held her. "It's going to take a few days to get the paperwork in order." He was still crying too.

"I'll go to London right away," she said, as though it would make a difference. But this time it wouldn't. The worst had happened. Candace's chances had run out. It was too late.

"Don't come, Mom. There's nothing you can do. I'll meet you in New York. Maribeth is coming with me." Kait nodded, unable to speak for a minute. "We should be back in New York in a few days."

"I love you. I'm so sorry. . . . I kept telling her to stop. She wouldn't listen."

"It's how she wanted to live her life, Mom. She

wanted to make a difference, and maybe she did. She had a right to make that choice," he said, re-gaining his composure.

"Not if it killed her," Kait said in a whisper. "Did you call Steph?"

"I just did. She'll be home as soon as she can. When I get back from London, I'll help you make the arrangements."

"I can do that before you get home," she said, looking dazed. She felt disoriented as she glanced around her trailer and saw Maeve. "Thank you for telling me," she said softly.

"I love you, Mom. I'm so sorry. For all of us. I'm so glad we had that vacation together."

"So am I," Kait said, and after they hung up, she fell into Maeve's arms and sobbed. "They bombed a restaurant she was in. They were flying back to London today." Maeve didn't ask her what country she had been in, or who had killed her. It made no difference now. Kait's assistant on the set stuck her head in the door then, saw what was happening, and retreated immediately. And after a long time, Maeve came out and went to find Agnes to tell her. The news was all over the set within minutes, and they stopped filming.

Maeve went back to see her then, Agnes went with her, and then Nancy joined them. And Abaya a little while later. The four women sat together and took turns comforting her and holding her, and tell-ing her how sorry they were as Kait just cried and nodded. All she could think of now was how beautiful Candace had been, what a sweet child she was, her first daughter. It was unthinkable, unimaginable that she was gone.

The others left the set long before Kait left her trailer with her four friends right behind her, and they drove her to the hotel. She had thought of going back to New York that night, but there was nothing there except her empty apartment. She was better off here with them, until Tom called her to say he was ready to leave London. Kait called Stephanie from the hotel, and the others left her alone to talk to her daughter and cry. Stephanie said she'd come home in two days. And this time, Agnes said she was spending the night with her.

"You're just trying to get even with me for sobering you up," Kait joked through her tears, and Agnes laughed.

"No, I just like your hotel better. And your TV is bigger."

They all sat with Kait until long after midnight, and she felt like she had her family with her. Zack called and she talked to him, but afterward she couldn't remember anything he'd said except that he was sorry, and he was crying. Everything that happened to her was a blur. And finally, at sunrise, she fell asleep as Agnes sat watching her.

They canceled shooting for the day, with Zack's permission, and he told Nancy he didn't care what it cost them. They could afford to take a day off.

Kait never left her hotel room, and the women she was close to came and went all day and sat with her. And Tom called her to say he was in London, and would be in New York in two days.

Two days later the whole cast gathered around in silence when she left, and she saw that some of them were crying. She was planning to take a week off, until after the funeral, and Zack told her to take as much time as she wanted.

It was hard for the others to go back to shooting without Kait. Her absence was sorely felt, and her sorrow weighed on them, but their performances were moving and wonderful, and all their compassion for her came out in how they acted. Maeve and Agnes particularly did one of their best scenes since they'd started shooting.

When Kait got home, she called a funeral home and started to make arrangements. They were going to hold the service in a small church near the apartment, and Kait was working on the obituary when Stephanie walked in, rushed into her mother's arms, and burst into tears.

Tommy landed at midnight that night with Candace's body, or what remained of it, in a casket. Kait had a hearse waiting for them at the airport to take her to the funeral home. They had decided to keep the service private. Kait couldn't face her daughter's childhood friends. Tommy and Maribeth were at the apartment by one A.M., and they sat around the kitchen table, it was nearly four when they went to bed. Kait couldn't sleep, and neither could Stephanie, and finally they climbed into Kait's bed together, and were still awake when the sun came up.

Kait sent the obituary to **The New York Times** the next morning, and the BBC was planning to deal with the British papers. They made an announcement on the air, with a touching tribute to her, which they sent Kait by email.

The church service Kait had arranged was a brief agony compared to all the rest. The shock of her death had been brutal. The family spent the weekend together. And on Monday, barely able to tear themselves away from each other, Stephanie went back to San Francisco, Tom and Maribeth flew to Dallas, and Kait sat in her living room, lost. She felt as though her life was over. Nothing mattered anymore.

The cast was back in the city by then, and they were planning to start shooting on Long Island on Wednesday, but she felt too disconnected to talk to them or go back to work. Carmen and Paula Stein from **Woman's Life** had called her when they saw the obituary, and were devastated for her. Jessica and Sam Hartley sent her flowers. And so did Maeve, Agnes, and Nancy. Zack had sent a huge arrangement of white orchids to the funeral home, from him and the entire cast.

Kait felt as though a part of her had died with her daughter. Tommy had arranged for Candace's things to be packed up at her London apartment and sent home to her mother. She couldn't bear the thought of going through them when they arrived. Every inch of her soul seemed broken. They had not only blown Candace's life to bits, but Kait's as well.

Agnes called her that afternoon to make sure she was all right, and Maeve shortly after. They were relieved to be back in New York, and so was Kait. Both women offered to come over, but Kait said she wanted to be alone. She didn't have the strength to see anyone. Suddenly everything except Candace seemed unimportant.

Kait was sitting in her kitchen two days later, thinking about her friends in the cast, when suddenly she wanted to be with them. They were her family now too. She put on jeans and a T-shirt, didn't bother to put on makeup or do her hair, and, wearing a pair of sandals, drove out to Long Island. They were shooting at the airstrip that day. It was Phillip Green's final scene as Loch. Everyone looked shocked when they saw her get out of the car, and they all rushed toward her. Candace had been gone for a week by then, and Kait felt as though she hadn't seen them in months.

Agnes walked toward her as the crew went back to work, and she smiled at her. "Good girl. I knew you'd come. We need you. And that asshole is cheating on Abaya again," she said to bring her back to the present, and Kait laughed. She felt decimated inside, as though a part of her were torn where Candace had been ripped from her, and the rest of her was just a shell around the wound, but it felt good to be with them. She had brought a bag so she could stay at a nearby hotel if she didn't want to go home that night. And after she watched Phillip Green's last performance, she thanked him before he left.

"Nick Brooke will be here tomorrow," Maeve reminded her, as they walked along the airstrip during a break.

"Oh shit, I forgot." Meeting him seemed so far away now.

"He'll only be here for two days to shoot his part in the final episode." They had booked him at a time that worked for him since he had a busy schedule. And they would continue shooting other episodes after he left.

"How's Charlotte doing?" Kait asked, concerned.

"Still bitchy, but impending motherhood has improved her slightly," Maeve said with a grin. She didn't like her, but she was a decent actress, and a necessary evil on the show, just as Dan was.

"Agnes says Dan's cheating on Abaya again. Who's he after this time?" Thinking about it was a good distraction.

"One of Lally's assistants. The one with breasts the size of my head."

"And Abaya doesn't suspect it?" It was a relief to talk about the problems of the set, instead of thinking night and day about Candace.

"Not yet. She's convinced he's changed and she's

madly in love with him. She has a nasty shock in store when she figures it out."

Maeve went home to check on Ian that night, which was what she liked about working on Long Island, and she was glad to relieve her daughters for a while, so they could get out and see friends. Agnes and Nancy had dinner with Kait at the hotel. They didn't mention her daughter, but they could see how ravaged Kait was. She still wasn't herself.

She went for a long walk alone on the beach the next morning, before she came to the set, and when she returned, she saw a crowd of people around a car, and a man in a cowboy hat get out. There were often fans hanging around the outer perimeter of the set once they knew who the stars were. A moment later, as they cleared a path for him, she saw that it was Nick Brooke. He looked no different than he had in Wyoming, and he smiled when he saw her at the edge of the crowd and approached her with a serious expression. He waited until the others had given them some space.

"I'm so sorry to hear about your daughter, Kait. I read it in **The New York Times.** I'm glad I met her." Kait nodded with tears in her eyes and couldn't answer him, and he gently touched her shoulder.

"Thank you" was all she managed to say, and accompanied him to his trailer so he could drop off some things.

"I want to write to Tom and Stephanie if you give me their email addresses." She nodded in answer, and

they went into his trailer. He looked satisfied as he
glanced around, but he was anxious to see the old
planes and went to find the hangar where they were
kept. She followed along with him, and they walked
in silence until he saw the planes, and gave a whoop
of pleasure. "I like planes almost as much as horses."
He examined each one, and they were there for a
long time before they wandered back. By then she
had regained her composure. It felt like seeing an
old friend, and it meant a lot to her that he had
met Candace on their Wyoming trip. Kait smiled
remembering that Candace had wanted to fix him
up with her mother, which Kait didn't tell him. But
the warm, easy connection they'd had in Jackson
Hole had followed them to Long Island.

She introduced him to the rest of the cast when
they got back, and he and Maeve chatted for a few
minutes, and he told Agnes how honored he was to
meet her. He liked Abaya immediately, and was gracious to everyone he met. At lunch, she told them
about watching him ride the bucking bronco, and
he laughed.

"I got nailed by a good one two weeks ago. I think
I may have cracked a rib," he said, putting a finger
on it gingerly. "Maeve had better be gentle with me
in our love scene or I'll cry." The others laughed
when he said it. Maeve was in good spirits because
Ian had been doing better when she saw him that
morning.

Lally got Nick's costume pinned and rapidly sewn

for him, and by one o'clock, after they lit the scene, they were ready to start shooting. It was his opening scene with Maeve, and they were breathtaking together as she saw him for the first time when he came to meet her, as a friend of her late husband's, and asked her for a job flying cargo. The moment was electric and by the end of the episode, passion had overwhelmed them. There was instant magic between them on the set. It ended just as quickly when Nancy gave them the sign to cut, and started again with the next take. It was fascinating watching them work. They were the best actors Kait had ever seen, with the exception of Agnes, who left everyone speechless every time she had a scene to perform, but she had none today. All the action was between Nick and Maeve. They worked straight through till six o'clock with only one brief break, and Becca and Kait sat on the sidelines following the script. Neither one of them ever missed a single line.

"They're amazing," Becca whispered to Kait, who nodded in agreement. She almost wondered if they'd ever had a spark of romance between them in real life, they were so convincing in their roles, and the chemistry between them was like fireworks. They were a joy to watch as they brought the characters to life, whether fighting or falling in love. All of Anne Wilder's years of loneliness erupted in passion in the scene with Nick.

"That was a great, great day," Nancy compli-

mented them both, as Maeve headed to her trailer
to take off her makeup. The head of production
ran up and shouted that he had an important announcement to make, and everyone stopped in
their tracks and waited to hear what it was.

"Zack just called from L.A. The network just
greenlighted us for season two!" He was ecstatic. It
was big news. "They didn't even wait for the ratings.
They love us! They want a full twenty-two episodes
right off the bat this time!" It meant that the network was thrilled with what they were doing and
thought the show would be a hit. Becca and Kait
were already writing the second season and had
several scripts complete. "Congratulations, everyone!" There was a hubbub of conversation as people
talked about it and hugged each other, and Kait was
delighted too. At least the show was doing well, even
if she felt as though she'd been hit by a wrecking
ball. It also meant that Nick would be with them
for the second season.

He had dinner with the principal players that
night. They went to a seafood restaurant nearby
and drank a fair amount of wine, except for Agnes and
Kait. Agnes was solidly sober again, and Kait didn't
think she could handle alcohol in her fragile state.
Nick sat next to her and kept a close eye on her
all night, and afterward walked her back to her
hotel. The others had either gone ahead or lagged
behind, and Nick and Kait found themselves walking alone.

"I've thought about you a lot since your trip to Jackson Hole," he said quietly. "I had a wonderful time with you and your family at dinner."

"So did we," she said, remembering it, and what a gracious host he had been at his ranch.

"You'll be going on hiatus soon. Maybe you could come back again. Wyoming is beautiful in the fall," he said, but she didn't want to think about traveling at the moment, she wanted to stay close to home. And she had promised to visit Stephanie in San Francisco, and Tom in Dallas. "I'd like to see you again, Kait. Not just at work." He was making his interest in her clear. "We're going to be busy when we start shooting again. And maybe you could use some downtime now."

"I'm feeling kind of lost at the moment," she said honestly, "like everything inside me is broken, since last week." He nodded, and his eyes were kind when he looked at her. "It's going to take time." She wondered how much time, if Agnes was still heartbroken about her son forty years later. Kait had the sense that there would always be a part of her missing now. The piece that had been her daughter.

"I've got things to do here occasionally. Let's try to get some time together, and you have an open invitation to the ranch if you want to get away," he said, as the others caught up. Dan walked by with an arm around Abaya, and Nick spoke softly to Kait. "What's with that guy? I get a bad feeling about him. He feels as phony as a three-dollar bill to me."

"You're right on the mark," she whispered back. "He's cheating on her, and she's the only one who doesn't know it. She's madly in love with him."

"She won't be for long when she figures it out." It made Kait think about the story he had told her, about the wife who broke his heart. It happened to most people at least once, and hopefully never again.

Nick was staying at the same hotel she was, and he walked her to her room and said good night with a warm smile. She knew she had long hours ahead, wide awake. She hadn't had a full night's sleep since Candace died. "A walk on the beach in the morning?" he asked her. "It clears my head before I work."

She nodded and disappeared into her room, and it was another painful, restless night, but she got a few hours' sleep before the sun came up. He called her in her room then, and reminded her of their walk. Ten minutes later, she was outside waiting for him, and they headed for the beach.

"Bad night?" he asked her, and she nodded. He wasn't surprised. "Are you feeling guilty, like there's something you could have done to stop it?"

"No, not really, just sad. She had the life she wanted, and she knew the risks. Her life just wasn't long enough for me. I don't think she'd have given up her job, even if she knew how it would end. I've been thinking a lot about it, and Tom is right. It was a choice she made, just not one I liked. Your kids are who they are, right from the minute they arrive. She wanted to change the world all her life."

"Is that what you want to do with the show? I've read all the scripts. There's some great stuff in it."

"Thank you. I just want to pay tribute to how brave some women are, how hard they fight to do the right thing, even in a world that doesn't understand them or want them there."

"Isn't that what Candace was trying to do?" he said gently.

"I never thought about it that way," she said pensively. "My grandmother was that kind of woman."

"So are you," he said. "Women have to fight a lot harder to get where they want to go than men do. It's not right, but that's the way the world is. You have to have the strength to open the doors you want to walk through and then have the guts to walk in. It's still a man's world in a lot of ways, although most people won't admit it. I've been reading your agony columns. You give good advice." He smiled at her. "Maybe Candace was trying to do what your grandmother did, in a different way. Maybe you are too. You raised a great family, Kait."

But now part of it was missing. Candace would never be there again, that was what hurt so much. She was never coming back. She had gone to fight her wars and died trying.

"Your story about the Wilder women is about winning when no one will let you play," Nick continued.

She liked the insights he had into her story. "My grandmother fought to save her family. She gave us all an incredible gift. Not the money, although that was nice, but she refused to give up and be beaten, and she saved all of us, not just her children, but three generations. She wasn't lucky with her own kids."

"It works that way sometimes," he said, as they turned back. He had to be in hair and makeup soon. "Your kids are great. All of them. Candace was too."

Kait nodded, and they walked along until the hotel was in sight again. "Thank you for saying it," she said softly.

"Thank you for picking me for this project," he said, and she smiled at him.

"Thank you for accepting it."

"I almost didn't. But something told me to do it. Maybe my intuition." They went back upstairs to get what they needed for the day, and he drove her to the set in the car he'd rented. She left him in hair and makeup and went to her office in the trailer, and was startled to find Abaya waiting for her, crying. Kait suspected what was coming. Long overdue.

"I think he's cheating on me. I found a pair of red women's underwear on the floor of his car last night. He tried to act like he had no idea how they got there. He must think I'm an idiot."

"Maybe they'd been there for a while, and you never noticed." Kait didn't want to confirm or deny

it. It was up to Abaya to be realistic, and the evi-
dence was blatant.

"A red thong? You think I wouldn't notice that
sitting at my feet? I think it's that bitch in makeup
he was sleeping with before. I think he's a liar, and
always was."

"Yes, he was," Kait agreed.

"What should I do?" Abaya looked as lost as Kait
felt.

"Open your eyes and ears, Abaya. See what he
does. That's stronger proof than words. Don't be
too trusting and think he's what you want him to
be. See who he really is. Then you'll know what to
do." The decision had to be hers.

Abaya nodded and left a few minutes later. She
went straight to hair and makeup and confronted
the girl she hated, right after she finished doing
Nick's makeup. Abaya waited until he left, and she
took the red thong out of her pocket and handed it
to the makeup assistant.

"Are these yours?" she asked her. The girl looked
nervous at first and then shrugged. There was no
point denying it. He wasn't married, after all.

"Yeah, they are. I left them in your boyfriend's
car."

Abaya's heart was pounding. "Recently?"

"Yesterday, while you were working."

Abaya felt like she was going to faint, but she
didn't, she just turned around and walked out.
The girl in makeup was as sleazy as Dan was, but

she wasn't a liar like him. He came running to Abaya's trailer ten minutes later, after the makeup girl reported the conversation to him. He looked panicked as he faced Abaya.

"Get out of my trailer," Abaya said fiercely. "I have nothing to say to you." She had finally woken up and come to her senses.

"Wait, let's talk. I can explain."

"No, you can't. You had sex with her yesterday. I was right about you in the beginning."

"I'm in love with you."

"No, you're not, and you made a fool of me. Now get out."

"We have a big scene together in an hour. You can't leave it like this."

"Yes, I can. Now get out of my trailer, and my life." She looked as though she might throw something at him, and he turned around and left. He felt like someone had let the air out of him as he walked away and realized what an idiot he had been. She was the only woman he knew worth having, and he had screwed it up out of habit. He always did. And women made it so easy for him. He could have anyone he wanted. He walked past Becca on the way to his own trailer, and she glared at him in disgust.

"You're a jerk," she said under her breath, and he didn't answer her. He walked into his trailer, locked the door, and burst into tears.

* * *

When Nick and Maeve shot another scene from the last episode, the magic happened again as Kait watched them. Everyone was mesmerized as they played the scene, as anger turned to passion and then love, the emotions portrayed in the scene were convincing and raw. They were both amazing actors. Their performances were powerful and deeply moving, and Kait found herself remembering the things he had said to her on the beach that morning, about Candace and herself. He understood who the players were, and about life. There was something incredibly genuine about him, there was no artifice, which was why the part he was playing rang so true. They did it in three takes, and there were tears in everyone's eyes when they were finished.

They had only one more scene to play together that afternoon, and Kait was sorry he wasn't staying longer and there weren't more scenes to do. The rest would have to wait till they started shooting the next season.

He stopped by her chair as he left the set and looked down at her. "How did that work for you?"

"It was perfect," she said, smiling at him.

"Good. That's how I want it to be. It felt good to me too."

She wasn't sure if he was talking about them, or the scene he had just played with Maeve. He could have meant it either way. And so could she.

Chapter 14

All the members of the cast were sorry to see him go when Nick finished his two days of shooting. He made a point of meeting all the lighting and sound men, with a word or two, a handshake, a friendly pat on the back. He had been well liked on all the sets he worked on. And Agnes commented that he was a gentleman. He had told her what a great honor it was to meet her, although he hadn't worked with her yet. His scenes had all been with Maeve, and one with Abaya. For an instant, Kait had thought that there was chemistry between them, but after what he'd seen of Dan and knew from Kait in an abbreviated version, she realized that he was just being kind.

They would be shooting the rest of Nick's scenes, for the second season, after the hiatus. He stayed to have dinner with Kait and was planning to drive to New York City for meetings he had with a literary agent before going back to Wyoming. He was trying to option a book he had read that he loved and wanted to produce as a feature film. Even if he stayed on the show, he, like the others, would have time to do other projects during the hiatus. They were all counting on it, for extra money and so that they wouldn't get too identified with only one role, which often happened when actors continued for a long time with a series. But it was a desirable problem they all hoped to have, if it ran for many seasons.

His dinner with Kait was quiet and simple. They didn't talk a lot. She was still feeling flat and badly shaken after losing Candace. She had come back to work quickly, but she wasn't herself yet and wondered if she ever would be again. She was tired all the time now, couldn't sleep at night, and the memories of her daughter haunted her. She wished now that she had tried harder to stop her, and to insist that she quit her job in London. But Candace never would have. She was too committed to reporting injustices and changing the world. No one could have stopped her. Nick could see the torment in Kait's eyes. He didn't expect her to talk a lot. Just being with her was enough, and Kait felt calmer when she was with him. He had a tranquil aura around him, and gave her the sense that he was protecting her, although she didn't know from what. The worst had already happened. There was nothing he could do now except be there and let her be silent.

When they talked it was about the show and the

future episodes. She and Becca had outlined most of them and written some. And Zack and the network loved them. It was going to be a strong show and hopefully run for years. Kait wanted to make the second season even better than the first.

"Does Grandma Hannabel like me?" he asked in a teasing tone. He couldn't wait to work with Agnes, just to say he had. He thought she was a remarkable woman, the grande dame of feature films from another era long before his time.

"Not at first," Kait answered, smiling at him. "You have a huge showdown with her, which turns things around. Becca just rewrote the scene for the third episode. After that, Hannabel's a fan. She thought you were too arrogant at first, in the show," she corrected quickly, "and sometimes you are, but you're there to help her daughter and protect her from the guys who are trying to shut her business down. Everything changes once you get there. You help her make a success of it, and Hannabel gets that, in time."

He nodded. He was crazy about the role, the actors he would be working with, and the planes. It had everything he loved.

"We've still got to get a horse in there somewhere," he teased her, and she laughed.

"I'll work on it," she promised, knowing he was only joking. "But old planes are pretty sexy too, and the guys who flew them."

"Yes, they are," he agreed, and then he looked at her seriously. "When am I going to see you again?

Before we go back to work?" There was an inexplicable connection between them, as though they had known each other for longer than they had. He seemed to understand how she thought and how she reacted, and why, without talking about it. His instincts were to shield her. He could see how much she had on her plate and how it weighed on her, and how much she worried about her children and what was happening in their lives. He wanted to know her better and spend time with her, away from work. Their morning walk on the beach had touched his heart.

She was the kind of woman he would have liked to have children with, if he'd found her in time. The ones he had met along the way never seemed to him like they would have been good mothers, more like his own and Kait's, who had run away. He didn't want children now, at the eleventh hour or to make up for what he'd missed, but he did want a good woman in his life—one he could talk to, respect, share warm times and even bad times with. Kait was that kind of woman, although she didn't seem to want a man in her life. It was the one thing about her he wasn't sure of—if she would let him into her private world or not. She seemed unsure about it herself and she was so shattered now. But they had to start somewhere, and he didn't want to wait months to see her. He believed that the right opportunities were meant to be seized and explored, independent of the show.

They would know how the ratings were in November and December and if they had a hit on their hands. They were all on pins and needles even now, waiting to find out. But all the signs were good and the network had faith in them, which was an excellent predictor of success.

"What are you doing during the hiatus?" he pressed her.

"I'm going to try and get out west to see Tom and Stephanie," she said vaguely, but Wyoming wasn't on her flight path. "I don't know how busy I'll be with postproduction. It's all new to me. I'm thinking about giving up my column. I wanted to wait and see how the ratings are, but it's been really hard to keep up. There's always some crisis on the set, it's not just about the shooting schedule," which she had thought in the beginning.

"It never is when there are humans involved." He smiled at her.

"Charlotte threw us a real curve when she told us she was pregnant. She's going to keep the baby with her in the trailer while she's nursing. That will probably slow us down too." She looked apologetically at him, but he didn't seem bothered by it. He'd worked with nursing women before, and dealt with almost every situation. "And if Ian starts to go downhill, Maeve is going to have a hard time keeping up. We're prepared for that."

"I'm not sure she is, though," he said sympathetically. "It's going to be very hard on her."

Kait nodded, just as losing Candace was on her. They were the dramas that happened in real life.

She liked talking to Nick about the show. Usually she talked to Zack about it, but hadn't had time lately. And he was busy too. He had been in L.A. most of the time since they'd started shooting, working on other projects and setting up promotion and advertising with the network for **The Wilder Women,** and making the deal for their second season.

There was going to be a big ad campaign in September. It had just started in earnest, and it looked good so far. Nick was still a big secret, but at the end of the first season, there would be ads and billboards of him with Maeve. They had shot the still photography for them while he was on the set, and they looked great together. Casting him in the role of her new man had been inspired.

Talking to Nick, she could see what sharing her life with the right man would be like, like Maeve and Ian. She had never had that, and for the past few years had thought it was too late. But she was beginning to wonder now. Or was that just an illusion because he was a handsome man and a movie star? She wasn't sure and didn't know him well enough to decide. That was what he wanted from her now, the time to find out if there was something there for them or not, and she could sense now that it was what he had in mind.

"Candace thought we should go out together,"

she said shyly. "And Steph." She smiled. "Tommy just wants you to himself. He's been surrounded by women all his life. A mother, two sisters, now a wife and two daughters. He worships his father-in-law."

"Hank is a good guy," Nick said since he knew him, although he didn't know him well. He had met him several times while buying horses, and he had some remarkable ones himself. "Maybe we should honor Candace's request," he said, gently treading on what he knew was hallowed ground and not wanting to offend her. "Let's just see what happens," he said, and she nodded. He didn't want to force anything or rush her. He made it seem like they had all the time in the world.

She walked him to his car when he left for the city after dinner.

"I'm going to miss walking on the beach with you tomorrow morning," he said, and she nodded. She had liked that too, and sharing the sunrise with him as they went barefoot in the sand, with their guard down, and their defenses, before the day began and others crowded in. "I like riding in the foothills early in the morning. It has the same kind of feeling as the ocean. It makes you realize how small you are, and no matter what you plan, God has a bigger idea, and you're not the one in charge."

But she couldn't figure out what His idea had been when Candace died, or why it had to happen. It still made no sense to her. But maybe it didn't have to, and she just had to accept it for what it was, which was the hardest part, and understand that her daughter would never come back, and Kait would never see her again. Kait looked up at Nick with a lifetime in her eyes.

"I'll be around if you need me, Kait," he said softly. "I'm just a phone call or an email away. You can send me a text. I don't want to crowd you, but I'll come running if you call."

No one had ever said that to her before, and she had the same sense of well-being she'd had with her grandmother when she was a little girl. Someone she could trust who would be there to protect her.

"I'm okay," she said, trying to sound brave.

"I know you are," he said confidently, "but it never hurts to have a friend in your corner, or on the same team." Zack had been that for her since they put the show together, but it was different. There was something else lurking beneath the surface with Nick, which was impossible to ignore. Candace had felt it, and even though Kait had denied it at the time, she had too, and thought it was her imagination. Nick gazed at her. He touched her hand and then got into the car and waved as he drove away. They had made no plans to meet again in their off time, but she had the feeling that they would. She walked back to the hotel, thinking about him. Then Candace crowded into her mind again, and she spent a long, lonely, sleepless night. And the next morning, at dawn, she walked the beach alone.

* * *

Everyone talked about Nick on the set the next day. They all liked him, it was hard not to, and Nancy commented that he was a hell of an actor and so easy, like Maeve and Agnes. They were all people with enormous talent who were a privilege to work with.

Abaya and Dan had their final scene together the next morning, and it was a nightmare. They got into a ferocious argument on the set. Nancy had them break for lunch and told them to go duke it out on their own time, and that they were costing the network money. All she needed was this last day on set with both of them. Dan followed Abaya to her trailer after that, and she wouldn't let him in.

"I told you, I'm done. You're not going to play this game with me, of who you're cheating with today. I hated you from the minute I met you, and I was right. You're a slimebag, a dirtball. Take your fucking red thong and get lost. And don't call me after you leave the show."

He could see she meant it, and he could sense what a huge mistake he'd made. But she refused to give him another chance, and he didn't blame her. Her shutting him out made him want her all the more. He had cheated on women all his life. But he realized now that she was different. Not being able to have her was making him fall in love with her. Too late.

She didn't believe him now and didn't want to hear it. "I have better things to do with my life." She was a whole person and respected herself, even if she had been naïve at first. She knew that now.

"I don't know what happened. I really did fall in love with you. And what I did was very, very wrong," he tried to explain, to no avail.

"You'd do it again if I gave you the chance." She was sure of that now, and it was true.

"I swear I wouldn't. Give me one more chance. If I fuck up again, I'll walk away myself." She shook her head at him, and slammed the door in his face.

Their performance for their final scenes together on the set that afternoon was slightly better, but not by much. They were both tired, frustrated, and emotionally overwrought. Abaya couldn't wait for his part in the series to end so she wouldn't have to work with him anymore. His character was about to die so she wouldn't have to see him again. And he knew he wouldn't see her afterward. She wouldn't let him near her after the red thong incident. His part in the series was about to end with his death. They were shooting out of order, and Nancy had shot all his scenes by then. He had managed to lose Abaya right at the end, with no time left to try and win her back.

Dan was planning to go skiing in Europe during the holidays, and he was going to model during fashion week in Paris, and then had a part in a movie. And Abaya was going home to her family in

Vermont. She wanted to spend time with her parents and siblings, and do some skiing later. She'd
had enough of Hollywood behavior and people for
a while, with Dan on top of that list. She could
never respect a man like that, and told him so again.
Nancy wasn't thrilled with their performance in
their final scene together, but she knew it was the
best she could get out of them now. His part on
the show was over, much to Abaya's relief.

Maeve went home to Ian that night, and called in
the next morning to say that he was running a fever,
so she had to delay the scenes she was in. They re-
scheduled to shoot with Brad and Charlotte. She
was visibly pregnant now, five months. They shot
around it as much as possible, and Lally had done
some clever costuming, and mostly they were filming the episodes now with the newer scripts, where
Chrystal and her family were facing her disgrace.
Charlotte had been in the tabloids recently with
the drummer she thought was the father, but he
had demanded a DNA test when Charlotte asked
him for support for the child. He was already paying support for two other children he'd had with
two different women as a result of paternity suits
they'd brought against him, and he wasn't anxious
for a third, especially since neither he nor Charlotte
were entirely sure it was his. But she was in good
spirits, and the pregnancy had been easy for her

after the first weeks. It hadn't slowed her down, and Kait thought she looked beautiful. They were talking about auditioning the babies they were going to use with her in the second season. They would use identical twins, as most shows did, to save time. Twins gave them longer shooting hours, and an alternative if one of them got sick.

They shot the last scene of the season in September on a beautiful Indian summer day. It was an emotional scene between the three lead women, and they all noticed that Lally hadn't come in. She had been called off the set the previous afternoon when her partner called to tell her that her water broke. Their big moment had finally come, and Lally raced back to the city. She'd been going home to Brooklyn every night in case her partner went into labor. They had decided not to know the sex, and wanted a surprise. Lally had texted the associate producer at six o'clock that morning and all she'd said was that the baby had been born and weighed ten pounds.

"Ouch!" Maeve said when she heard about it. "Thank God my girls were small. I was on bed rest for seven months, and Thalia was two months premature. She weighed three pounds."

"Stephanie was a big baby like that," Kait said, and then looked sad, thinking of Candace. Everything led her to thoughts of her daughter. She was still struggling with the initial stages of overwhelming grief, but she was grateful for the distraction of the show. She would have been lost without it, and she was worried about what she was going to do during the hiatus. Kait dreaded it, and knew that her painful memories would find her there, and her loss, without the show to fill her time every day.

Kait had no firm plans yet for their months off, both her children seemed to be too busy at the moment to have her visit them, although she planned to, at a good time for them. Stephanie had just gotten a big new promotion, and Tommy was negotiating to buy another chain of restaurants for his father-in-law. And even her granddaughters had a million lessons after school every day. No one had any time. Instead, for the moment, Kait and Agnes had agreed to go to the theater together and catch up on some Broadway shows. Maeve wanted to spend all her time with Ian. He wasn't doing well, and had taken a slow turn for the worse in the past few weeks. It was a huge relief to Maeve that filming was over for now.

Lally showed up at lunchtime, looking jubilant. "It's a boy!" she shouted, and handed out cigars to the entire cast. It touched Kait to see her, and she remembered as though it were yesterday when her own babies were born. They were the happiest days of her life. Charlotte was terrified at the idea of a ten-pound baby that had been delivered naturally without drugs. She said she wanted a Cesarean so she didn't have to go through labor, which Kait thought sounded much worse. And Charlotte was planning to have a boob lift when she finished nursing. She didn't want it to spoil her figure or her perfect breasts.

"You really have to wonder sometimes," Kait said to Maeve as they walked to her trailer.

"Actors are incredible narcissists," Maeve agreed with her. "It never ceases to amaze me. Charlotte is more interested in her boobs than her baby. I can't imagine her as a mother."

"Neither can I," Kait agreed.

"What's the latest with Romeo and Juliet?" Maeve asked, referring to Dan and Abaya.

"They're done. He's off the show. It's over. She's going home to Vermont in a few days, after she does some reverse shots. She says she won't give him another chance."

"He deserves that," Maeve said matter-of-factly. "He's another one. The sole inhabitant of Planet Dan. I'm lucky Ian was never like that," she said with a sigh. She worried about him all the time now, and her heart stopped every time her cellphone rang. "Any word from Nick Brooke?" she inquired discreetly, not wanting to pry, but they had all noticed how taken with her he was and how attentive. "He's such a great actor, and a decent person. Ian loves him. He wants to see him when he comes back. He was having a couple of really bad days when Nick was here, or he'd have seen him then."

"He's back in Wyoming now." She'd had a few

texts from him and an email after he left, and enjoyed hearing from him.

"He'd be great for you," Maeve said gently, knowing how private Kait was, and that her whole world was upside down after her daughter's death, but in a few months, she'd feel better, and maybe have come to terms with it.

"My girls said the same thing when we met him in Jackson Hole last summer." Kait smiled at the memory. "I don't know." She sighed. "He's very appealing but I'm not sure I need the headache of a relationship. In a lot of ways, I'm comfortable alone."

"Comfortable isn't always a good thing," Maeve reminded her. "We need a boot in the behind sometimes, though I can't imagine dating again either. I know I won't when Ian's gone, I would never find another man like him, and I don't want to."

"I'm more in the situation of the adage 'I miss having a husband sometimes, just not the ones I had,'" Kait said, and they both laughed as Maeve put all the personal belongings from her trailer into two big tote bags. A little while later, she drove back to the city and gave Agnes a ride, after they said goodbye to everyone. And feeling sad to leave, Kait drove home alone. It was going to be lonely without seeing her friends every day on the set, until they started shooting again, if the ratings were good and the show did well. Zack was sure it would be a hit, and Kait hoped he was right.

Chapter 15

Kait was going through a stack of papers on her desk after finishing her column. It felt like the old days, and as though the last months had been like a dream, especially the three months on the set. Her cellphone rang, and she saw that it was Stephanie when she picked it up. She hadn't seen her since Candace's funeral in August. She still wanted to visit her in San Francisco, but Stephanie and Frank were always busy, and so were Tom and Maribeth in Dallas. There was never a good time for them. Kait had thought of taking a trip during the hiatus, but it wasn't fun traveling alone.

The reality of what had happened to Candace had begun to set in. Kait kept expecting her oldest daughter to call her from London, or picked up her phone to call her, and then remembered.

"Hi, sweetheart," she said to Stephanie.

"How are you, Mom?"

"I'm okay," Kait said quietly.

"Sleeping any better?"

"Sometimes. It gives me more time in the night to do things and catch up," she said wryly. Her nights had been short and painful since Candace's death. People told her it was normal, although sometimes the agony of the loss was brutal. "What about you? How's the new promotion?" She was proud of her as always.

"It's good, it's kind of an adjustment, but I like the money. Frank and I are thinking about buying a house together."

Kait frowned as she thought about it. It wasn't an idea she liked usually. She didn't believe in commingling funds or making important investments with partners you weren't married to. It hadn't come up so far with the others. Candace had never had a long-term partner she was serious about at twenty-nine. And Hank had given Tom and Maribeth a ten-thousand-square-foot house on his estate as a wedding present, in both their names, so there had been no decision to make. Kait didn't need to worry about him. And Stephanie still had a small trust fund from her great-grandmother that had enough left in it for a down payment for a small house, after she paid for her education, which had been expensive, but she had gone to great schools. Buying a house now would empty the trust, if the bank trustees would allow it. It wasn't up to Kait, which Stephanie knew, but she wanted her advice. She always consulted her on major decisions, and Kait was flattered.

"You know how I feel about it. Investing in a house with someone you're not married to is complicated. Why don't you buy on your own? You could buy a condo."

"We want a house outside the city, like the one we're living in and renting now. And we can get a better house together. Frank's dad said he'd help us."

Kait didn't comment for a minute, she still didn't like the idea. Frank was a nice guy and they were well suited, but the way things were now, if they broke up, it would be relatively simple to dissolve their living arrangement. But buying a house could be a messy situation if either of them wanted out. Stephanie didn't think that was going to happen, but one never knew, as Kait had discovered. Although she and Adrian had parted on civil terms, and he had left her, she still had to pay him spousal support for a year after the brief marriage. You never really knew someone until you divorced or broke up.

"Frank's dad told us pretty much the same thing. So we talked about it, and we're going to get married, Mom. I called to tell you. Neither of us really believes in marriage, but it seems like a smart investment decision."

Kait was shocked as she listened. "That sounds a little cold-blooded, doesn't it? And not very romantic." She was disappointed for her daughter.

"Marriage seems like an outdated institution to both of us, and it has a sixty percent chance of not working. Statistically, that's not very attractive."

Kait couldn't argue with her but hated to hear her sound so blasé and negative about it.

"But it seems like it makes sense if we want to buy real estate," Stephanie said practically. Kait had said as much herself, but not to convince her to get married.

"Do you want to be married to him?" Kait asked.

"Sure. Why not?" Stephanie said blithely. "We get along really well." They'd been together for four years. "We'll have a prenup of course, and a contract for the house. And we don't want a big wedding," Stephanie assured her.

"Why not?" Kait asked her, sorry to hear it sound so practical, and only motivated by the purchase of a house.

"I'd feel stupid in a big white dress, after living with him for four years. Besides, we both hate dressing up. We thought we'd go to city hall sometime at lunchtime."

"Could I be there?" Kait asked hesitantly. It sounded like a depressing plan to her. She wasn't feeling festive at the moment, but she wanted her only surviving daughter to have a nice wedding. But Stephanie had been gone from New York for a long time and no longer saw her old friends, and they seemed to have a very small social life in San Francisco, which consisted mostly of others who worked at Google.

"Sure. I guess we could get married at city hall in New York if you want. Like over Thanksgiving."

They were coming home for both Thanksgiving and Christmas this year, for their mother. They knew the holidays would be hard on her after losing Candace. It had been Tom's suggestion. "I'll talk to Frank. We found a house we like, while we were on a bike ride on Sunday. The price is right, and it's in pretty decent shape."

It was all about the house for her. The rest was unimportant, and it really bothered Kait. She couldn't resist saying something to her. "Steph, do you love him? Is he the man you want to spend the rest of your life with? Do you want children with him?" All of that was way more crucial than a house.

"Of course I love him, Mom. I wouldn't live with him if I didn't. I just don't think of it the way you do, as the be-all and end-all of life, guaranteed to last forever. And I don't want kids with anyone, nor does he. Our work is more important to us." She was honest about that and always had been, and she'd found a man who felt the same way. "Kids are more commitment than I'll ever want to make. It's too consuming. Look at you now with Candace, the heartbreak that is for you."

It shocked Kait that Stephanie saw it that way, as a commitment not worth making because you might lose one day. "But I don't regret having her for a minute, or any of you."

"That's nice, but it's not for me, or Frank."

Kait knew Candace had felt the same way. She had been far more dedicated to making her documentaries than she could imagine being to children. She was glad that Tommy didn't feel that way.

"So what do you think?"

"I think you're of a whole different generation of people who see things from another perspective. But I love you, and I want you to be happy."

"I am happy, and we love the house," she said simply.

"Would you marry him if you didn't want to buy the house?"

Stephanie thought about it for a minute before she answered. "Yeah, I think I would. Probably not for a few more years, like when I'm thirty." She was turning twenty-seven, and Frank was the same age, which seemed young to Kait, although she and Scott had been younger when they married and had kids, but that was a long time ago and the world had changed since then. Marriage didn't seem to have the same meaning. "But I'd rather buy the house now, when the interest rates are low, and we found one we like." She was a businesswoman above all, and not a romantic. There was no getting around it.

"Should I put the interest rates on the announcement?" Kait teased her, and Stephanie hesitated and then laughed.

"So what do you think about Thanksgiving, Mom? Does that work for you?" Kait realized that it might take the edge off the sadness of the holiday, although Candace hadn't come home for Thanksgiving in years.

"That's fine. Will Frank's parents come?" Kait had never met them.

"No, they can't come then. And they want to give us a party later in San Francisco. They know the plan. And they're coming out in January." Stephanie seemed satisfied with that, and she said Frank was too.

"Should we look for a dress? Do you want me to come out so we can shop for one?" She hoped that she'd say yes. It would be a good excuse to see her.

"I can't, Mom. I'm too busy. I'll see you on Thanksgiving. And I'll figure out something to wear. I don't want a white dress, and I can look online." Shopping and fashion weren't Stephanie's strong suits, and didn't matter to her.

After they hung up, Kait sat silently for a while, thinking about the conversation. It wasn't what she had wanted for Stephanie, but Kait knew that her own ideas weren't relevant. Her children had to do things their own way. Just as Candace had, right to the end. Maybe that was the message here, that they were each their own people, with their own ideas and lifestyles, and they didn't have to be the same as their mother. Kait would have liked to see more romance in her daughter's life, but that wasn't who Stephanie was, and she had to do it her way.

What they wanted was to spend Thanksgiving together, and the day after, Stephanie and Frank would get married at city hall, in whatever she chose to wear, with only her family present. Tom and Maribeth had had a huge wedding, with eight hundred guests, thrown by her father in a massive tent with crystal chandeliers hanging from the ceiling, three different bands, and a singer flown in from Las Vegas. To each their own. And now it was Stephanie's turn to do it her way, no matter what Kait thought of it, or what her dreams for her daughter were. At least Stephanie had called to tell her, and wanted her mother at her wedding. Kait was grateful for that. She thought about it and realized that she would have advised a mother who wrote to her column to go with the flow of what her daughter wanted. So she took her own advice.

Stephanie was a very modern young woman, with a mind of her own. It was what the TV series Kait had written was all about, modern women who tossed aside tradition and did what they believed in, in their own way. It was what her grandmother had done, out of necessity. The difference now was that women were doing it by choice. It made Kait realize that if she believed in the theory, now she had to stand behind her daughter. It was a brave new world for Kait, and not about her.

Kait called Maeve frequently to see how Ian was doing, and it seemed as though he started to spiral down at a rapid rate right after they stopped filming the show. They took him to the hospital with a respiratory infection, and after massive doses of

IV antibiotics to stave off pneumonia, they had to put him on a respirator. He wanted to go home, so Maeve made it possible, with a respirator at home, double shifts of nurses, and her daughters' help. Maeve sounded stressed when Kait spoke to her, and said he was slipping through their fingers. The inevitable couldn't be reversed, and he slept a lot now. Maeve was sitting by his bedside night and day, trying to spend every moment with him, and she had a bed set up in his room, so she could be with him at night. It didn't sound good to Kait, and she knew it wasn't. Maeve had braced for the worst, and was relieved they were on hiatus. It was as though Ian had waited until she was, to begin drifting away.

A few days after they'd last spoken, Maeve called her at six in the morning. Kait had a sixth sense when she answered the call.

"He went peacefully two hours ago," Maeve said, sounding strangely calm, as though the reality of it hadn't sunk in yet. After losing Candace, Kait could imagine only too well what she was going through and how it felt. Although they'd had time to prepare themselves for Ian's death, the loss was no easier than it had been for Kait, the sudden absence of someone that one loved and couldn't conceive of never seeing or speaking to again, their voice and laughter silenced forever. Maeve would never again feel his arms around her.

They announced Ian's death on all the news channels that morning. There were tributes to him in every newspaper, with the long credits of his distinguished career. The obituary his press agent wrote said that he had died after an illness, and the funeral service and interment would be private, with only the family present. A brilliant mind had been snuffed out, a talented director and loving husband and father. The funeral was in three days, to give them time to get organized and make all the arrangements. They were not disclosing the location, to avoid being mobbed by fans, and Maeve was having his body cremated, which was what Ian had wanted, since he felt his body had betrayed him.

Nick called Kait from Wyoming the night Ian died, after speaking to Maeve. She had invited him to the funeral, as one of Ian's oldest friends, and she had sent Kait an email, telling her she would be welcome too.

"I'm flying in tomorrow," Nick told her.

"How do you think Maeve is doing?" she asked Nick, concerned.

"She's an incredibly strong woman, but this is going to be very hard on her. They were married for a long time, and they were crazy about each other. They were the only people I ever knew who made me wish that I was married. Ian had an older brother who's flying in from somewhere. I offered to take Maeve to the funeral, but he's going with them. Would you like me to go with you?"

She thought about it for a minute and realized she

would. The whole experience was still very fresh for her after Candace and would be even harder than it would have been otherwise, and she felt desperately sorry for Maeve and her daughters, although they had been prepared. But Maeve had admitted that none of them had expected him to go so quickly. It was a mercy for him, instead of lingering for years on a respirator, frozen in his own body, with his mind intact. Kait couldn't imagine a worse way to die, but Maeve said he had been peaceful in the end, and died in her arms. It broke Kait's heart to hear it.

Nick said he was staying at the Pierre, not far from her apartment, and would be on his way to Europe after that, to meet friends in England and look at some horses he wanted to buy. He was tempted to ask her to go with him, but he didn't dare. But Ian's death was a reminder to all of them that life was short and unpredictable. He promised to call her when he got to the hotel, and he invited her to dinner the night he arrived. He was sad about his reason for coming, but happy to see her again.

She talked to Zack after that and he wasn't coming. Maeve hadn't invited him. He admired her immensely, but they weren't close. And then Agnes called and said she was going on her own.

The following day, Nick called her in the late afternoon once he was in his suite. There had been paparazzi outside, and he wasn't pleased about it. Someone had tipped them off when they saw his reservation. But he had gotten through them po-litely and took refuge in his room.

"That must get tedious. People come up to Maeve all the time to ask for autographs when we have lunch."

"You learn to live with it," he said simply, and said he'd pick her up at seven-thirty for dinner at 21, which was his favorite New York restaurant.

She was wearing a navy dress and matching coat when he arrived at her apartment. She felt very grown up and respectable after months of wearing jeans and T-shirts on the set, which was the only way he had seen her so far. The dress was short enough to show off her legs, and she had worn high heels. He was wearing a dark blue suit and looked like a banker. He smiled when she got into the car.

"You clean up pretty good," he teased her. She looked beautiful with her red hair loose and long. And he got the royal treatment when they got to the restaurant. It reminded her that she was with a major movie star, which was easier to forget at the rodeo or on the set. She suddenly smiled when they sat down, thinking of him on the bucking bronco. "What's funny?" he asked her after he ordered bull shots for both of them, which was mostly beef bouil-lon with a shot of vodka.

"I was thinking about you at the rodeo on the bronco."

He laughed at the memory she conjured. "My ribs

are finally feeling better after the last one," and he told her that Maeve had asked him to sing "Amazing Grace" the next day, which had been Ian's favorite hymn. It had been sung at Candace's funeral too.

They had a quiet dinner tucked away in a back corner, talking about some of his movies and her children, the magazine, and her column. She told him she was planning to quit after they saw what the ratings looked like.

"I'm going to miss it. But it was hard keeping up with it this summer. I wish they'd find someone else to write it. I hate to let people down, they count on that column."

"To everything a season," he quoted, smiling at her. "You've already started a new chapter, Kait. You've got to go with it, and be free to do that. You can't drag the past along."

"I hate to stop, and they asked me to finish out the year. I wanted to honor the commitment, but I didn't realize how hard it would be to do. **The Wilder Women** has eaten up all my time. Everything that happens on the set is so consuming."

He nodded in agreement and knew it from his own experience in movies. "I can't wait to start shooting the next season," he said, smiling warmly at her, and she felt that way too. He said it seemed like forever, waiting. "I feel like I'm part of the show already." He looked pleased. And he was going to be their big surprise for the viewers. A very big one, and no one had squealed so far. There had been no leaks to the press, and Zack was happy about that. Once the word was out, Nick and Maeve were going to do a press conference. And before that, they wanted Charlotte, Dan, and Abaya to do one. There was going to be a big press push for the show, to drive the ratings. It made Kait think of **Downton Abbey** again. She hadn't had time to watch it in months, she'd been too busy. She admitted her passion for it to Nick, and he laughed.

"I love it too." And then he mentioned three others that he liked too, which were more hard-edged and male oriented: a police show, one about an undercover drug agent, and one that was pure science fiction. They were the shows that everyone watched and would be their competition for the ratings.

He took her back to her apartment after dinner, and she didn't ask him to come up. They were both tired, he had flown in that day, and they had two hard days ahead of them. He was going to see Maeve in the morning, and had promised to take her to lunch to give her a break from the funeral arrangements.

"Do you want to come to dinner tomorrow night?" she asked him. "I'm a lousy cook, but I'll pick something up. I haven't really cooked since the kids left, except on Thanksgiving and Christmas."

"That would be great." He was pleased at the chance to see her again. He hugged her and kissed her on the cheek when he left her and went back to his hotel. And the following night he showed up at seven, and she had a spread on the kitchen table of roast chicken, vegetables, and a salad. He took off his jacket and rolled up his sleeves and sat down to eat with her. She was wearing slacks and a sweater, and he told her how Maeve was doing. The funeral was the next day.

"I think she's on autopilot, but she's a remarkable woman. The girls are pretty badly shaken up. But given what he had ahead of him, it's a mercy," Nick said solemnly.

"I know. She warned us that we might have to shoot around her. She didn't think it would be so soon."

Nick told her over dinner about the horses he was going to buy in England, and a shooting weekend with British friends, which was a tradition he enjoyed. He had a very pleasant life when he wasn't working, and always went back to the ranch for the lifestyle he enjoyed most. That much was clear. He was still a Texas boy at heart, despite living in Nashville, L.A., and Wyoming since then, and occasionally New York. He told her that at one time he had tried doing Broadway and it wasn't for him. He preferred the movies to the stage. He found stage acting too limited and stilted.

"I won't tell Shakespeare you said so," she teased him.

They made it an early evening because of the funeral the next day. He came to pick her up in the morning wearing a black suit and black tie with a white shirt, and she was wearing a black suit too, with black stockings and high heels. They said very little in the car on the way to the church where the service was being held. It was a small church near Maeve and Ian's home, and Maeve had hired off-duty policemen, just in case they needed them. But the service was exactly what Ian had wanted, his family and a few close friends to say goodbye to him. Both Tamra and Thalia spoke at the funeral. And, as promised, Nick sang "Amazing Grace," without a quaver in his strong, beautiful voice as tears rolled down his cheeks. And then a procession of men carried the urn out of the church, and they all watched it placed in the hearse, and drove behind it to the cemetery where he was to be buried. Maeve and the girls had picked the plot together in a small garden, under a tree, with room enough for his wife and children, and a little fence around it. And there was a stone angel looking over him. They each left a white rose on his grave, and Maeve read his favorite poem before they left.

On the ride back to the city with Nick, Kait didn't speak for a long time. She couldn't. It had been too moving, too painful, and too poignant with Maeve and the girls there, and the ache in her heart for Candace was too strong. It had reopened the wound that hadn't even healed yet, and Nick understood.

They just sat in the car together, holding hands, as she felt his strength running from his arm into hers.

They spent two hours at Maeve's apartment, talked to Agnes for a while, and then slipped away. Maeve looked exhausted, and it felt like a cruelty to her to linger. She needed time alone or with her daughters. Nick took Kait back to her apartment, and she heaved a sigh when they sat down on the couch. The day had been so emotional, it had worn them both out. Nick knew he would sleep on the flight. He was leaving for London that night on his plane.

They didn't mention the funeral again before he left, it was just too much for Kait, and he sensed that. They talked quietly for a while, and then he had to leave. She walked him to the door and thanked him for going with her.

"Have a good time in England." She smiled at him, and he looked at her and gently touched her face.

"Take care of yourself, Kait. And good luck with the show." The premiere was only a week away, and the tension was nauseating. Then he bent toward her and kissed her on the lips, and she put her arms around his neck while he did. She hadn't expected it, but after he kissed her she was glad he had. "To be continued . . ." he said, smiling at her. "In season two."

"I think you have me confused with Maeve," she said, with a warm look in her eyes.

"No, as a matter of fact, I don't. I know exactly who you are, Ms. Whittier." And he liked her just the way she was. With that, he rang for the elevator and was gone a moment later. And Kait walked back into her apartment with a broad smile.

Chapter 16

A week after Ian's funeral, Kait, Maeve, and Agnes had agreed to watch the first episode of the show together at Kait's apartment. Maeve still looked rough, and didn't want to see anyone except her two friends. But none of them wanted to watch the show alone. It would be more fun together. **The Wilder Women** was due to air at nine P.M. Maeve and Agnes arrived together at eight, and Kait had set out things for them to eat while they watched, including her grandmother's 4 Kids cookies, which were a staple in her home, and most people's, and everyone loved. Both her friends smiled when they saw them. They were too nervous to eat anything, but excited. Zack and Nick had both called Kait right before her guests arrived. Tom and Stephanie were watching that night too.

At exactly nine o'clock, all three of them were in her living room, watching the television intently, and didn't say a word to one another as the show came on. This was serious business, and they were both thrilled and terrified. The ratings for the first night would set the tone. There had been massive advertising for the past two weeks. The advance reviews had been positive, particularly for the all-star cast. And word of mouth would enter into it after the first night, as people told each other about the show and if they loved it or didn't. Rather than starting slow, they had a dramatic first-night episode, with all the principal members of the cast involved, so people could get to know them. The big names were featured in the opening credits, except for Nick, and were a dazzling array of major stars. Nick was still their surprise being saved for later in the season.

Kait was sure that the rest of the cast were watching that night too and would be just as anxious to see the ratings and reviews. And her children had sent her texts with good wishes. The three women sat mesmerized as the first episode began, as though they'd never seen it before and were first-time viewers. There wasn't a sound in the room until the first commercial break, since the show was on a major cable network.

"Jesus, I look a hundred and two," Agnes finally commented, took a sip of her Coke, and helped herself to a 4 Kids cookie. "Do I really look that old?"

"Older," Maeve teased her, and Agnes guffawed. "Your wig is really good, though, and your delivery is flawless, and your timing," Maeve complimented her.

"You made me cry in the second scene," Agnes returned the compliment. "I hate to admit it, but Charlotte looks incredible on screen. No wonder every guy on the planet wants to go to bed with her."

"Not lately," Maeve said tartly, and all three of them laughed. "Besides, she's twenty-three. When we were that age, they all wanted to go to bed with us too."

"Speak for yourself," Agnes shot back at her. "At this exact moment every man over a hundred in a nursing home is lusting after me." The threesome laughed again as the show came back on. They all agreed that the pace and editing were excellent, and Becca's script was fantastic, even better than Zack had promised. She had polished it till it shone.

Watching it on television at the same time as the entire country made them realize that their show had a certain magic to it. It flowed beautifully, and the casting was flawless. Each actor was totally believable in their role, their lines delivered perfectly. And Kait smiled as she looked at her two friends and wished she had a photo of the three of them. They had all worn jeans, their hair was a mess, none of them had worn makeup, Agnes and Kait were wearing glasses, and Maeve had contacts. They didn't look glamorous that night, but like middle-aged viewers with a mission to watch their favorite show and hang on every word.

The first episode of **The Wilder Women** passed

quickly and ended on a high note, with suspense about what would come next. Kait's phone sprang to life the minute it was over, and so did Maeve's. In both cases it was their kids, raving about what they'd seen, while Agnes helped herself to another Coke and more cookies.

Tommy told his mother how proud of her he was, and said that Maribeth loved it and was already hooked, and he liked the male characters and the actors who played them. He thought Charlotte was spectacular looking, even if slutty, and that Abaya was amazing for an unknown and was headed for stardom with the show. According to him, it all worked, and Stephanie called as soon as Kait hung up, and said that she and Frank had loved it. So did Maeve's girls. Carmen texted her, and Zack called again to tell her that it was a sure winner. He was waiting for the ratings and the reviews the next day.

After the calls, the three women talked animatedly about the show, critical of minute details they wanted to improve in the next season. But on the whole, it looked good to them, though the competition was stiff in that time slot. Nick texted Kait a few minutes later. He was back at the ranch after his brief trip to England. He said he was proud to be part of it, and was sure it would run for years. "We're going to grow old together with this one," he wrote, and Kait smiled when she read it.

The three of them hung around and talked for another hour, and then Maeve and Agnes went home.

They were just as nervous as when they arrived, since they wouldn't see the ratings and reviews till morning, which would tell them how they scored. It would be a long night of waiting for them.

Zack called Kait at nine the next morning, six A.M. in L.A. "Try this," he said, without saying hello. "'In first place for best new show of the year, or old one for that matter, **The Wilder Women** exploded onto the air last night with a star-studded cast of current and previous movie greats: Maeve O'Hara, Agnes White, current hotties Dan Delaney and Charlotte Manning, and brand-new dazzling talent Abaya Jones, Brad Evers, and a cameo by Phillip Green. An all-star cast, flawless script by Becca Roberts, compelling story by Kait Whittier, about women in aviation in World War II and beyond. This writer's prediction: seven seasons, at least, maybe eight or ten. Watch it once and you'll be hooked. And beware to the competition. **The Wilder Women** will give everyone a run for their money this season. Kudos to all!'

"How do you like that for our first review? And we had a seventy-one share last night for the first half hour, eighty-two for the second. We knocked 'em dead!" Kait had tears in her eyes as she listened, and thanked him for calling her. When she called the others after he did, Agnes was chortling with glee, and Maeve sounded human again and was immensely pleased. She was just sorry Ian wasn't there to see it. He had believed in the project immediately and convinced her to do it, after she met Kait.

Kait had calls from friends all day, including Sam Hartley, who introduced her to Zack on New Year's Eve. The next day she called Paula Stein at the magazine, who sounded glum.

"I figured I'd be hearing from you. I watched your show last night. It's fabulous. I guess we're history in your life, Kait." After twenty years.

"But very precious history. I'm going to miss it terribly, but it's been really tough keeping up once we started shooting. I don't want the column to slip, and I can't do a good job at both. It wouldn't be fair to you." Kait had a long hiatus ahead of her, but she had made her decision and was ready to give up the column.

"I'm grateful you tried," Paula said generously. "When do you want to stop?"

"I can do it till the end of the year if you want, as I promised. But I really want to stop by then. It'll still be sad for me. Let's say I'll do it till Christmas. I could do a farewell column for the holidays."

"That's more than fair," Paula said gratefully. It was two months' notice, and Kait had managed to do both jobs since February, and through three months of shooting the show.

"What are you going to do with it?" Kait hated to see them end the column, but she knew they might.

"We thought you would decide to quit, and we made a decision to end it then. There will never be another 'Tell Kait' like you. We're going to replace it with a beauty column Carmen is dying to write, 'Carmen Cares.'"

"She'll be great at it!" Kait said, sincerely happy for her friend.

"Well, good luck with the show. You've got a winner on your hands. We're proud of you," she said, and Kait smiled. It meant a lot to hear it. She had taken a big risk writing the bible for the show. And Zack had believed in her, which made it happen. He had gone to bat for her.

She rode the wave of praise and great reviews all week. She emailed Carmen to tell her she had quit, and wished her luck with her new column. They promised to have lunch soon, but they were both busy and had no time for now. As Kait thought about it, after she read more good reviews, she realized that she really had started a new chapter, just as Nick said. She had a new career, a new talent to develop, a host of new friends, and suddenly a very exciting life. And there was always real life in every mix. She had lost her daughter, which was a major tragedy, just as Maeve had lost Ian. But along with the blows life dealt them were the joys, and Kait had more than her fair share of those now. There was always the bitter and the sweet to contend with to keep one off-balance. But this new time in her life was very sweet. And she realized with an ache in her heart that Candace would have been proud of her too.

Chapter 17

Nick called her almost every day after the first episode aired. And the second one was even better. With the reviews they'd had for the first night, the ratings went through the roof for the second, and kept climbing week by week. And they had more great reviews. But even more important, people all over the country were talking about the show and loved it. And the social media were buzzing with it.

She had just finished planning her family Thanksgiving when Nick called her just to check in. She had invited Agnes to join them, because she had nowhere to go, and Maeve and her daughters, to keep them from having a mournful holiday without Ian for the first time, and she decided to ask Nick if he wanted to come to New York to join them. He thought it sounded like fun. She warned him that she'd be busy the next day, because Stephanie and Frank were getting married and it was family only. But they were flying back to California the night of the wedding, and Tom and Maribeth and the girls back to Texas, so she'd be free on the weekend.

"That works," he said, sounding intrigued by the plan. "I was thinking about going skiing in Aspen, but I'd rather spend it with you. Would your children mind if I come?"

"No, they'd love it," the holiday was going to be challenging for them too, without Candace. They had all had their losses that year, so some new faces in the mix would boost everyone's spirits. Kait was sure of it.

"Just check with them to be sure. I don't want to step on anyone's toes." He was very considerate about not intruding. She asked both her children the next time they spoke, and they thought it would be fun to include the others. As Tom pointed out, they had something to celebrate with a hit show. It was a better perspective than mourning Candace and Ian, which Kait had been dreading. She loved the idea of Nick joining them, and so did he. And Maeve liked it too, when she mentioned it to her, since Nick and Ian were old friends. They would be twelve at her dining room table, which was perfect, and she booked a caterer for the holiday. And they were going to the Mark, which was Stephanie's favorite restaurant in New York, for a wedding lunch on Friday. It was going to be a busy weekend.

By the time Thanksgiving rolled around, six episodes had aired, all of them resoundingly successful. Kait had been working hard on scripts with Becca all month, for the second season. Now they had a standard to live up to, which was driving all of them. Only the cast really had time off, Kait and Becca didn't, and Zack was always busy with the production aspects of the show.

Kait had one hard blow two days before Thanksgiving, when Candace's furniture and belongings finally arrived from England. It had taken time to get them packed up, they came by ship, and were slow clearing customs, and it almost tore Kait's heart out to see them at the storage company where she had them delivered to sort through them. Her clothes, her desk, her books, some teddy bears from her childhood she'd taken with her. Boxes of photographs from her travels, letters she had saved from her mother until they switched to email. It was hard to see it, and before it destroyed her, she left it all in storage to go through more thoroughly another time. She wasn't ready to deal with it yet, and it would have spoiled the holidays for her. She was shaken after she saw it.

Frank and Stephanie arrived on Tuesday to get their marriage license, and had a quiet dinner with Kait that night. Tom's family arrived on Wednesday night. Nick flew on his plane and was staying at the Four Seasons this time. The guests were invited for four o'clock in the afternoon on Thanksgiving, with dinner at six. Kait had always liked being together as a family on holidays, and they all looked immaculate and elegant when the guests arrived.

The table gleamed with crystal and silver on one of her grandmother's embroidered tablecloths, with rust-colored flowers in the center. And the smells from the kitchen were delicious.

Maeve and her girls were the first to arrive, and Tamra and Thalia thought Tommy's daughters were adorable, and played with them while they waited for the others. And everyone talked and ate the hors d'oeuvres the caterer served on one of Kait's silver trays.

Agnes showed up next in a black velvet Chanel dress with a high neck and white cuffs. Nick was last with an enormous armload of roses in fall colors. The caterer helped Kait find a vase big enough, and she put them on a side table, while everyone chatted animatedly, and the men slipped into Kait's bedroom to watch football until dinner. The atmosphere was everything Thanksgiving should be. And when they finally got to the table, Kait said grace and mentioned both Candace and Ian, and dabbed at her eyes afterward with her napkin, as did Maeve. But the rest of the dinner was high-spirited, and the turkey and trimmings were excellent.

Nick talked about his recent trip to England, and Tom and Maribeth about a photo safari they wanted to take in South Africa in the spring, without the children. And Nick suggested that they all come to stay at the ranch with him next summer.

"It's not as fancy as the Grand Teton Ranch," he

said to Kait with a grin, "but I'll do my best to entertain you." Tom loved the idea, and nodded agreement to his mother, who said it sounded like fun to her too.

Maribeth put Merrie and Lucie Anne to bed after dinner, and the adults stayed till after ten o'clock and then finally dragged themselves to their feet after a lot of food, and started to leave. Before he did, Nick wished Stephanie and Frank a beautiful wedding and a happy life together. They both were touched, and thanked him. They had mentioned at dinner that they were closing on their new house as soon as they got back to San Francisco. And Kait noticed that they had held hands through most of dinner. Frank had given her an antique engagement ring, which he had told her was the best he could do, and Stephanie loved it.

Everyone kissed and hugged when they left, and Kait teased the bridal couple afterward and told Frank to close his eyes in bed that night, since he was not supposed to see the bride until the wedding, and said they were planning to blindfold him at breakfast.

"For real?" He looked at his future wife in a panic, and Stephanie laughed at him.

"Don't pay attention to my mother." He was looking somewhat daunted after sharing Thanksgiving with a table full of major movie stars, his future mother-in-law, and the prospect of staying at Nick

Brooke's ranch the following summer. Nick had invited Maeve and her daughters too, he had enough room for all of them.

"What a nice evening," Tommy complimented his mother, as he poured himself a brandy and handed one to his future brother-in-law after the guests went home. Kait was tired, but pleased with their Thanksgiving meal together.

She had missed Candace, but in some ways it was no different than the years she hadn't come home. Kait tried lying to herself and pretending that she was in London, but at other times she was acutely aware of the truth, and she could see that Maeve was too about Ian. There had been tears in her eyes more than once, but she had fought to maintain her composure, and Nick had kept the mood light for all of them with funny stories. He had wanted it to be a good Thanksgiving for Kait, and he thought it had been.

Nick called her when she was in bed that night, thanked her for letting him join them, and said he'd see her on Saturday. He had rented a car, and they were going to drive to Connecticut for the day and find an inn to have lunch. And he was flying back to Wyoming on Sunday. She was touched that he had come so far to spend Thanksgiving with them. He told her he had loved it.

The day dawned cold and clear the morning of Stephanie's wedding. She and Frank were awake early and went jogging in Central Park around the reservoir before the rest of the family was up. They returned red faced and invigorated as Kait was pouring coffee for the adults, and milk into cereal bowls for the two little girls. They were playing games on their iPads, and Tommy wandered in with **The New York Times** under his arm.

"What time is the wedding?" he asked casually, as the joggers went to Stephanie's bedroom with a glass of orange juice.

"We have to leave at ten-thirty," Kait told him. "The ceremony is at eleven-fifteen." Without telling Stephanie, she had ordered a bouquet of phalaenopsis orchids, and it had just arrived. She still hadn't seen her daughter's dress. By all familiar standards, it was a very unusual wedding.

They gathered in the living room at ten, the girls in the dark green velvet-smocked dresses they had worn the night before with white organdy collars and white tights, and black patent leather Mary Janes like Kait's children had worn at their age. Tommy had opted for a blazer and gray slacks, with a navy coat over his arm, and Maribeth was wearing a beige Chanel suit. Kait had chosen navy blue, which she thought suitable for the mother of the bride. Five minutes later, Stephanie walked into the room in a white wool suit that was dressier and more traditional than anything her mother had seen her wear in years, and Frank was in a dark suit Stephanie had helped him pick out, and his beard was neatly trimmed. Kait went to get the florist's box and handed Stephanie the beautiful bouquet, and pinned a sprig of lily of the valley to Frank's lapel, and then she handed two tiny pink bouquets to her granddaughters. They looked like a very respectable group as they took the elevator downstairs to an SUV with a driver Kait had hired for the occasion, and they headed downtown to city hall right on schedule. Stephanie checked that Frank had the license with him that they had picked up on Tuesday. Frank said he had it in his pocket, as Stephanie turned to look at her brother.

"Will you give me away?" she asked him as a last-minute thought, and he nodded, touched, and patted her shoulder.

"I would have given you away years ago, if Mom had let me. Mostly when you were around fourteen." They all laughed at his comment. They followed one another into city hall with Kait leading the way, holding her granddaughters' hands, and the two couples right behind her.

And at precisely eleven-fifteen, Frank and Stephanie stood before a city clerk after Tommy had handed her over, said their vows to each other, and were pronounced man and wife. They exchanged rings while Kait held the bouquet, Frank kissed the bride, and then it was over. They took photographs of the ceremony and emailed them immediately to Frank's parents, and then on the front steps of the courthouse they posed for more photographs, and then headed uptown to lunch at

the Mark. Kait looked at her daughter proudly. It
had been an instant wedding, but suddenly Stephanie was married and it brought tears to Kait's eyes.
She blew her nose as her son patted her shoulder.

They sat at the table at the Mark until three
o'clock, drinking champagne, while everyone
chatted and laughed and the bride and groom were
happy. Tommy brought up the visit to Nick's ranch
again.

"I'd love to go there next summer, Mom. Do you
think he meant it?"

"It sounded like he did." She thought it would
be fun too, and so did Stephanie and Frank. It was
unanimous. At three-thirty they were back at the
apartment, and, standing in the doorway, Stephanie
tossed the beautiful bouquet over her shoulder and
her mother caught it, more as a reflex than a desire.

"You're next, Mom," Stephanie said, laughing
at her, and she and Frank went back to her small
bedroom to change. They had stayed in her childhood room behind the kitchen, next to their nieces.

"Don't hold your breath for that," Kait said about
the bouquet, and set it gently on the table. She
wanted to have it preserved for Stephanie. And when
Stephanie and Frank reappeared they looked more
like themselves. Frank was wearing an old army surplus jacket with a fleece lining, jeans with holes in
them, his favorite hiking boots, and a sweater that
had seen better days, and Stephanie was wearing
a purple parka she'd had since college, jeans, and

a matching pair of hiking books to Frank's. She looked totally happy and at ease, and Kait smiled when she saw the gold bands on their left hands that were bright and shiny and new, and didn't have the patina of age yet.

The bridal couple hung around with the others until six, and then headed to the airport for an eight o'clock flight to San Francisco. Stephanie thanked her mother for the perfect wedding, and said it was exactly what they had wanted. She was touched that her mother had respected all of her wishes, and added a few details of her own, like the bouquet and groom's boutonniere. They all waved from the doorway as the newlyweds left and got into the elevator.

"That was perfect," Kait said, collapsing into a chair, as Maribeth went to change the girls into play clothes for their flight. Kait made sandwiches for them to eat before they left, and at nine o'clock, Tom and his group left for the airport to fly back to Dallas. The Big Event was over. They'd had Thanksgiving together, and Stephanie's wedding, and when the door closed behind the last of them, Kait put on her pajamas and lay on her bed, and did something she'd been dying to do for weeks. She put on an episode of **The Wilder Women** that she had recorded, just the way she had with **Downton Abbey** for several years. Now she could watch her own show, and she loved every minute of it. It was even more fun watching it again. She watched three episodes before midnight. And then Nick sent her a text, afraid to call her. All it said was "How was it?"

She called him back and told him all about the wedding, and admitted that she was dead on her feet, but couldn't wait to see him in the morning.

"Do you still want to go to Connecticut, or do you want to stay here?"

She wanted to go, but the weather made the decision for them. It was pouring rain the next day, and they decided to stay home in her apartment, eat popcorn, and watch movies. She forced him to watch two of his own because she hadn't seen them. He groaned but sat there with her, and as darkness fell, he turned to her and smiled. "I always have so much fun with you, Kait. And I don't even like watching my movies. But I do like watching you," he said as he leaned down and kissed her, and she pulled him back onto the couch with her. They lay there, kissing, and then she took his hand and walked him into her bedroom, which was what he had wanted to do all day, but didn't want to scare her if she wasn't ready.

They peeled off each other's clothes in the twilit room, and slid between the cool sheets, as passion overwhelmed them and they made love. They lost all track of time and where they were, and afterward, they dozed in each other's arms and woke up hours later. It was dark in the room, and he turned on the light next to the bed and looked at her.

"Do you have even the remotest idea of how

much I love you?" he said to her, and she smiled at him.

"Maybe half as much as I love you."

"Not a chance," he said and they made love again, and a long time later, they got up and cooked dinner, as he grinned at her. "I don't think my old films have ever had that effect on anyone before." He laughed. "We'll have to watch more of them."

"Anytime you like, Mr. Brooke," she said and kissed him, and then they went back to bed and talked and whispered in the dark, until they fell asleep. And she realized, as she drifted off with Nick pressed next to her, that he was an important part of her new adventure. In a single year, her whole life had changed, and she loved it.

Chapter 18

December was an insanely busy month for Kait and Becca. They were getting the scripts ready and polished for the second season. They had time, but wanted them to be perfect. They had twenty-two new episodes to start shooting at the end of January. The network had confirmed their second season as soon as the show went on the air and the ratings went crazy. There were fan sites on social media dedicated to the show and the stars.

Kait had stopped writing the column the week before. It was an enormous relief not to have to do it anymore, and it would be nice not to have a demanding schedule during the rest of the hiatus. She was going to be developing more story lines for the scripts.

Kait had gotten Christmas presents for her family and the members of the cast that she was close to, and small token gifts for the entire cast and crew. She gave each of them a fun red plastic watch and a big chocolate Santa Claus. And now she had to get the house ready for Christmas.

She bought the tree and had it delivered, and brought out the same decorations she used every year. She decorated the mantelpiece, and put the wreath on the door. She wrapped the gifts the night before her family arrived. They were coming the morning of Christmas Eve and spending one night, and then Tommy, Maribeth, and the kids were joining Hank in the Caribbean as they always did on Christmas night. Frank and Stephanie had decided to take a belated honeymoon, and were going to Florida to be with Frank's cousins. And this year, Kait had plans of her own on the night of the twenty-fifth. She had invited the principal members of the cast to her house for a party. Maeve was coming and bringing Agnes. Zack was in town, and she had invited him. Abaya had said she would come and asked if she could bring a date. Charlotte had accepted and said she was ready to pop. Lally and her partner were coming with their baby, who would be three months old on Christmas Day. They had to bring him because Georgina, "Georgie," was nursing. And Nick was arriving to see her, and she had invited him to stay with her once her kids left on Christmas Day.

The cast was her second family now, and instead of feeling abandoned when her children left for their vacations, she was expecting a second wave.

She was going back to Wyoming with Nick for two weeks, and going skiing in Aspen with him for a week before they came back to New York to go back to work.

As Kait finished wrapping her gifts for her children, inevitably she thought of Candace, who was going to miss another Christmas with them, and Kait was trying to make her peace with it. She turned off the Christmas music so she didn't get too nostalgic, and on Christmas Eve morning, when her family arrived, they said the house looked beautiful and the tree was perfect. That night at dinner, they talked about the show again, and the rave reviews it had received. People were already addicted to it, and Maribeth said that all her friends in Dallas watched it and loved it.

"Season two is even better," Kait said proudly. "And Nick is in it."

"How's that going?" Tommy asked her, giving her a quizzical look. Nick was the first man he'd seen his mother with for a long time, and it was easy to see they were crazy about each other.

"We're having a good time," she answered primly.

"Why didn't you invite him tonight?" he asked. He liked him, and Nick was fun to have around.

"Because this is family," she said, thinking of Candace. "I'm having a party for the cast tomorrow night. He'll be here then."

"You left him alone on Christmas?" Stephanie

teased her. Marriage was agreeing with her, and she looked happy. They had gotten their house and were moving in after the trip to Florida.

"He's spending it with friends. He said he doesn't mind. I'm going to Wyoming with him for two weeks, and Aspen, before we go back to work. And he still wants you all to come out to his ranch next summer."

"Sign me up," Tommy said enthusiastically, and Stephanie and Frank nodded. And Maribeth was game. "Is it serious, Mom?" her son asked her.

"I don't know what that means at my age," she said honestly. "We're spending time together. We're going to work together. We'll see what happens. He's a major movie star and likes being a bachelor. And I'm set in my ways. What will happen remains to be seen. You have your own definitions about relationships these days, so do we. Nothing is quite the same as it used to be," though Tom and Maribeth had a traditional marriage, but Stephanie and Frank didn't. The doors were open now to create the relationship one wanted.

"I'm glad you're having fun, Mom," Tom said quietly, and a little while later, Kait went to get the cookies and milk ready for Santa with Merrie and Lucie Anne, and the carrots and salt for the reindeer. They loved their rituals and traditions. At midnight she was in her room. Nick called to say good night, and tell her he loved her.

"Merry Christmas," she said softly, and wished that he could be with them, but it hadn't felt right to her, or to him either, especially so soon after losing Candace. Maybe next year. Thanksgiving was meant to include friends. But Christmas was about family and more intimate.

"Merry Christmas, see you tomorrow," he said, enjoying the anticipation. He still couldn't believe his good luck at having found her.

In the morning, Kait and her children and grandchildren opened their presents, and the children opened their gifts from Santa. And after their traditional leftovers-in-pajamas lunch, they all got dressed and, after much kissing and hugging, left for their other destinations. Instead of feeling bereft as she had for so many years, Kait raced around the apartment, tidying up, throwing away wrapping paper and bits of ribbon, and lighting the lights on the tree. She jumped in the shower, and Nick came over to spend the afternoon with her and brought his suitcase. They made love, and exchanged gifts naked in bed. She had bought him a sturdy Rolex watch he could wear every day. And he had gotten her a gold bracelet, and black alligator cowboy boots that fit her perfectly. They showered and dressed together and at seven-thirty her guests arrived, and she looked glamorous in black velvet pajamas with black satin mules. And he wore a blazer and jeans and his own well-worn alligator boots.

Charlotte was the first to walk in, and her enormous belly preceded her. Kait thought she had never seen anyone so pregnant.

She settled uncomfortably onto the couch and reminded Kait of Agnes Gooch in **Auntie Mame.** "We had a DNA test, it's not his baby," she said, referring to the suspected father who had turned out not to be, "so now I don't know who the baby daddy is," she said but didn't seem upset about it, which was definitely an example of new wave motherhood to Kait.

Maeve and Agnes arrived together, and Maeve said her girls had left that afternoon to go skiing in New Hampshire. Becca was away too and had gone to Mexico. Zack walked in and gave Kait an enormous hug and started talking to Nick, who had been chatting quietly with Maeve.

"You know, I was very jealous at first when I heard the rumors about you two, if they're true," Zack said. "For about five minutes, I thought Kait and I were going to have something when we met last year, but then she wrote the bible and we started working together, and missed the boat by becoming friends."

Kait was intrigued to hear it because she had felt an undercurrent initially too, but it had petered out just as quickly, and he was always in L.A. Now he was like a brother to her, a wonderful person to work with, and they were friends.

"I'm happy to hear you 'missed that boat,' " Nick said with a slightly possessive glance at Kait. "I would have been very upset if you hadn't missed it." He looked at them both with relief, and Kait laughed as Nick put an arm around her, staking out his turf just in case Zack needed to be reminded of it.

Lally and Georgie arrived with a mountain of equipment and their baby sound asleep in his car seat. He looked just like Lally so they knew whose egg had won out, since they had both contributed. And Abaya stunned them all when she walked in with Dan Delaney. She looked more than a little sheepish, and said he had "reformed." He'd come to Vermont and begged her for another chance, and she'd finally agreed.

"One slip and he's out, though," she said, looking at him sternly, and everybody laughed. It was Christmas and Agnes said that everyone deserved a second chance but no more than that. None of them believed Dan could stick to it, but they wished the best for Abaya. He was off the show now since he'd only been signed for the first season, and the character he played, Anne Wilder's older son, Bill, was dead now. He said he was auditioning for a part in another series.

The baby woke up then and Georgie went into Kait's bedroom to nurse him, while Lally wrestled with the port-a-crib so they could put him down after his feeding.

Nick helped Kait pour eggnog and serve wine. She had hired the same caterer she had before, and there was a buffet in her dining room, and the same Christmas plates she had used for the family dinner.

Everyone was chatting and talking and laughing. She put the Christmas music on and Nick smiled at her, and kissed her when they met in the kitchen.

"Nice party," he said admiringly. "Beautiful hostess."

"Great cast, incredible leading man. Just don't fall in love with Maeve during your next love scene with her. I think I'm already a little jealous," she admitted.

"Good. Because I don't trust Zack for a second. You'd better stay away from him." He laughed as he said it.

"You have nothing to worry about," she promised.

"Neither do you," he said and kissed her again. He could hardly wait for the others to go home so they could make love again. He was having a good time, though, and had come to like the cast he'd be working with, and felt comfortable with them. They were all good people.

It was after midnight when the guests started leaving. Someone commented that there was more major talent in the room than at the Oscars, and it was true.

"I hope we win a Golden Globe or Emmy with the show," Kait said, and Zack said he did too.

Dan and Abaya were the first to leave, for obvious reasons. They couldn't keep their hands off each other and had been glued together all night. Maeve took Agnes home. Zack left to go to another party and meet up with his latest girlfriend. And Lally and Georgie were getting the baby ready to leave. Kait had the feeling he had been nursing all night, when Charlotte came out of the bathroom with a towel wrapped around her and a look of panic and astonishment.

"My water just broke. It's all over your bathroom. I'm sorry, Kait. What am I supposed to do now?" She looked like she was about to cry, and Lally stared at her in amazement.

"You don't know? Didn't you take any classes?"

Charlotte shook her head. "I didn't have time. I've been learning my lines since Becca sent me the new scripts. Everybody yelled at me when I missed my lines this season, so I've been working on it early this time."

"You're having a baby, you needed to pay attention to that too. Are you having contractions?" Lally asked, as Georgie finally got their baby into his snowsuit and back into his seat and strapped him in. He looked drunk from nursing.

"I think so. Kind of like really bad cramps, right? I've been having them since this morning. I thought it was something I ate last night."

"Oh my God, you're in labor. Call your doctor. Do you have his number with you?"

"It's in my phone," she said and then couldn't find it. Nick and Kait took the couch apart looking for her phone, and finally found it under a chair. Charlotte was looking more like fourteen than twenty-three, and Kait couldn't imagine how she had been through this before and knew so little about it, but that was eight years ago and she was just a kid then.

"Georgie and I can take you to the hospital if you want," Lally said, trying to be kinder. "I don't want to take the baby inside, but we can drop you off. Where are you having it?"

"The birthing center at NYU," Charlotte said, clutching her enormous belly, which looked like a beach ball under her dress.

"We'll take you there on the way to Brooklyn," Lally said as Charlotte struggled into her coat. She had to sit down before she got it on. Kait had been watching the exchange between them. She couldn't just let them drop her off alone.

"I'll go with you, Charlotte," Kait said quietly. "Give me your phone, I'll call your doctor." All she got was his answering service, but she left Charlotte's number. "I'll get my coat," she said and went to tell the caterer that she was leaving to take one of the guests to the hospital.

"Was it a problem with the food? Is it an allergy?" He was instantly panicked and Kait pointed at Charlotte, sitting at the edge of a chair, wincing and clutching her belly.

"I don't think the food did that to her," she said, and he looked shocked.

"She's having the baby?"

"Looks that way. Just close the door behind you. I'll be back soon. And everything was perfect." She had already paid him before the party.

As she turned, Nick handed Kait her coat and put on his own. "You're coming with us?" Kait asked Nick. "You don't have to."

"This is our first baby," he said seriously. "I'm not letting you go to the hospital alone." Kait burst out laughing, and they helped Charlotte into the elevator as she leaned on Nick's arm. Lally and Georgie had already left by then, when Kait said she'd take her. And the doorman got them a taxi. Kait timed Charlotte's contractions on the way to the hospital. They were regular and two minutes apart. Nick raised an eyebrow with a question. This was all new to him. "We're cutting it pretty close," she whispered as Charlotte started moaning and clutching Kait's arm with every pain.

"Wow, this is awful," she said through clenched teeth. "It wasn't this bad last time . . . it really hurts like hell." Kait didn't want to tell her that this baby was probably bigger. She was huge. "Could we go a little faster?" she said to the driver.

"Is she gonna have it in my cab?" He glanced at Kait.

"I hope not," Kait said, keeping an eye on her. The contractions were a minute and a half apart now, and they were still ten blocks away.

"Am I going to have to deliver the baby?" Nick

asked her. "I played a doctor in a movie once. I was pretty good at it. And I help deliver horses all the time."

Charlotte was crying and had screamed with the last pain as the driver ran two red lights, and three minutes later, had them in front of NYU.

"Get a nurse and a gurney . . . fast!" she told Nick, and hung out the window to call after him. "Make that a doctor." An attendant ran out with a wheel-chair a minute later. They were parked in front of the ER, and Kait helped get her into the chair, and they sped her inside with Charlotte screaming.

"It's coming . . . it's coming!" They got her into an examining room, pulled up her dress, and took her underwear off as Kait stood with her. Nick waited outside, and Charlotte let out one long never-ending ear-shattering scream worthy of a horror movie, and the nurse caught the baby girl that slid out from be-tween Charlotte's legs, and held her up as the baby cried and so did Charlotte. "Oh my God, I thought I was dying," she said to Kait.

"You have a beautiful baby girl," the nurse said to Charlotte, wrapped her in a blanket, and placed her in her mother's arms as Charlotte looked at her in wonder. "She's so beautiful," she whispered. "She looks like me." With that, two doctors and a nurse ran into the room to examine mother and child, and cut the cord. Kait kissed Charlotte on the fore-head and smiled at her.

"You did a great job."

"Thank you for coming with me," she said, and looked gorgeous despite mascara and tears on her cheeks. Kait nodded and made a quiet exit to find Nick waiting in the hall.

"My God, that sounded awful." He looked shaken. Charlotte had screamed like she was being murdered.

"The baby must weigh nine or ten pounds. Anyway, she did it. God knows who the father is, but she has her little girl. We can go home soon," Kait said and hugged him. Charlotte was going to call her mother and have her fly in from Southern California, and she'd be fine at the hospital until then.

Nick was vastly impressed by what he'd seen Kait do that night. She had gone from perfect hostess to labor nurse in the blink of an eye, and nearly midwife. And she laughed when she told him what Charlotte said when she saw her baby, about it being beautiful and looking just like her.

"That's about right for an actress. The kid will probably grow up to be an actress too or a serial killer."

Kait was still laughing when she looked at him. "This is a little bit like having fifty kids. I used to say I missed my children. I don't have time to now," except Candace, "I have a whole cast of them."

"You're a very patient woman, or a born mother or both. Where were you when I still wanted to have kids?"

"Busy with my own. And don't ask me to have a

baby now. I gave at the office. And we have the cast to deal with."

"I don't want to have a baby, and I never did. I like things the way they are," he said as he put an arm around her.

Kait went to say goodbye to Charlotte and admire the baby, who was already at her mother's breast. Charlotte reminded Kait that she was going to have a boob lift when she stopped nursing.

When they got to Kait's apartment, the caterer had left and everything was immaculate. Kait and Nick got undressed and climbed into her bed, exhausted after the emotional night, and she smiled at him.

"It was a beautiful Christmas, Kait. Even the little bit of it I got to spend with you. I love you."

"I love you too," she whispered as he turned out the light. It had been a beautiful night. For Charlotte too, and her new daughter. She had said she was going to call her Joy. It was the perfect name for a perfect day.

Chapter 19

Nick and Kait spent New Year's Eve at Sam and Jessica Hartley's New Year's Eve party that she went to every year, where she had met Zack the year before. Zack was in Sun Valley by then, with a new woman he had met recently. Meeting him had changed Kait's life. The partygoers were shocked to see her walk in with Nick Brooke. Everyone in the room recognized him. And it was obvious to anyone who saw them that Nick and Kait were a couple. They exuded that quiet, unspoken intimacy that couples have when they get along and are in sync with each other. Jessica whispered to Sam that they looked very much in love.

Once Sam told everyone at the table that Kait had written the story **The Wilder Women** was based on, they all told her how much they loved it, and had been glued to it since October.

"Nick is the star of our second season," she said proudly. It was no longer a secret and had been announced, so she could tell them.

They had fun at the dinner party, and stayed long enough to kiss at midnight, and then they went home so they could be together and make love peacefully. They were leaving for Wyoming the next day, and Kait was excited about it. She loved the life they were starting together. They were going to spend a night with Stephanie and Frank in San Francisco after Aspen, and the weekend in Dallas with Tom, Maribeth, and the girls, while the rest of the cast could do other projects if they wanted to. And then they'd be back at work on the show. Kait hoped it would continue to be a hit and the ratings would go through the roof next season, more than ever with Nick on it.

And whenever they got a break, she would go to Wyoming with him. That was the plan, although what happened in real life was often different.

Kait called Maeve and Agnes before they left her apartment. She promised to call from Wyoming, and then they drove to the airport in New Jersey where he'd left his plane. They took off half an hour later, settled into the comfortable seats, with Nick relaxed in his cowboy clothes, looking fatally handsome. It was still hard for her to believe that she was part of his life now. And she could see everything he felt for her in his eyes. She was wearing the cowboy boots he'd given her for Christmas.

She was in a whole different world now. The past had drifted behind her like scenery, and everything around her had changed. It was a new chapter and a whole new life. Kait thought about how lucky she was. Everything that had happened was so different from what she'd expected, and so much better than she had ever imagined. She wondered if her grandmother had felt that way.

As she thought about it, she took a pack of her grandmother's 4 Kids cookies out of her purse. She always traveled with them. She handed one to Nick, and he looked at her and smiled. They both knew that Constance Whittier had taught her that life was exciting and you had to face its challenges and opportunities every day. You couldn't hide from them, and Kait didn't want to. She wanted to experience it all, with Nick and on her own. It was what brave women did. They embraced life.

She gave him another cookie, and he kissed her. Their life together was going to be an adventure, and they were ready for it. The plane took off a few minutes later, and gained altitude quickly, as they circled over the airport and headed west. She smiled, remembering that a year before she'd begun writing the show that would change her life.

About the Author

DANIELLE STEEL has been hailed as one of the world's most popular authors, with over 650 million copies of her novels sold. Her many international bestsellers include **Accidental Heroes, Fall from Grace, Past Perfect, Fairytale, The Right Time, The Duchess, Against All Odds, Dangerous Games, The Mistress,** and other highly acclaimed novels. She is also the author of **His Bright Light,** the story of her son Nick Traina's life and death; **A Gift of Hope,** a memoir of her work with the homeless; **Pure Joy,** about the dogs she and her family have loved; and the children's books **Pretty Minnie in Paris** and **Pretty Minnie in Hollywood.**

daniellesteel.com
Facebook.com/DanielleSteelOfficial
@daniellesteel

LIKE WHAT YOU'VE READ?

If you enjoyed this large print edition of
THE CAST,
here are a few of Danielle Steel's latest
bestsellers also available in large print.

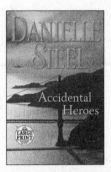

Accidental Heroes
(paperback)
978-0-5255-9037-8
($31.00/$41.00C)

Fall from Grace
(paperback)
978-0-5255-0128-2
($31.00/$41.00C)

Past Perfect
(paperback)
978-0-5255-0126-8
($31.00/$41.00C)

Fairytale
(paperback)
978-0-5255-0127-5
($31.00/$41.00C)

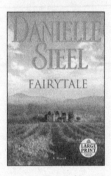

Large print books are available wherever books
are sold and at many local libraries.

All prices are subject to change. Check with your
local retailer for current pricing and availability.
For more information on these and other large print titles, visit:
www.penguinrandomhouse.com/large-print-format-books